About the Author

J.C. Grey is the author of the rural romantic suspenses *Southern Star* and *Desert Flame*. Born and raised in the UK, J.C. trained as a journalist in London before moving to Sydney. She is known for her high-voltage love stories and atmospheric evocation of uniquely Australian settings.

Also by J.C. Grey

Southern Star, 2013
Desert Flame, 2015 (writing as Janine Grey)

LOST GIRL

J.C. GREY

First Published 2017
First Australian Paperback Edition 2017
ISBN 9781489220417

LOST GIRL
© 2017 by J.C. Grey
Australian Copyright 2017
New Zealand Copyright 2017

Published by
Harlequin Mira
An imprint of Harlequin Enterprises (Australia) Pty Ltd.
Level 13, 201 Elizabeth St
SYDNEY NSW 2000
AUSTRALIA

Cataloguing-in-Publication details are available from the National Library of Australia www.librariesaustralia.nla.gov.au

Printed and bound in Australia by McPherson's Printing Group

MIX
Paper from
responsible sources
FSC® C001695

Prologue

Days become weeks, weeks months, and seasons turn as the house waits.

Spring showers and rich soil see green things sprout, tentatively at first then with enthusiasm, as if they sense the absence of hard, yanking hands. Common jasmine tunnels below ground, thrusting upwards where it will, twisting and twining up the hardy old camellia, suffocating it. A killer dressed in angel's clothes.

A high wind one night scatters leaves into the gutter above the high window of a bedroom, blocking it. A small waterfall forms, creating a relentless drip, drip against the wall. A menacing green-black stain begins to spread.

Hail fractures a slate tile on the roof, and it hurtles to earth. The impact on the old cobblestones creates a thousand splinters. One ricochets like a bullet into a rear window, producing a spider's web of cracks.

A shutter comes loose and slams bitterly, soon accompanied by its partner. Wind whistles down the chimneys and the interior doors join the resentful chorus.

At the end of the drive, rusty fingers creep from the lock in the gate, freezing it shut.

Twice, people come. One puts up a 'For Sale' sign, only for a sudden squall to strike it down later that night. The other takes one look, shakes his head and carries on past. Even animals do not linger long here.

The house sighs and whispers mournfully to itself as it listens in vain for a heartbeat. Spring ripens into summer, summer turns to autumn. The house is now all but hidden by shadowy vegetation. Yet still it stands. Still it sighs and whispers to itself.

And still it waits …

One

July last year ...

The four other women in the fertility specialist's waiting room stare at me in envy, despite their bellies ripening while mine remains flat. Some of it may be the loss of their girlish figures but a bigger part of their resentment has to do with me being Sydney's current It Girl. I know I should hate the way that word objectifies me—an 'it', a girlish thing, not even a womanly one—but in a perverse way, I love it too, as it means I am something they are not. So I tolerate their stares.

The other reason for their covetousness sits by my side, oblivious as always to the attention we are attracting. He is Marc McAllister, my husband, wealthy funds manager—the guy who predicted the global financial crisis, in fact—and all-round good guy. He looks the part: sharp navy suit, crisp white shirt, red abstract tie. His blond hair is cut close to his head around beautifully shaped ears. I love his ears.

In this setting—as in any—he looks completely at ease, regardless of the fact that the quality and/or commitment of his sperm are being called into question—by me, anyway. As far as the

3

specialist is concerned, ours is a case of no-fault infertility, though she suspects me. I can tell.

Deep down, I suspect me too. After all, Marc is, well, Marc. As the son, grandson and great-grandson of wealthy, socially connected McAllister movers and shakers, his provenance is known and celebrated whereas my pedigree is less exclusive.

I realise I haven't yet introduced myself. Marc calls me Em but my real name is Emerald Reed-McAllister. For the moment, anyway. I'm not going to give away all my secrets this early in our relationship—yours and mine, that is. Even Marc doesn't know everything although I'm sure he suspects that my background is not exactly gold-plated. It doesn't seem to put him off. At least, I don't think so.

Of course, as an It Girl, I do have some points in my favour, including a face that transforms from odd to extraordinary when filtered through a camera lens, and one of those long, lean bodies that exhales 'yoga', even though I've never done a downward dog in my life. I also have a talent for choosing and wearing clothes now referred to by the gossip rags as 'Em-chic'.

You're already starting to hate me, aren't you? Give me some time and you'll hate me a whole lot more. Most women do.

Marc denies he married me for any of my physical attributes. Instead—get this!—he announced to all and sundry during his wedding speech that he married me for my wicked mouth. He was a little nervous and stuffed up the delivery so everyone got the wrong end of the stick. Anyway, you could have heard a pin drop, then someone cleared a throat and another tried a nervous titter that was strangled at birth. What else was a girl to do? So I stood up, shrugged nonchalantly and said I thought it was for my money. That was a joke. Everyone knew I didn't have two cents to rub together while Marc had pots of it. Fortunately, at this point his rugby mates—bless them—started laughing uncontrollably and saved the day.

Okay, so he's not really perfect because that sounds sickly and fake and just impossible to live with. Marc is none of these. Right now, he looks up from the *Financial Review*, takes off his reading glasses, grins and squeezes my hand. My granite heart has a sandstone moment.

'Reckon you'll be up the duff before the ASX reaches 6000?' he whispers. If, like me, you can barely count to ten, the ASX is the Australian Stock Exchange, and its ups and downs are Marc's bread and butter. Mine too now that my wagon is hitched to his star I suppose.

I squeeze back. 'As long as you keep *your* end up.'

He grins, the creases around his dark eyes crinkling, and I have to look away to get a grip on my treacherous emotions.

In the days that follow the appointment with the specialist, who tells us to keep trying and bills us three hundred dollars for the 'consultation', Marc does and still I'm not. Nothing we try works, although we certainly enjoy the trying, even when a hint of desperation starts gnawing around the edges of our conjugal bliss.

On one occasion, I ask the specialist if our problems are because pleasure is somehow a barrier to procreation. Is our enjoyment of sex a signal that we are not treating our mission seriously enough? Marc rolls his eyes and even the doctor struggles to keep a straight face. But, in the end—when even technology fails—all we have left is pleasure.

When I begin to suspect that he might leave me, I do the only thing I can. I leave him first.

I go back shortly afterwards for reasons you'll soon find out. But Marc learns something about me he didn't know before. I'm a bolter, not a stayer. The trace of a shadow begins to lurk behind his eyes.

Yesterday, not even a year after that first bolt, I left him again. And now I am here. Which is where, exactly? I wish I knew.

Present day, in the still of the night

Wake up!

My eyes snap open as if pulled by strings and I am staring up into the shadows. An elaborate ceiling rose is all twists and turns and curlicues. It is dead quiet outside. Not even the birds are up.

My ears are attuned to every sound the old house makes, the grumble of water in the pipes and the contraction of the old boards in the cool of early morning. I'm sure I heard something more, something that sounded almost human.

It is possible I am not alone here. When I stumbled in dog-tired last night after driving aimlessly all day, I didn't exactly announce myself. Squatters, the homeless—others like me—might also be in residence. When I get up I will search the crumbling house, but at the moment I am inclined to stay put.

I am warm and relaxed on the ratty red velvet chaise, covered by the picnic blanket from the car. More to the point, I am safe for the moment—both from Marc's bewildered disbelief and the terrible, eviscerating pain that has torn at my vitals these past five weeks. Eventually, both will catch up with me, but for now the weight has lifted a little. I sleep.

When I wake again, sunlight has chased away most of the shadows. This is not necessarily welcome. In my current state, shadows are my friends.

Too warm, I push back the picnic blanket and immediately feel a sting of loss. At first I am unsure of the reason, but then I realise it holds a trace scent of Marc's cologne. We once made love on it, a lifetime ago. I push the thought away and rise, wobbling a little. Properly awake now, I feel an urgent need to pee. I stagger barefoot across the drawing room out into the hallway that runs down the centre of the ground floor. The first door I open reveals a library, but the second is a powder room. Relief!

The toilet has an old chain flush but it works. As I pull up my panties and jeans, I wonder briefly who pays the water rates. I wash my hands and, startled, catch a glimpse of a face in the tarnished mirror above the basin. Who is that woman? She could be me if it wasn't for the limp reddish hair, chalky skin and puffy eyes. The too-wide mouth is identical, though, as are the chisel-cut cheekbones.

Not wanting to look at her—me—too long, I splash water on my face. There is no towel, so I shake my hands and head, and carry on down the hallway into a vast kitchen, where a double set of French doors leads out to the backyard. One pane of glass is badly cracked.

Burnished copper pots hang from a ceiling rack, an old pine dresser holds a full set of china and the timber bench, inset with a huge butler's sink, is thick with dust. A chopping board and knife lie on the bench as though waiting for someone to begin breakfast preparations.

'Hello?' I call out, remembering the whisper I'd heard earlier. My voice is a strangled croak and I realise I have a raging thirst. The cold tap on the sink grumbles as it turns, sputtering out irregular gushes of water. It is cool, though, and tastes fresh enough. My hands create a dish, from which I lap like a dog until the water runs down my chin into my singlet, dampening my breasts.

I am hungry too, but first I need to know if I have company. I peer into the large pantry and the adjacent laundry. But they are empty, likewise the gloomy dining room with its heavy drapes and vast, banquet-sized table. From there I circle back around to

the library, where I eye the long heavy drapes. They would make
the perfect hiding spot for a knife-wielding madman but when I
yank on the cord, all they reveal is a window-seat where a thread-
bare stuffed bear lies at an uncomfortable angle. I straighten him
and turn away.

Shelves run right up to the ceiling either side of the marble
fireplace, stacked none-too-neatly with both fiction and reference
books. *Jane Eyre* is sandwiched between a book on military history and Kenneth Clark's *Civilisation*. The spines are ragged, the
pages dog-eared. All have clearly been read and re-read. This is
a real library, not like the one at the concrete Mosman mansion
of Marc's colleague, Toby Meyer—and Toby's wife Griselda (I
kid you not! Marc calls her Grisly, which she is)—which seems
to have been purchased in a job lot from one of those publishers
that specialises in the collected works of writers no one ever reads.
The Meyers certainly never have, judging by the pristine covers.
Marc and I used to laugh about it, in the days when we still found
life funny.

Unless someone is concealed up the chimney, there is no one
in the library, so I return to the drawing room. It is as I left it:
the tall shutters closed against the light, rug in a pile at one end
of the chaise, a cushion at the other. My bag is next to my sandals on the hardwood floor, mobile perched on top. It pings to
announce an incoming message. Perhaps this is what woke me
earlier. Without checking, I know it is him, but we have nothing
to say to each other so I force myself away and climb the staircase
that curves elegantly from the entry foyer to the first floor where
it branches into two.

Upstairs, the rooms are similarly vast with four-metre ceilings
that make them seem even larger, as does the absence of furniture.
In the master bedroom, my attention goes immediately to the
wide bay window and the French doors next to it. The doors

open easily onto a small balcony and I step outside and catch my breath, but not from the cold of the stone against my bare feet.

I am at the rear of the house, which seems to be surrounded by green. The original landscaping is a memory imprinted on the soil rather than fact. I can hear the rush of water somewhere in the distance. Topography, humidity and neglect have conspired to produce a jungle that is fast encroaching on the house. Spindly palms tower over the tangle beneath. I recognise lantana and morning glory among the ground covers. Clivia has multiplied unchecked in a great swathe of orange and dark green, but the camellias, leggy and yellowing, are at the mercy of the all-conquering jasmine.

From the position of the sun, I am looking north and beyond the trees I can see tin rooftops and the glint of sun on glass, a wisp of smoke. I suspect it is the small town of Lammermoor, which was where I was heading last night when the mist suddenly emerged from nowhere, crawling along the low-lying road in front of the car, herding me here.

I explore the other bedrooms and a bathroom, all of them empty. It is all but conclusive that I am the only life form in this house, possibly bar the odd mouse or two. In any case I am in need of a shower and getting hungrier by the minute so I decide to abandon the search.

As I walk back to the stairs, past the master suite, the fine hairs on my arms prickle—a draught maybe, but it is enough to make me step back inside the room. I have not secured the French doors and one of them has blown open. As I shut it tight and turn the lock, the door to the dressing room clicks shut. I have already peeked in there and scanned the empty racks and hanging space, and the en suite bathroom beyond. But now I go inside and see that there is a small door tucked around the corner.

Curious, I turn the old-fashioned ball handle. It moves easily in my grip but the door does not budge. This can't be right. I turn it again, putting my full weight against it. But it is as if a heavy mass lies on the other side, and it doesn't shift one centimetre.

When I put my ear down to the handle and listen, my arms prickle again, but though I stand, half-crouching until my back aches, I hear nothing but the drum of my pulse.

Two

Present day

Lammermoor is a bustling small town that has retained its old-world charm. Clearly the local chamber of commerce has ideas of grandeur—a banner across the high street claims Lammermoor is Australia's favourite country retreat—but most people I pass on the street appear to be local. There's not a selfie-stick in sight.

The good thing, from my point of view, is there is a deli-butchery with a decent cheese selection—my weakness before my appetite vanished. The downside, from the proprietor's point of view, is the fact that he has likely sunk every cent he owns into a business on the brink of failure. The over-eager welcome and the half-hearted gourmet sausage special is a dead giveaway. I almost think he would have manhandled me into his shop had I lingered one second longer outside. His smile is stretched; his willingness to describe in miniscule detail the characteristic of each cheese is overwrought. Then there is the desperation to make a human connection.

Where am I from? Am I here for Easter? How am I enjoying Lammermoor?

I am Sydney, not born but bred, and I know how you get to those with a gourmet fetish and deep pockets. It is not by trying to suck up to your customers. The typical Sydney shopper prefers to be ignored or condescended to. Treat them as equals or, worse, betters, and they will run a mile. One shops to be enhanced by the experience, as a high-profile model once told me, not to do the enhancing.

I respond vaguely to his questions, take my package of Jarlsberg (excellent with crisp, green apples) and open the door. When I glance back at him, he looks up hopefully. 'The lamb sausages should be in the window on a bed of rosemary,' I say. 'And you need a blackboard easel with a handwritten menu for sausages, mash and sautéed red onions.' He stares at me so I shrug and leave. As an occasional model, I have been around photographers and stylists enough to know how things should look without thinking, but he is welcome to take or leave the advice.

The afternoon market is thick with locals and a handful of tourists. I am noticed. Some try to hide their stares by rummaging in shopping bags or stopping to wipe small, snotty noses but I don't think they recognise me. Not really. But they recognise that I don't belong in town, despite my jeans and checked shirt and pony tail. I try not to make eye contact, but as I hand over a twenty for my vegetables, the rosy-cheeked vendor says, 'I liked your last movie.'

I am bamboozled until I catch on that she has me confused with a well-known arthouse actor, with whom I share nothing but height. I let the confusion clear from my face and smile. 'Oh, you mean *her*. I get that sometimes. Sorry.'

The stall-holder looks embarrassed so I pat her hand. 'It's no problem. We can't all be famous.'

She laughs, makes a light-hearted reply and pops a pack of raspberries into my bag, on the house.

Suddenly in her eyes, I am one of them. Ordinary. Chameleon-like, my specialness is gone. I may not be a movie star but I am a fabulous actor when I need to be.

I am nearly back at the car when something catches my eye in the window of a real estate agency. It is the house, *my* house, as I have already begun to think of it. The advertisement is curled with age, half hidden behind a newer, glossier picture of a newer, glossier home. The weekly rent quoted is ridiculously low for a walloping great pile of stone, even if the ad is several years old and the place is a wreck. Mind you, everything seems cheap compared to Sydney prices.

A woman, wearing a skirt suit like armour and hair like a helmet, comes out of the shop. Before I can stop to consider whether this is really the best move, I am half blocking her path.

'The house,' I say and point at the ad.

'Yes?' She is what you might call well-preserved—or mutton dressed as lamb if you're a rude bitch like my friend Brendan.

'In the window.'

She looks at me with shrewd eyes, up and down, as used to sizing people up by their clothes as I am, albeit for different reasons. Mine are simple but good, and I know how to wear them. Her eyes fix on the chunky resin band on my wrist. It is one of a kind, and I can see she has sensed its value, and the opportunity to land a good deal in a weak market. She's also seen the antique wedding ring that is still on my finger, and has me pegged as the wife of a wealthy self-made man, not realising that she is a day too late.

'Most of the holiday accommodation around Lammermoor has been taken through to Anzac Day,' she says. 'But you're lucky, that one is available. It has great green credentials.'

She thinks I mean the new and glossy pictured next to the old and crumbly.

'I—'

'I'll be back in about twenty minutes,' she says, skirting around me. 'I have to drop some keys off. Please make yourself comfortable inside. Sally will make you a cappuccino.' She rushes off, hips straining the tight skirt. She would do better in loose layers.

I beep open the car, and stash my shopping. Having caught the scent of the cheese, my stomach is protesting its increasing hunger, a good sign as I have eaten little for weeks, but it will have to wait a little longer.

Inside Lammermoor Realty, Sally is a freckle-faced strawberry-blonde a year or two younger than I am, with gap teeth and an endearing terror of the new coffee machine, with which she has been entrusted. She looks even more fearful when I request not a cappuccino but an espresso. Thinking she might burst into tears, I take over the coffee-making duties as we have the machine's big sister at home—correction, Marc has it in his home. Sally finds me a Tim Tam.

'I'm renting the place by the river,' I tell her, flicking idly through a property catalogue as I lick the chocolate off one end of the biscuit. 'Your boss sent me in to pay and pick up the keys.' Okay, it is a stretch but a harmless one.

'No, you can't!'

I swallow a mouthful of Tim Tam and look up. This is not a response I had anticipated, unless it is an inexpert attempt to drive up the rent.

'Someone else is interested?'

Sally shakes her head, curls bobbing wildly. 'You don't want to stay at that place.' She is emphatic. 'It's creepy. Everyone says so.'

I nearly smile. With so many ghosts of my own, a few more will simply blend into the crowd.

'It's just an old house. A few creaky boards, that's all.' As I pull my credit card from my wallet, platinum flashes. 'Four weeks rent all right?'

'But everyone says—'

'You're advertising it in your window.' I go over to the window and reach for the photo. It is gritty with dust, and I shake free a dead moth that has stuck to it. It makes its last flight to the floor, crumbling to nothing. 'I'm sure your boss wouldn't advertise a property she had her doubts about.'

I'm dead sure she would; even Sally, young as she is, is a little uncertain about the depth of her employer's integrity. But what can she say, especially when the exclusive credit card is winking at her?

'Well,' she says. 'If you're sure.'

'I am.' Actually, I am surer of this than I am of anything else in my life at this moment, so I may as well go with the flow.

Sally's boss has trained her better in processing rental payments than she has in using the coffee machine. I key in my PIN, realising that I may soon have to drop the McAllister from my name. Maybe the doing will be easier than the thought of having to do it. Sloughing off identities past their use-by date is not something I have struggled with before.

Sally and I both agree that a damages bond would not be appropriate given the state of the place. She has to hunt up the keys, which are eventually located at the back of the bottom desk drawer. Not that I need them to get in, but I would like to be able to lock the door at night.

'I'll ask Val about getting the power and water switched on,' Sally promises.

'Don't worry about that. They've been left on.'

'Oh, we never do that,' she assures me. 'Not with places empty for so long. Even out here we can get … the wrong sort. You know, squatters.'

Actually, I do know, although you probably wouldn't think it. Once or twice I had to be … creative in my choice of accommodation, in another life before I married money.

'Well, they're on. Someone must have been paying the bills.'

She looks mystified, but as I am worried about Val returning and killing the deal, I postpone my questions about the place. I am just in time. As I drive away, Val is race-walking along the street, anxious to return to her waiting client. I hope she will be happy enough to have leased the place that she will forgive Sally for the lack of a rental agreement, or even a contact number.

On the way back to the house, I glance down at the house keys on the passenger seat. One is big and old, the others unremarkable.

When the river comes into view, I have to concentrate. There is no mist this clear, bright afternoon to force me off the road at just the right place. The track is near impossible to make out, concealed as it is by low-hanging branches. But I slow and make the turn, keeping to the middle of the track for the sake of the Audi's paintwork.

Almost immediately, I feel as if I have been swallowed whole by the valley. The forest towers over me, more protective than intimidating, and with the windows open I can smell the damp mysteries of earth, roots and leaves. Seconds later, the car is bumping over the narrow wooden bridge that crosses the stream. As I approach the open gates of the house, for the first time in daylight, I am jolted by the quiet dignity of the place. In the mellow afternoon light, the sandstone glows a rich gold, and the tall windows gleam through the dirt. Even the loose shutters and rusted locks are not so much flaws as an opportunity.

This house needs me, I think, as much as I need it.

I see there is a plaque on the wall just to the right. It is so dirty, I cannot make out what it says from the car, so I park and get out. Even close up, it's hard to decipher. I have to rub my hand across the metal to dislodge the dirt from the copper.

House of Lost Souls. My breath catches and I blink. The letters blur and rearrange themselves into Lammermoor House, and I let out a laugh. It's been a tiring thirty-six hours.

I continue up to the house, hauling in my groceries and new bed linen and towels, dumping them on the kitchen table. I have a month to make some decisions. But not now. I want hot soup, some cheese and then sleep. I have had as little rest as I have had food in the past weeks. Now my body is craving both.

But before I do either, I use the old key to lock the front door from the inside—keeping the outside world out.

๑ ๑ ๑

May, the year before last ...

It is the night of Brendan's show. He's my bitchy photographer friend, and I am one of his subjects. The photos of me are good. More than good. And I am ... something. *Intriguing*, says one art connoisseur, head cocked to the side in thought. *Bewitching*, says a womanising collector who wants me to hang from his arm as well as his living room wall.

'I will have you,' the collector says in his thickly accented voice, almost making me giggle, but he is too late. All four photographs bear red 'sold' stickers. Displeased, he storms off to rant at the gallery owner.

Wearing aloofness like a cloak over the green shot-silk cocktail dress that my fashion-student housemate, Claire, ran up this afternoon (striking in a sea of dreary black frocks), I find a quiet corner where I can observe the crowd. Even so, it is hard to escape the speculative glances. Everyone wants to talk about the woman in the photographs, the one with secrets in her dark green eyes. Quite how Brendan achieved the look, I don't know. The images are so leached of colour they are almost black and white, except for the eyes. My eyes.

I sip my champagne, knowing I appear more poised than I really am. Having been in Sydney for almost five years, I survived the lean, early days by sleeping on friends' and strangers' couches at times and attending any function like this where I knew there would be free food. I soon fell in with a creative crowd in Surry Hills and Darlinghurst, who see a kindred spirit in me, and so far I have managed to conceal my lack of any real artistic talent. I have modelled for Claire and other emerging designers to earn a little cash and exposure, had some short-term fashion retail jobs and lowered myself to café work during lean times. I have acquired the skin of a free spirit without the soul.

Apart from a couple of brief mentions in the social columns, I have flown under the radar. Now, I am truly noticed and it is both disconcerting and exciting. And, yes, it is also the realisation of something that I always knew would happen, sooner or later. It is this languorous 'knowing' that Brendan has captured so acutely in his photography, although I don't realise it until later.

'Em, darling,' he says now, rushing up, his eyes shiny with excitement and possibly something more chemical in nature. His jeans are so tight they make other men wince to look at them, and he is wearing the silver cowboy boots of a true artiste and show-off. 'You won't believe it. They've all sold.'

'I know. Congratulations.'

'To him.' He jabs a finger across the room towards a group of penguin-suited men, all of whom are looking at me, save one with his back to me.

'Which him?'

'Marc McAllister. Tall hunk, blond hair.' He describes the only man not looking my way. 'Investment banker. Rich. Straight, sadly.'

'How can you tell? Maybe he keeps his silver cowboy boots to himself.'

I am, I confess, a little put out that the hunk seems oblivious to me, and I stare at his back, just as he turns. He is strikingly handsome in a kind of fallen angel kind of way, the blond hair set off by eyes that at this distance look almost black. Mine lock on his, and a shiver runs through me. He jolts, as though responding to the same electric shock. Satisfyingly, his hand shakes a little as he places his champagne flute on a table.

I'm not sure which of us moves first. Maybe we move in unison towards each other. But I do know that we meet in the middle of the gallery and then walk side by side without touching, out to the top of the spiral stairs that curl down three floors to the street.

Until he mutters *what the hell* under his breath as we stand there, neither of us speaks. One look and our sophisticated shells have been smashed on the rocks of desire. Urgency buffets us like a windstorm. I feel too tight for my skin, let alone my clothes. I glance up at him as he tugs at his bow tie.

'My car is right outside.' His voice is a low rumble. 'We can be at my place in about fifteen.'

It is not far and yet it might be the moon. I grip the smooth banister and stare down the snail-shell curves to the tiled lobby below. This isn't how it works, I tell myself. How I know this, I am not sure, maybe it is instinctive or perhaps I have learnt more than I thought since I landed in Sydney, but I am certain that I must let him pursue me. A man like this will not value anything that falls into his arms too easily.

'What do you want to do?' he asks urgently.

'All right.' What can I say? When it comes down to it, I am not impervious to temptation.

We are careful not to touch on the stairs or in the street, both knowing that it will be cataclysmic. In the car, it is more difficult. Once, his hand glances off my knee when he shifts gears. We both freeze and stare straight ahead. A moment later, he pulls over and yanks on the handbrake. We are outside a two-star hotel, not the kind of place he would ordinarily patronise, I am sure.

I glance at his jaw where a muscle ticks wildly, and understand why he has pulled up here. We will make it no further.

Inside, the desk clerk asks no questions as he processes Marc's credit card and hands over a key. He must see this kind of wild fling played out in his lobby night after night.

Still we have not touched each other. He has not even asked my name although, given he has spent a small fortune on four photographs of me, he probably knows it already. In the lift to the third floor, we stand at opposite sides and let our eyes devour each other. I think I moan. He curses again.

At the door to our room, his hand is not steady enough to swipe the card that opens it. In the end I do it. We enter, and we are lost.

Three

Present day, early morning

Don't cry.

'What?' I murmur but only silence answers.

My eyes flicker open, and I realise the new bed linen beneath my chin is wet with salty tears. My throat and nose are clogged and I have to sit up on the chaise to grope around in my bag for a tissue. I blow loudly. When I'm done I feel wrung out but lighter, well enough to wrap myself in my robe and make coffee.

I should not have read Marc's messages before turning in last night, but fortified by red wine—drunk from the bottle as the glasses in the kitchen are stupendously ugly—I thought I should get it over with.

The first, left around the time the mist swallowed me on the day I arrived, read: *Where are you?* The second, sent when I was exploring the house, said: *Are you okay? Call me. Please.*

My hand clenches around my mobile in the pocket of my robe. I should not look at it but I cannot resist. There is another message and a missed call from earlier this morning. My hand trembles as I go to read the message and I accidentally turn on the camera instead. It clicks as a photo is taken, probably of my feet or the fridge door. My resistance to Marc is temporarily restored and I shove the phone back in my pocket without reading the text or listening to the message. Willpower is a muscle that requires exercise, I tell myself.

When I have made coffee in my new plunger, I pour it into my new mug and take it outside. On the back porch, a sturdy rattan chair holds a mildewed cushion, which I toss to the floor. The chair is generous and low, so I curl into it like a cat, observing the world over the rim of the mug. The coffee is rich and robust, and I decide I like it better this way, made with an old kettle and cheap plunger rather than a space-age machine.

The garden, bounded by a heavy stone wall, is becoming familiar. I can make out the four rectangles of an old kitchen garden; green bean canes remain standing in one of them though they tilt at odd angles. In another, mint has been left to run riot, bullying its companions into submission, although the stalwart rosemary survives. Basil has long gone to seed, and curly-leafed parsley is a ragged lacework left by an army of caterpillars. Fragments of fine green cobweb may be dill, but I am not sure. I am no gardener or gourmet, although when Marc and I first married, we booked into a weekend cooking course—thinking that was the kind of domestic thing couples did. But just the thought of preparing the oyster entree was so erotic we never made it out of bed that day, too busy feasting on each other.

My lips curve at the memory before I can stop myself. I am not paying attention and accidentally jerk my coffee cup. Only my swift reflexes ensure the hot liquid lands on the porch and not my lap. Before I can spill the rest, I drain the mug, put it down and step off the porch. The grass—more weeds than grass, in fact—is wet and slippery with dew. I hold my robe up as I wander through the kitchen garden. Despite its neglected state, it smells good—of dew and mint and rich soil.

Under a dark-red leaf, a hint of canary yellow catches my eye. Reaching down, I tug the piece of metal free of the dirt. It's the carriage from an old-fashioned train set, the type little boys play with—or at least they do in vintage movies. My heart twists a little but it is not too bad. To distract myself, I try to remember what toys I grew up with but nothing comes to mind. Did I have a bear? A doll? I don't remember. And yet there are other things about that time I wish I could forget.

Inside, I rinse my coffee cup and the train carriage, which I take into the library and place on the window-seat next to the bear, which has fallen on its face again. I set the bear to rights, adjusting it and the chair and carriage until I am satisfied their positioning cannot be improved on. It makes a charming scene. On impulse, I pull my phone from my pocket, using the camera to take two shots from slightly different angles. They are both good, thanks to the alchemy of my innate sense of style and Brendan's influence.

I remember the earlier shot, the one taken by accident. Surprisingly, it is even better than the others, a slice of pale foot against the aged patina of the wide kitchen floorboards.

In the shower, my mind probes around the edge of an idea that is forming. I haven't quite got a hold of it yet, but something is taking shape. It is the first time anything has fired my imagination in a long time—well, for the past few weeks. As I rinse conditioner out of my hair, I know that I was right to come here. It has been just a few days, and already I am eating, sleeping and living in the present. And if I cannot yet shake the recent past from my dreams, the burden is somehow lessened.

I spend several hours entertaining myself taking photographs of the house, which fascinates me. The splendidly ornate staircase and the front-door lock yield the most intriguing shots, but they all have something. One of a dark stain in the master bedroom, juxtaposed to the elaborately detailed ceiling rose, sends a shiver up my spine, and I delete it, not wanting to think what might have caused it. The locked door remains impassable, but I shrug. There is plenty more to capture my lens—the open door to the master balcony, drapes fluttering in the autumn breeze, the drawing room chaise a splash of deep colour against the grey marble fireplace, the copper taps of the claw-foot tub gleaming dully. I even venture outside and down the driveway to the gates. The old brass lock, stiff and rusted in reality, glows under the attention of the camera-phone.

That evening, I sit at the kitchen table, my empty soup bowl pushed aside and the pendant lights casting an intimate circle of light. I flick through the photographs repeatedly, wishing I could print them and spread them out on the table, scrutinising them for imperfections, identifying opportunities for improvement.

It strikes me that the pared-back elegance of the rooms would make striking backdrops for a fashion shoot. My friend Claire, the fashion designer, would be in seventh heaven. I can see her deceptively simple creations here: an ivory camisole draped over a kitchen chair, billowy Bedouin pants on a padded hanger hooked lazily over a window frame, a lacy bustier looped over the newel post. But I do not want her here. I do not want anyone here.

As I ready for bed—brushing, flossing and Listerine-ing—I stare at my reflection. The shadows are already less evident; either that or I am so used to them I don't see them. I realise the space, the silence is what I need, and what I didn't have before—what I craved without knowing it. Here, I need please no one but myself. I can put aside the grief to examine at a time when its bite is not so savage, or maybe not examine it at all. I imagine boxing it up, pushing the lid firmly down and tying tough brown string around it, then placing the box in the sealed cupboard or room or whatever lies beyond the locked door. It is close but not too close, there but not here.

Only at night does the door open, silently, letting grief roam free and unfettered, seeking out the dark places ...

I push the thought aside and settle down on the chaise in the dark, not yet sleepy despite my soup-warmed belly. Rather than think about locked doors, dark cupboards and sealed boxes of sorrow, I think about the photographs, and about angles and light and interiors and swathes of fabric fluttering in the breeze from an open window ...

🙠 🙠 🙠

Morning comes rudely, or at least I am suddenly alive to it. Immediately, I sense that something is missing but it takes a moment for brain to catch up with instinct. Then I put my hands to my face, which is free of tears or the salty remains. As my eyes look towards the light that sneaks in through the shutters, the doorbell clangs and I jump, my heart following a moment later.

Marc has found me.

On bare feet, robe untied and billowing behind me, I race up the stairs and peer from the narrow window that overlooks the front drive. I dare not attempt to open it for fear the sound will give me away. From here, I cannot see the front door, but I can see a car parked next to the Audi. It is white and conservative. Not Marc, then. I do not want to think about how this makes me feel.

The bell jangles again, but by the time I get downstairs and turn the big key in the lock, she has turned away, having given up. It is Viking Val, the real estate agent. She spins as she hears the creak of the door, her face settling smoothly into the professional smile of her trade.

'Hello!' she says with robust cheer. 'I thought you must be out gardening or walking on such a lovely morning.' She takes in my dishevelled state. 'I hope I haven't woken you.'

'No,' is all I can manage, suddenly gripped by the feeling I am about to be turfed out on my ear. I grab the edge of the door, just in case she plans to drag me from the house here and now, although this is unlikely. Val is more one for lawyers and bailiffs, I suspect.

Her eyes are now focused on the vestibule and I realise she expects to be invited in, but a flutter of fear ripples through me. My feeling is that it would be like inviting the enemy inside the gates, which is ridiculous, especially as she is now digging into her bag—one of those brands whose commitment to genuine leather is one-hundredth of a millimetre thick—and pulling out a sheaf of papers.

'Sally forgot to give you the lease to sign,' she is saying.

She hands them to me and I take them wordlessly, my mind a whirling dervish of confusion, fear and relief that leaves me speechless. When I realise my arm is still outstretched to take the papers, long after my fingers have clasped them, I shake myself together.

'Sorry.' I manage a smile to match hers. 'I overslept. Would you like to come in?'

She walks up the steps towards me. I have an urge to slam the door before she can step inside but I am too late. I close it softly and as we stand in the shadows she appears somewhat diminished. At least, I am no longer afraid of what she might do.

'Oh,' she says, staring around, a look of surprise on her face. 'It's nicer than I remembered.'

Of course, I immediately start to wonder if she means to increase the paltry rent, but she hasn't finished.

'It's amazing what a difference a few simple touches can make.' Now, that could have sounded like an estate agent trying to offload a lemon, but Val's eyes are on the sprigs of wild jasmine and mint curling from a jar on the table that I moved from the library to the foyer for my photo shoot, and—through the open drawing room doors—to the chaise-bed with the dove-grey waffle-weave picnic rug tossed over the end.

'Perhaps, the kitchen,' I say, dragging her gaze away. I am less in evidence in the kitchen, I hope. As soon as I sign her papers, she will have no reason to stay.

Yet she seems just as charmed by the kitchen with the soup bowl upturned on the drainer, and two blue-striped tea towels draped over the bench. A small bowl of eggs sits centre-table because their organic shape appeals to me.

'Clever,' Val murmurs, handing me a pen and walking to the windowsill where a row of late-season plums catch the morning sun. She turns and I know she watches me as I sign the papers. My hair falls over my face, concealing my expression, as I realise she no longer has control of this encounter.

She wants to ask me what my intentions are, I know, but is trying to get the framing right. So I plunge in with a question of my own.

'How long has the house been empty?'

Startled, she can't quite hide the truth in her eyes before I see a fragment of it. 'Oh, quite some time.' She waves a hand to indicate a time period somewhere between a month and a century. 'It became too much for the elderly couple who owned it. After that, there was an attempt to convert it for commercial use—possibly more than one—but ...' She shrugs. 'It's rather off the beaten track.'

'When was this?' I press.

'Well, before I moved to Lammermoor,' she says. 'And that was ... thirteen years ago. Good Lord, time flies.'

She knows more than this—much more—but is unwilling to be drawn. It surprises me as I had her pegged as someone who uses gossip as currency. I hand the papers to her and add some pressure.

'And the family? Do they still own the house?'

Something moves behind her eyes. 'No. It's been owned by a financial corporation for thirty years or so.'

I frown, wondering why a bank would let an investment like this moulder away untenanted for thirteen years or more. Marc would not approve. An investment that doesn't work for you is not an investment, it's a ball and chain, he would say.

Too late, I realise my distraction has cost me the chance to dig further. Val is shouldering her cheap yet capacious bag and making to leave.

'We can set up an automatic debit for the rent, if you prefer,' she says as I trail after her. 'You don't have to come into the shop each month.'

'It's no trouble,' I tell her as we pause by the front door.

'All right, Mrs Reed-McAllister.' As she says my name, heavily mascaraed lashes drop and I realise she has worked out who I am, and is weighing up the value of the information.

'Just Reed. I'm glad I found Lammermoor House,' I say. 'With the high walls, it feels very private.'

Again, something flickers in her eyes that makes me certain her thoughts are different from what she is about to say. Nevertheless, she has not missed my meaning. 'I understand,' she says and walks through the door.

I stand there uncertainly, watching her drive towards the gates, and wonder if she will blow my cover. Probability says not; she has a business to run and I am renting her white elephant. But just in case, I lock the front door from inside.

                              ๕   ๕   ๕

August the year before last ...

Winter falls softly outside the window of Marc's warehouse apartment. In the half-light of late afternoon, we sprawl lazily on the long suede couch. A log fire burns low in the hearth. Despite the open-plan space, it feels intimate. I have rearranged the furniture from its summer floor plan to make it so. It made Marc smile and shake his head, but he didn't stop me.

His fingers twine through mine and he raises our clasped hands to the meagre light, while his other hand strokes languidly down my spine. Everything in me stills with the realisation I am happy. Not in the scream-yourself-silly sense but in the quiet knowledge that there is nothing I would change about this moment. I am almost stunned at the realisation. Is it true? I do not ever remember a time when I was not thinking ahead to my next move. Yet now I want time to stop and this moment to last forever.

Marc chooses the moment to shatter my peace.

Looking at our raised left hands, he says, 'We should get married—'

It takes a moment for his words, their meaning, to make any kind of sense. Then, terrified out of my wits, I am off the couch and across the room before he can finish. I stand, shivering, by the fire, arms clasped around my middle. How long would it take me to reach the door? On my trembling, unsteady legs, would I make it before he stopped me?

He sits up slowly on the couch, seemingly untroubled by my abrupt departure. 'As I was saying, we should get married … next month.'

A terrible situation has just worsened. I do not like watershed moments that I have not instigated. One moment, I was content and in control; now I am off balance and trying to recover my wits as he adds a deadline to his declaration. It's not fair. No, more than that. He is being utterly unreasonable.

'Why?' I eventually stutter.

'I don't think giving you time to dwell is a good idea.'

'Not why next month, I mean why at all?' I clarify.

'You know why,' he replies, those fallen angel eyes on my face. And the truth is I do. The reason is in our every touch, our every look. It has been so from the moment we locked eyes across the crowded gallery, and nothing—not even his exposure to me twenty-four seven since I moved in six weeks ago—has succeeded in crushing it.

I am appalled by his recklessness, and begin to list all the reasons it is a bad idea. It is a long list that starts with the fact that he knows nothing about me. His lack of knowledge is because I am expert at diverting conversations as they approach treacherous territory.

'I assume you'll tell me in your own time,' is his reasoned response.

'I could be a ...' I am trying to find the magic word that will cause him to drop this insane idea. Inspiration strikes. 'I know, a bigamist! Yes, a bigamist with a whole string of husbands.' I sneak a look at his face. His eyes are alight with humour, which is not the desired result. Despite this, I can't help myself. 'Some alive ... and some who have expired in mysterious circumstances.'

'Are you?' he enquires with a quirk of an eyebrow.

'Well, no. Of course not.'

'Well then.'

'The point is, you don't know what you're taking on. I might have been to jail for fraud or money laundering. Imagine what that would do to your reputation!'

'Em, I've never even seen you look at a bank statement. You told me you were financially illiterate.'

'It could be my cover.' I tighten my arms around my waist, feeling this whole conversation getting away from me.

'But it's not.'

'No,' I mutter. 'I've never been to jail.'

'Well then,' he says again, his face calm. 'What is it about your past you're afraid of?'

'I'm not afraid of it. It's just irrelevant. Boring.' The sensation of being trapped in rising flood waters is overwhelming, and a bigger part of me that I want to admit would risk drowning to find out where this leads.

He smiles victoriously. 'There we are then. If it's irrelevant, there's nothing preventing our marriage.'

In desperation, I air a few other reasons, each more poorly articulated than the last. When I reach 'your mother hates me', he gets up, goes to his study area, opens a drawer, comes back and stands in front of me.

A small vintage ring box of faded olive green velvet is in his hand.

'Don't.' Childishly, I clasp my hands behind my back. 'Your mother *does* hate me.'

It's true. Yvette McAllister is haughty, well bred and half French. She recognises peasant stock when she sees it and has no problem letting me know she knows.

Marc shrugs. 'I know, but she has no say in this.'

I suck in a breath at this bold statement, but there is a light of almost holy invincibility shining in Marc's eyes.

'She'll make your life hell.' It is costing everything I have not to run, and almost as much not to snatch the box greedily from his hand.

He shakes his head. 'Not possible while you're in it.'

This wildly romantic statement, uttered with quiet intensity, shears straight through the first line of my defences.

'She'll make *my* life hell!' I counter.

'Quite possibly, but you'll have the satisfaction of knowing you stole her darling boy out from under her nose.'

I frown, thinking about it. He is right. How could I turn down the opportunity to rub her nose in it? An engagement will suffice to seriously piss her off but, tempting as it is, even I know it's not nearly a good enough reason.

Still, I'm not quite done yet. 'You've only known me three months.'

'I knew the day after that first night.' He is implacable, which means I will have to find a reason to turn him down rather than convince him to withdraw the proposal.

'What's the rock like?' I ask, jabbing a finger at the box. It offers the only way out I can think of right now. If it is ugly, I will take it as a sign that I should turn him down. 'Is it big?'

Marc smiles slightly as he shakes his head and flicks open the box. The Art Deco ring sits there, small and perfectly formed in silver with a square emerald a shade brighter than the colour of my eyes flanked by three diamonds on two sides.

My arms are wrapped even more tightly around my waist now against the compulsion to reach out and touch it. But I am done in—both of us know it—not by the gorgeous ring but by the fact he knows me well enough not to buy some expensive modern monstrosity. The second line of my defence is obliterated. Bastard.

'What will you do if I say no?' I wonder aloud.

'I'll love you just the same.'

It is the first time he has used the L word. My defences have been stormed. When my arms fall to my side, he takes my left hand in his and slips on the ring.

'All done,' he says. 'Now that really wasn't so bad, was it?'

I sniff. 'Baddish.' And I warn myself not to be surprised if he calls it all off in a few weeks.

Four

Present day, morning

The howl wants to rise up out of me, banshee-like, and it is so sudden and powerful that for a second I can't breathe. The panic attack is literally suffocating, and for a brief moment I am terrorised, before realising that, if this is indeed death, my troubles are at an end. I relax at the thought, and just as suddenly I can breathe again and the drama is over. I'm still alive, damn it!

The waffle-weave rug, carrying Marc's scent only faintly now, is tangled around my legs, trapping me. Frustrated, I tear it and the sheets off and hurl them to the floor. Rolling on to my belly, I thump the chaise with my left fist. But the thick upholstery deadens the sound, rendering it utterly unsatisfying. It seems even my rages are doomed to failure.

Grief has a trick or two up its sleeve, I am learning. Just when I think I have made progress, it sends me back to step one. Well, not quite. Nothing could be quite as terrible as those days when the initial numb denial turned to crushing despair as I realised nothing would ever be the same again. I would have ripped my

33

heart from my chest to be freed from the grief. The banshee is merciful in comparison so maybe I should be grateful.

Something cool and soft touches my little toe, wiggles it. For some reason, I think of little piggies going to market and wee-wee-wee all the way home, which is odd. The only time I remember my stepfather being playful was in the presence of social workers and cops, and never with nursery rhymes. My mother preferred other kinds of games altogether, switching affection on and off like a tap. Perhaps one of my sib … no, I don't think so.

The wiggling sensation comes again. With a gasp, I push myself up and I hear the soft pad of feet running away from the scene of the crime, the suggestion of a giggle trailing in the air behind.

Wildly, I throw myself from the chaise and out of the room but by the time I reach the doorway, the house is silent again.

'Who's there?' I call down the empty hallway. 'What do you want?'

I strain my ears and try not to imagine what could be lurking in the shadows, just out of sight, but all I can hear is the beating of my heart against my ribs, slowing with each moment of silence. My shoulders droop. I feel exhausted, although the day has barely begun, and defeated, as though my battery has run dry after the energy spurt of the past days.

Slumping down onto the chaise, I stare at the small toe of my right foot. It looks normal, untouched by a playful hand. My nail polish is badly chipped though. If for no other reason than pride, I will need to see to it.

A ping makes me jump and I nearly laugh at myself. And because it is already a bad day, I decide my estranged husband can barely make it any worse so I decide to check his messages.

This one isn't from him; it's from Claire. *Sweetie, Marc called me. I think he was crying. He just wants to know you're okay. So do I.*

There is one from Brendan, too. *Don't be such a selfish bitch, Em. Call Marc now!*

Good cop, bad cop.

Marc hasn't texted in the last twenty-four hours, but some of his older messages remain unread. I hesitate, then jab my thumb to call them up. I may as well rip off the bandaid all in one go.

It's the fucking worst, baby. But it will get better. Call me.

Em, tell me where you are. Anywhere. I'll come and get you.

You don't have to say anything. Just let me know you're alive.

For God's sake, Em! I'm going out of my mind. At least tell me you're okay.

I'm calling the police.

Shit! The last thing I want is cops turning up on my doorstep. I call him.

🙦 🙦 🙦

September the year before last …

'What about your family?' Yvette McAllister's purr bears the smallest trace of a French accent (it always conjures up an image of the guillotine) and all the venom of a taipan.

'What about them?' I shrug, feigning a lack of interest though every sense is on full alert. Marc is on the terrace, manning his parents' barbecue, but I can hold my own, secure in the knowledge he chose me and not her.

'It's customary for the family of the groom to meet the bride's people,' she points out. 'I'm looking forward to getting to know your mother.'

'You wouldn't get on,' I say suddenly, tired of her games. She's lost and it's time she acknowledged that.

Yvette gives a forced laugh. 'What a thing to say! Of course we'll get along.'

She won't have the chance to because I wouldn't let my parents within cooee of Marc. If she knew them, she'd be grateful to me. In any case, as I've already said to Marc, they're irrelevant.

She adjusts the slender gold bracelet on her arm. As usual, she is beautifully dressed in tailored pants and shirt, and her blonde hair is impeccably groomed. She has Marc's ears, I notice – or rather, he has hers. I soften towards her for a fraction of a second. Maybe she senses it because she clears her throat delicately and moves in for the kill.

'This is awkward, Emerald, but I have to ask if your parents will be paying for your wedding. The reason is, you see, that we have quite a large circle of friends and business contacts that we'll wish to invite, and—'

'Marc will be paying, and our wedding will be small and intimate.' I meet her cold brown eyes with an equally cool look of my own that warns the wedding party could easily become one person smaller still if she pushes things.

She gasps and puts a hand to her mouth. The drama is all for effect and it works. Immediately, Marc's father Gordon approaches, alert to his high-maintenance wife as only a man who has spent thirty-five years negotiating an eggshell-strewn path can be. Marc rolls his eyes at his brother Léo, hands over the tongs and follows his father across the lawn to where we stand.

'Everything all right, darling?' Gordon asks his wife in his hearty, hopeful way. 'You two girls enjoying talking weddings?'

Marc says nothing but his eyes are darkly amused. I smile sweetly but my shoulders are tense and I have to force them to relax.

Yvette has her hand to her throat as though she can barely speak, but in the end she manages. 'But it must be somewhere suitable, *oui*? Not … Las Vegas?' The question is directed at Marc in a voice filled with the kind of scandalised horror that might be appropriate if I'd suggested conducting our nuptials in the nude on Lady Jane Beach.

Marc roars with laughter as Gordon stares at the ground and Yvette presses her lips together. I fight the urge to tell her that when she does that the subtle cosmetic work she's had done becomes visible.

'If Em wants me to wear a silver jumpsuit and serve deep-fried peanut butter sandwiches at the reception, I'll do it,' Marc says when he recovers.

Yvette is not amused. 'It's no laughing matter, Marc! I just want to ensure a level of dignity. I do not want this family to become an embarrassment, a laughing stock.'

Marc hugs her. 'It'll be small and casual—very Sydney, Mum,' he says. 'No fuss.'

The attention from her first and favourite son mollifies her, although her mouth makes a moue of distaste at his choice of adjectives. She tolerates Sydney only slightly better than she does me.

'Marriage'—she pronounces it the French way, with the stress on the last syllable—'is not casual. It is solemn and serious. It is for life, Marc.'

'I hope so.' The devilish glint in Marc's eyes softens as they lock on mine, and my pulse kicks up. His lids half close as his eyes drop to my throat and I can see he has seen the tell-tale sign of arousal there.

The timing is terrible. The McAllisters' spacious Vaucluse home and garden is packed with about thirty people—an intimate gathering of business and social contacts. We cannot slip away unnoticed, particularly as Yvette has promised an announcement with dessert. I am dreading it—the dessert, that is, not the announcement, which I know is Marc's sister Sylvie's pregnancy. Yvette uses food as ammunition and this time is no exception.

'Do try some, dear,' she says when the waiter comes out with a confection that rivals the Taj Mahal. Yes, I know this is supposed to be a low-key event, but Yvette's tolerance for casual stops at her menfolk manning the barbecue. However, she has limited the wait staff to two.

'Thanks, it looks delicious,' I reply in reference to the pavlova.

'I'm sure you will want to slim down before the wedding,' she says lightly. 'But you have plenty of time for that.'

I'm ready for it but before I can respond, Marc is beside me, his arm around my shoulder as though he is worried I might run.

'Afraid not, Mum. We're getting married next month.'

Uproar.

❦ ❦ ❦

Present day, morning

The phone is answered before the first ring and I brace myself.

'Em, thank God.' His voice is low, intent.

'No police. Promise.'

'Anything. Right now, I'll promise you anything. Hold on.' I hear voices faintly in the background and Marc excusing himself. Then there is only the sound of his breathing and mine.

'Are you all right?' he asks, the simple words belying the meaning invested in each syllable.

'Yes. No. I don't know.'

It may be the first honest thing I have said to him in weeks and we both know it.

'Me too.' His voice is raw and, as usual, I retreat, as poorly equipped to manage his feelings as I am my own.

'I shouldn't keep you,' I say. 'You're obviously at work.' I imagine all the suits around the boardroom table whispering about the CEO's flaky wife.

'It doesn't matter. Nothing matters except us, Em.'

'Don't! I can't do this.' My voice is sharp as I deflect his emotional intensity. 'I can't do this, Marc.'

'I know, baby. I know.' Down the phone, I can feel the almost superhuman effort it requires for him to back off. 'I know you need time. No police, I promise.'

It is an impossible situation. He needs his wife to share his grief. I need solitude. If there is a way forward, it is shrouded in fog.

'Don't try to find me.'

'Just promise you'll call me or text me every few days. And if you need anything ... *anything*.' His voice is as fierce as it is low.

'I need to be away.'

'I know. Claire sends you her love, and Brendan.'

'But not Yvette?' Even feeling the way I do, I can't resist prodding.

There is a rumble of reluctant laughter. 'Not Yvette. But Dad, Sylvie and Léo ...'

I know what he is trying to say. They can't quite like me for me, but they will love me for Marc.

'You should get back to your meeting.'

'It can wait.'

'Marc ...' I am seized by the desire to say that I don't mean to hurt him, but the truth is that I always knew there would be a price to pay.

'What?' His voice is gentle, unthreatening, and I wish I could just let it all go, but I don't even know how to start.

The closest I can get is to ask: 'Have you seen Will and James?' They are his closest friends. They played rugby together at uni and are still tight. He needs them right now.

'Yes.'

'Good. I'm glad.' The words are stiff. 'Marc, I have to go.'

'I know, love.'

As I end the call, I wonder how he can know when I don't even know myself.

Five

Anzac Day has been and gone, yet the weather remains mild and soft. There was a service at the cenotaph. The entire town turned out at five in the misty morning to gather in the square, solemn children holding candles aloft. Even I went, although I stood a way off, observing rather than participating.

This time of year—the slow slide into winter—suits me. I occasionally venture into the forest, but mostly I roam the house and garden. Before I came here, I would have said that the routine, the confines, would have driven me mad, but surprisingly it is not so. Every day, there is something new to see, something different to discover.

Some days I am filled with purpose, whether it is to find where the rain has been getting in to stain the ceiling or to study the vintage wallpaper in the library. Others, I am content just to be, adrift and wandering. Often I feel as if I am in a half-dream state, a limbo-land. I have taken a step forward but the door behind me has now slammed and I can't go back. Yet the way ahead is not clear.

41

Today, I am cross-legged in the chair on the verandah, my phone in hand, watching two birds play chase through the shrubs. They streak across the lawn, dodging all obstacles in their path, and before I realise, I am smiling and then laughing. They are too fast for a photo, even if I had thought to take a shot. By the time I do they are gone.

Once again, I flick through the photos I have taken. Something nags at me but whatever it is remains elusive, and with a sigh I put my phone aside. Inspired by the birds, perhaps, although at a slower speed, I weave my way across the lawn. My hand brushes the mint and freshness fills the air. Crouching down, I crush a stalk of lavender between two fingers and breathe the pungent scent.

Little is flowering now except for the doughty clivia, and even its fiery flowers are fewer than when I first arrived at Lammermoor House. But there is no end to the greenness, and after the autumn showers we've had, the garden appears lush and fertile. As I walk, I pinch off dead flowers and untangle the jasmine wending its way up a stripling. My first gardening bee, I think, looking at the greenery in my hand. I do not intend to take it any further; I like the garden as it is—a place wild and unkempt where only the fittest survive.

The sensation of being watched prickles my skin and I glance up. Out of the corner of my eye, I see a dark blur move across a small top-floor window. My breath catches and the greenery spills from my hand. Counting the windows across, I frown as I realise the house has an attic level, beneath the eaves.

Is somebody—something!—up there? My heart is racing but just as I am pondering what it could have been, the birds return, ducking and darting. I catch their reflection in another window and release a breath. Mystery solved.

Since I have been here I have not seen too many animals. In fact, I struggle to think of one. The birds are welcome visitors.

I may not be ready for human company but I am glad not to be entirely alone.

Ready or not for people, I must venture into Lammermoor today for supplies. Not looking forward to it, I trudge reluctantly to the shower and later dress carefully in a long-sleeved bronze tunic, jeans and brown boots. My long hair I pile on my head. A fringed scarf in dark green and bronze goes around my neck, dangling jade earrings in my lobes. Apart from lip gloss, my face is bare but for the mask I slip into place as I shut the front door behind me.

In Lammermoor, I notice that the deli window has been transformed. The chalkboard menu spruiks a recipe for fishcakes with a Thai dipping sauce, and a middle-aged woman is scribbling it on the back of a grocery receipt. The teenager standing next to her rolls his eyes, plucks out his phone and snaps a shot of the window blackboard. 'Dude,' he says, handing it to her with the sigh of someone used to dealing with a Luddite.

'I'm your mother, Dylan,' she says. 'Not a dude.'

'Whatever.'

I know their eyes follow me as I walk into the store, and a second later they are at the counter. As the woman asks for more information and buys the ingredients she needs, I consider the cheese counter, planning to make a gruyere and leek tart. With a large, if dated, kitchen and eons of time at my disposal, I have been experimenting with reasonable success. I find the careful measuring, weighing, chopping and mixing therapeutic. Providing I follow the recipe carefully, the results follow and it feels as though I have some control, as though there is something I can do that does not end in catastrophe.

When they have gone, the deli owner turns to me with a smile of recognition. 'Haven't seen you in a while. I thought your holiday must have ended.'

I just smile and congratulate him on the window. He nods enthusiastically, and I notice the worry lines are fainter across his brow. He confides that trade has slowly been increasing and he is breaking even.

'It's not great but it's a start. But every time I do a blackboard special, the supermarket drops its prices.'

Shaking my head, I list the gruyere and a few other things I need. 'Don't compete on price. You'll never win.' He looks suddenly defeated. 'Your point of difference has to be your quality and service. Your ... knowledge of the produce and the customer. Supermarkets are there to make money for shareholders. You are here because ...?'

'I dunno. My grandad opened the shop in 1958, and then Mum took over. Then me.' He packages up my shopping and rings it up.

I hand him a twenty. 'You are here because you come from a long line of deli owners with a passion for great produce and service.'

Enthusiasm is back on his face and he repeats the words as another woman pauses outside to read the recipe.

'Keep one step ahead. Open late one night a week and do a cooking demonstration. Invite a celebrity chef to do a book signing. Talk to customers about how to use different ingredients.'

The bell over the door jingles. It's time for me to go. 'Wait ...' he starts to say, but his new customer is speaking to him and I slip away.

Apart from Marc, Harley the deli man—his name is on his uniform as though he might forget it—is the first human I've spoken to in nearly two weeks. It looks as if he may be the only one for the next two weeks as no one in the supermarket or florist shop speaks to me, until a voice calls to me as I am loading up the car.

'Miss! Ms Reed!'

It is Val's offsider, Sally. Panting, she hurries up to me, half-eaten sandwich in her hand. She must be on her lunch break.

'Hi.'

'Thanks for showing me the coffee machine.'

'Sure.' I look at her enquiringly. She has more on her mind than cappuccinos, I think. Her face glows with ruddy good health and curiosity.

'I love your boots.'

'Thanks.' I start to turn away.

'It's just, I mentioned to my uncle about you living at Lammermoor House and he said you should leave right away.'

At her words, I stiffen, not sure if this is a threat of some sort.

'He said it's not safe. I wanted to come and tell you but he wouldn't let me go on my own and he wouldn't come with me.'

I laugh. 'It's pretty shabby, but it's perfectly safe.'

'No, I don't mean that … Uncle Bob says …' Her voice trails off and she looks uncomfortable.

'What?' I prompt her, resisting the urge to sigh and keep walking.

An uneasy shrug is the only response. She looks down at her half-eaten sandwich.

'I've been there a while now and lived to tell the tale.'

'Anyway, the house is going to be sold. You'll have to leave,' she blurts. Her flush deepens with guilt. 'I wasn't supposed to tell you.'

Shocked to silence for a moment, I consider this. It should not surprise me. The house is a sandstone beauty that deserves something better than its current fate. Someone else has discovered its appeal and snapped it up.

The money in the account that Marc set up for me when we married, which I have forced myself to ignore until now, flashes across my mind. Would it be enough for a counteroffer if the ink is not yet dry on the sale? Almost certainly not. I almost ask Sally the sale price, but cut off the thought before it can take breath. The money is Marc's. I have done nothing to earn or deserve it, and evidently even I have some scruples. One, anyway.

By now the mask is in place. 'Well, I'd better start packing,' I say lightly to Sally. My fingers tighten on my car keys. 'Who's buying it, by the way?'

'Oh some superannuation fund in the city, I think. The bank was happy to let it go, Val said, even though they got a lot less than they wanted. Anyway, you should move out. I can show you some other places we've got that are available after the June long weekend.'

'I'll think about it,' I tell her. 'It might be time for me to move on anyway.'

As I drive off, I give an absent wave out the window, wondering if I should expect another visit from Val in the next few days to give me notice. Then I remember the six-month lease that she had me sign and something in my stomach settles. I don't know much about these things but I assume it gives me some protection. I resolve not to worry about it until the Viking turns up on my doorstep.

A few metres down the street, I notice an old-fashioned hardware store. On the spur of the moment, I pull the Audi over. Less than three minutes later, after a brief transaction with a silent, long-haired man who regards me with a blank expression from behind the counter, I am back in the car and continuing on towards Lammermoor House.

As I drive slowly through the gates, the wind catches them and blows them shut, almost as though the house and I are of the same mind. Again, I stop the car and pull the new padlock from its packaging. I get out of the car, and click the lock into place. I rattle the closed gates to make sure they are secure against the agent or new owners. They are. I turn towards the car. The gates rattle again, and I spin on my heel. The gates are silent but a quick wind shivers through the trees and scuffs the gravel on the drive. As I stand there, it drops as suddenly as it rose so I climb back in the car and drive up to the house.

Hauling my groceries inside, I notice that great swathes of purple clouds are forming overhead, and wonder if the long, healing days of autumn are coming to an end and, if so, what winter will bring.

❧ ❧ ❧

November, the year before last …

It is little more than a week before our wedding and Marc is distracted. He has been for days. His normally easy expression is troubled and there have been several phone calls to the apartment that have caused him to apologise and retreat to his study.

The open-plan layout doesn't lend itself to privacy; his study is really just a space marked out by open bookshelves and a long, low leather sofa. So when this happens for the third time, I decide to listen in case it concerns me.

It does. Marc's voice is lower than usual. Clearly he is as worried about being overheard as I am by the content of the call, which I gather is about money. His or the business's, I'm not sure, but it doesn't really matter. Marc is the business.

When he hangs up, I brazenly walk in and plonk myself down on the sofa, arms spread along the back. I cross my legs clad in loose printed pants and admire my pedicure.

'So,' I say brightly. 'Have you lost all your money? Are you poor?'

'Shit!' Marc looks up. He must have been miles away not to hear my heels on the hardwood floors but he recovers quickly.

'If I have, what would you do?' he asks, sitting back in his desk chair and feigning the same nonchalance.

'Oh, I don't know. I suppose it would make sense to reappraise my options,' I tease. Inside, though, I quake. What would I do?

'Well, you don't have to. I ... we are not poor.'

'So ...?' My eyes stray to the mobile phone discarded on his desk.

His eyes follow mine and he leans back against the desk, his dark eyes speculative. 'My lawyer and accountant are concerned about your intentions,' he says. 'They want to set up a prenup.'

'I see.' On the surface I am calm but inside this revelation has cut a gaping hole. Why this should be I do not know. I expected it as a matter of course in the days that followed his proposal, if you can call it that, but when it didn't materialise I forgot all about it.

'You should,' I say, finding the insouciant tone I'm aiming for. 'This is exactly the sort of situation a prenup is made for: to protect a wealthy man from a grasping, gold-digging whore.'

He is around the desk and over to me in a flash, his hand on my jaw raising my eyes to his. 'Don't ever say that again.' His voice is gritty and dangerous. 'I won't have anyone speak about my wife that way.'

There is such cold steel in his voice that I shiver. I have never, ever heard him speak like this to anyone, certainly not to me. I figure it is not the moment to remind him that I am not yet his wife, that I still have nine days, two hours and forty-eight minutes to change my mind. I have already pushed out Marc's one-month deadline to a little over three; he will not delay another minute.

His fingers slowly relax on my face, stroking my chin. 'There will be no prenup,' he tells me.

'And your money men?' I ask.

'They get a bonus.'

I gape at him.

His face relaxes, the anger gone as if it had never been. 'They said what they did to protect my interests even when they knew it would piss me off.'

'Loyalty.' I nod as if it is a concept I have had passing acquaintance with. 'It's not my strong suit. I think we should get a prenup.'

He smiles, and those devil eyes are a dark chocolate. 'I think not.'

My heart is disintegrating while it continues to beat. I cannot bear it, and even as he kisses me I know that it must all end in tears.

❧ ❧ ❧

Present day, early morning

There is something I have lost, something important. Even though its identity is vague, I know I cannot find it anywhere and yet I must.

Looking, looking, looking. I am muttering to myself as I scour the house. I open all the kitchen cupboards one by one, peer into the dark hole of the old washing machine, sweep back the drapes in the library. It is in none of these places. Absently, I right the bear on his window-seat and stomp upstairs, my footsteps loud on the hardwood treads.

Coming ready or not! I hear the words echo as I reach the landing. I am getting warm now, I can feel it. In the smaller bedrooms, I make a show of peering under beds and inside wardrobes, even though I know where I will find it.

As I walk to the master suite and through into the dressing room, I hear a shuffling and a whisper. I smile to myself, knowing what I will find. Just as I open the door to stroll in, another nearby slams shut and I am propelled from sleep with such force it leaves me gasping.

Dreaming. I must have been dreaming, so deeply asleep ... but, no, that can't be right. We dream when we are in shallow sleep, don't we? Anyway, it was a dream. The house has virtually no furniture, certainly no beds to peer under.

I am chilled—the autumn nights are longer and cooler now—and reach to pull up the sheet and rug that must have fallen away. It is then I realise that I am not on the chaise. I am in the master bedroom's dressing room, standing in front of the small locked door that is still shuddering slightly from the force of its closure. Sleepwalking.

Closing my eyes, I put out a hand to the door knob, even as the lock clicks into place on the other side.

'Let me in!' I mutter, twisting the knob repeatedly. 'Who's there? Let me in now!'

Of course, the door remains shut, and the fact that I am terrified just makes me angrier.

'I know you're in there!' I yell at last. It is childish, but that is the way fear makes me feel. Excluded from a game I did not know I was playing. 'Be like that!' I kick the door, not hard as my feet are bare but it is enough to stub my toe a little. 'I don't care!' I grumble in retreat.

But I do, I realise as I retreat, hobbling.

As I walk from the room towards the stairs, I pass the long landing window and my gaze flies out and down the long drive as watery light glimmers over the trees.

A man is standing outside the gate.

November the year before last …

Four-and-a-half days before the wedding on the first of December, I finally come to my senses and tell Marc it's all off. It sounds brutal but it is the culmination of hours spent floundering in a rising sea of panic. What on earth am I doing? Marriage isn't something for half-formed creatures like me. It's for grown-ups, or it should be. Why isn't there a marriage test? You shouldn't be able to embark on something this serious until you've earned the right in some way, proved you have the mettle. Someone should have stopped it before now.

Feeling as though I can't breathe, I give it to him straight as he comes through the door, exhausted after the series of sixteen-hour days he has been working in order to take two weeks for our honeymoon in Morocco. The wedding can't go ahead.

'Okay,' he says agreeably, shrugging out of his jacket and loosening his tie. 'I need a beer.'

'Not until we phone everyone and cancel it.' I stand, one hand on either side of the doorway to the kitchen, preventing him from reaching the fridge.

The venue is not a problem, I know, as we are being married at Palm Beach on the sands outside Marc's small weekender. Still, there are around twenty-five guests, caterers, florists and myriad others who will need to be notified. He has organised much of it, although I changed the floral arrangements and menu when I recognised his mother's hand in the arrangements.

'Em,' he warns before lifting me bodily out of the way. He drags a beer from the fridge, twists the top off and downs it there and then in front of the open fridge.

I find the movement of his throat compelling and find myself staring, fixated by both the sensual undulation and by the implicit admission that Marc is feeling the pressure, too. He has never, to my knowledge, exhibited any prior need for an alcoholic prop.

A little uncertain, I stand there, not sure how to react to this Marc and how fair it is to do this to him right now. I recall that on the day he proposed, I had half-expected him to call the whole thing off before things got out of hand.

'Possibly I should have mentioned this a few days ago,' I acknowledge aloud. 'But you do see that we can't go ahead for all sorts of reasons.' I waft my hand through the air to indicate multiple insurmountable barriers.

'Name one.'

I smile. I only have one but it's a biggie. 'I don't have a wedding dress.'

Admittedly, it's because I deliberately haven't been looking.

He comes across to me where I still lurk by the door, and drops a friendly peck on my forehead.

'No prob,' he says and drains his beer, wandering past out onto our deep balcony that looks north over the city sprawl.

'No prob? That's all right for you to say!' Following him, I am working overtime to manufacture horror, even though I think my heart might never recover if he calls my bluff. When I wring my hands together theatrically, he bursts into laughter.

'Gorgeous girl, your never-ending delays and attempts to extricate yourself from our impending nuptials are both charming and amusing, alas utterly without hope of success.' As he sinks tiredly onto a wooden bench and props his right ankle on his left knee, he pats the seat beside him.

Fuming silently, I slink into it as he throws a casual arm over my shoulder. 'In any case, you do have something to wear.'

It's true, I have any number of things suitable for a beach wedding; long floaty numbers are my signature look. Then I consider the shock value of wearing a bikini. Or board shorts. Or strategically placed seaweed. My mood picks up at the thought of Yvette's response.

'Claire will bring it over on Saturday morning.'

'What?' I am visualising Yvette's face when I appear before the celebrant in a wetsuit.

'Claire has your wedding dress,' he repeats, far too smugly for my liking. 'You really don't think I'd failed to notice you hadn't bought one, do you?'

Six

Present day, morning

He is gone, the man. By the time I dash downstairs, shrug on a long cotton cardigan over my pyjamas and unlock the front door, he is nowhere in sight. To be sure, I go to the gates where the rusty chain is still padlocked. There appears to have been no attempt to cut through it.

A bushwalker, perhaps. Maybe someone else funnelled in by the mist—except that the weather is crisp and cool today, with little trace of humidity. Yesterday's wind seems to have swallowed it whole.

I know for sure the man wasn't Marc. My brief impression of the man was of someone middle-aged with a receding hairline and too-short trousers. It occurs to me that perhaps this is Lammermoor House's new owner come to inspect his acquisition. But I dismiss the possibility. The man I saw hadn't looked like the representative of a superannuation fund, either, more like someone who worked for a living. Instant guilt strikes me at the thought. Marc's company runs investment and superannuation funds, and I know the hours he and his senior management team put in—constantly alert to any tiny upturn or downturn in the financial markets. There are just different sorts of work.

What I mean is that Harry High-pants appeared like a man who worked with his hands, and maybe outdoors. Now I think of it, his face had a weather-beaten look about it, his shoulders slightly hunched as though against inclement weather.

I consider whether to open the gates and walk as far as the road, but my feet are bare and, if he means me ill, out in the green wood I am at his mercy.

Instead, I retreat down the drive on my cold feet, carefully relocking the front door behind me, and rush through my shower. When I have finished and at intervals throughout the following hours, I peer from the steps or the upstairs window, but there is nothing to see. By the afternoon I am still jittery, the morning cooped up inside having worn on my nerves.

My phone memory has all the photos it can take. I will need to offload some before I can take more. In any case, I have an urge to be outside in the weak sunlight. There is a shed in the western corner of the back garden. To date, I have done no more than stare through the window but today I slide the bolt and push open the door.

Inside, the loamy smells of potting mix and mulch make me cough. As I stand, gazing about me, a ray of lemony light thrusts through the dusty window, illuminating thousands of motes that hang suspended in its beam. How long have they remained that way, floating? An errant breeze spots the open door and buffets its way in, and instantly the dust motes are flung hither and thither. I am an agent of the first change this place has seen in at least thirteen, or possibly thirty, years.

A pair of wellingtons captures my attention. They are a murky olive green, a point in their favour as I cannot abide leopard-skin and floral wellies. Although they are on the large side, when I tip them up, only a little loose soil comes out so I put them on. As I knew I would, I feel differently when they are on, purposeful.

People say that clothes don't matter, but they are wrong. Moreover, they are ridiculous. Would Queen Elizabeth have held on to her position for sixty years had she preferred balaclavas to designer millinery? Would Gandhi's message have resonated so profoundly had he worn Armani instead of a loincloth? Of course not.

Clothes, for me, are more than a skin or a disguise. They allow me to see the possibilities, and allow me to act the part until I am it. They can fit you in or keep you out. They are not to be underestimated.

In leopard-skin print boots, I might not have felt the confidence to grasp the cumbersome old rake and spade and trowel—hung neatly side by side on hooks and decorated with spider webs—and heave them outside. Wearing olive green is a sign, to the world and to myself, that I am about to do more than smell the roses—not that there are any, but you get the drift.

Until this moment, I had never intended to make a project of the garden, and I am a little surprised to find myself in this position. I am not given to taking pointless action and the chances are that I will be here no more than a few weeks or months. Really, I don't even know enough to be effective, although it takes no experience to see that some plants are strangling some others. Removing their chokehold will give their victims a fighting chance.

I tell myself it is a one-off act of mercy rather than a gardening project.

Where to start is the immediate problem. I suddenly realise how big the garden is and how small my armoury of ancient tools. In fact, none of them is of any help with what I decide is my first task—dealing with the smothering jasmine. It is one of the few plants I know the name of. In Sydney, its pink buds tumbling over fences across the city seem to summon spring in their wake. Now, though, at the opposite end of the year, its slender twining stems disguise a ruthless strangling machine.

Without shears, I tug and the jasmine tugs back, burning my palms as the stems slip free. But I am not defeated. I stomp inside and return, brandishing a pair of kitchen scissors, with which I snip and slash industriously at the killer, partially freeing the three plants within its snare—shrubs with broad flat leaves, some turned to copper. For good measure, I chop off the end of each stem to remove the browning leaves. Of this I'm sure; the old must go for new life to grow.

After an hour wrestling with the jasmine, I turn my attention to the weed-filled herb bed, clearing out any growth that looks as though it has no right to be there.

The work is sweaty but addictive. Before I realise it, the sun has almost set and a sharp little breeze whips my neck and cheeks. I will need a serious scarf to go with the serious boots. Standing back, I take a second to admire my work before returning the tools and boots to the shed.

As I walk back to the house, clutching the scissors in hands that tingle with recent activity, I feel buoyed by the physical exertion. The house is in darkness as I enter the kitchen, thinking that I feel together enough to text Marc tonight to assure him all is well. He has kept his word and has not called the police or … I remember the man at the gate. A spy? I doubt it, but I will ask him.

I shower and pull on a clean T-shirt and loose yoga pants. Back in the kitchen, I put a serve of chicken and vegetable stew on the stove to heat and clean the scissors before returning them to the drawer. Casting my eye around for my phone, I cannot see it in its usual place on the kitchen table. Neither is it in my bag, the pocket of the jeans now in the washing basket or anywhere else I look.

Frowning, I try to remember if I had it in the shed. I don't think so and I really do not want to go hunting for it in the dark. I will check in the morning.

It means I cannot phone Marc and he is on my mind as I turn in. Little surprise, then, that he appears in my dreams.

ᴥ   ᴥ   ᴥ

Wedding day, December the year before last ...

'But *oo* is giving *er* away?' The whisper is pitched perfectly for me to just hear as I arrive downstairs from the attic bedroom of Marc's weekender. Yvette makes me sound like an unwanted microwave but this moment, this day is not hers to ruin.

'I am, but—a word of warning—I don't come free,' I answer. I would have preferred to glide down an elegant staircase as I make my entrance but the weekender is just a beach shack and the stairs are little better than a ladder tucked inside the front door, so I have to make do with gliding into the living room.

'Go away, *Maman*,' Marc murmurs, sparing not even a glance for her. His attention is riveted on me in the dress he asked Claire to design and make, and the look in his eyes makes me forget not just his mother but the whole world. In that moment, there is only us.

'You look ... you are ...' Marc falters and cannot finish. With horror, I see his eyes fill and his hand shake as he brushes the tears away.

'That bad, huh?' It is inane but it is all I can manage to lighten the awkward moment. It is enough to allow him to get a grip.

'That bad,' he agrees and he's not wrong.

The moment I opened the dress box, I knew it was right. In my heart of hearts, I was certain they wouldn't sentence me to some meringue or, God forbid, a Little Bo Peep outfit. But this is so me, it seems impossible that I have not had a hand in it.

Deceptively simple, it consists of layer upon layer of tissue-thin silk in various shades ranging from ivory to oyster, skimming from fine spaghetti shoulder straps to just above my ankles. Something about it pays vague homage to the twenties, while being utterly right for a modern beach wedding. A wide ivory band studied with tiny pearls and a small cluster of palely perfect roses at one side holds my hair off my face so that it falls rippling down my back. My feet are bare, save for pearly nail varnish. My only jewellery is my engagement ring and small pearl earrings.

Marc's clothes are even simpler, an open-neck white shirt and light brown chinos. He has had a haircut, which sets off those perfect ears of his, and when we step out hand in hand onto the shack's wrap-around verandah, the sunlight turns his eyes from devil-dark to a warm golden-brown that is free of the strain that has been there of late.

A cheer and a smattering of applause go up as we make our way down the steps and onto the beach, along the informal aisle created by the small crowd. The scent of salt and sun is heady, and I press my feet firmly into the sand in order to anchor myself.

'About bloody time,' one of the rugby boys says.

'So sexy I could scream,' Brendan whispers to Claire, his eyes all for Marc.

'Mummy, I need to pee,' Sylvie's toddler announces urgently.

'Last chance to escape,' Marc murmurs, and my fingers tighten reflexively in his as we face the minister.

But it is already too late, for both of us.

≈ ≈ ≈

Present day, early morning

Today, I wake laughing and crying at the same time, though I did neither at my wedding, my feelings too enormous to be let loose on an unsuspecting world. Instead, I had slipped easily into my performance as the It Bride—smiling, making small talk and dancing cheek to cheek with my husband. Marc, of course, was not fooled. He knew what my control was costing me, and the precise moment when it all became too much.

Determined not to wallow, I push the heels of my hands into my eyes and visualise the heavy garden spade tossing all the memories into the box of sorrows, before I press the lid down hard and deposit it with everything else in the locked room.

Maybe this is not the right moment to speak to Marc. If I feel up to it, I will text him later. The problem is my phone is not in the shed when I check, and I can think of nowhere else to look. I take my frustration out on the jasmine, and after another burst of work, the three brownish shrubs are finally free. I also make a discovery, down low and half hidden by larger branches—a short stem bearing a small mauve-blue ball of a flower, just beginning to die off.

I have an idea and take one of yesterday's cuttings into the house. Running low on groceries and with next month's rent due soon, I need to take a trip into Lammermoor in any case. I'm pretty certain the town does not boast a garden centre or nursery, but I recall the hardware shop where I bought the padlock has a small plant selection. It is possible that they will know what these brown plants are, whether they can be salvaged and what I can do to improve their chances.

The real estate agency is unusually busy. As I am waiting, I listen to the talk around me. There has been an interest-rate cut, a signal for people to dust off their mortgages and look for holiday homes before prices start rising again. I am just glad that Val has little time to chat when it is my turn to be served.

'How is everything?' she asks, pushing the card machine towards me.

'Good, thanks.' I key in my PIN. 'I heard the house has been sold.'

Her eyes slide away from mine and she busies herself with the receipt. 'Yes.'

'I trust it won't affect my lease.' I am clear to make it a statement and not a question.

'I shouldn't think so.'

'Good.' I take the receipt and thank her. Sally catches my eye as I break free of the jostling crowd on my way to the door. I can see she would like to say something, but I do not wish to hear it. The house has a history, that much is clear without anyone spelling out the details. And now, to add to it, I have dumped my terrible baggage in its hall and hidden my memories in its mysterious locked room.

In just a few weeks, I have come to know the house. I may not know everything but I know it better than most of the townspeople. I even feel a little defensive. The house has protected me, now I must protect it, as long as I am able.

In contrast to the real estate office, the hardware store is empty except for a man in a beanie, who is stocking shelves behind the till as I walk in. My footsteps echo along the aisles as I find lightweight shears to replace the scissors and a large tub of something called slow-release fertiliser. I would prefer something quick but this stuff seems to be suitable for everything. The plants I remembered from my earlier visit turn out to be indoor species, and I see nothing that resembles the twig with its coppery leaves. I do spot a hose, however, and it occurs to me that despite the showers last week perhaps my shrubs are water deprived, cloistered as they have been under the rampaging jasmine.

Taking a coiled hose from the display, I lug it up to the single check-out at the end of the store. The fertiliser nearly slips from my grasp but I manage to dump all my purchases on the old-fashioned desk.

'Credit, thanks,' I say, card in hand and looking up at the sales assistant, expecting to see the long-haired man from before. But this one is older, more worn, and his watery blue eyes flare in recognition as they meet mine. I smile and prepare to deny I am that girl, until he steps out from behind the counter and I see the slice of pale skin between his socks and the hem of his pants. It is the man from the gates, today modelling a beanie.

Does he know who I am?

I back up as he comes towards me but he simply goes to a shelf, checks the price of the hose and returns, still having said nothing.

'I wonder if you …' I begin, brandishing my twig and leaf. 'Do you know what this is and what it needs to thrive?'

He spares it and me barely a glance. 'Hydrangea macrophylla. Cut it back to the first pair of buds.'

I pick up the slow-release fertiliser. 'No good?'

'Won't hurt.'

'Anything else?'

'Needs shade. Better on the southeastern side.'

That wasn't what I meant and I'm sure he knew it. If he wants to say something, this is his chance. But he says nothing more, not even to acknowledge he had been outside the gate that day. Perhaps he is embarrassed to have been caught staring at the house. Or was he hoping for a glimpse of me? Unlikely. He doesn't appear the type to read the social pages.

Impatiently, I grab my card, gather up my purchases and turn to leave.

At the door I realise I have no free hands to open it and glance back at him. He is clearly reluctant to approach, as though I am toxic in some way. He begins to open the door and awkwardly I try to shuffle past. When he does not move his arm, I look up.

He moves his mouth almost experimentally as if he is trying to find the right words or frame them in the right way. When they come, they are hardly worth the effort.

'Don't wait until it's too late,' he warns.

I nod. Even I know transplanting plants is best done while they are dormant. 'Thanks.'

It is only while I am driving home, thinking of other things, that I wonder if his warning had anything to do with gardening at all.

Seven

Present day, early evening

The sneaky wind has turned to showers and the showers have turned the soil to mud. The trees drip chilly droplets down my neck, vines cling limpidly to any exposed skin and the tall grasses manage to deposit mud inside my boots despite the tie tops.

After a miserable morning of gardening, during which I seem to achieve nothing except wet feet, I retreat inside and wander aimlessly from room to room.

With my phone still missing, I castigate myself for not buying a camera while I was in town. The gloomy day has transformed the house into a study in shadows, and I journey between the subjects of my last shoot, imagining how I would photograph them today. The curving bannister in particular teases me, and I walk up and down the stairs twelve times, investigating various angles until I have identified the one that delivers the most intrigue.

By mid-afternoon, I am almost stir-crazy and consider a last-minute dash into town, but the showers have turned into something more insistent. Instead, heavy socks on my feet, I wander into the library, switch on the lamp, pluck *Jane Eyre* from one of the bookshelves and settle in, the bear on my lap.

I read a few classics after moving to Sydney, inspired by a bookish girl I once shared a house with. *Jane Eyre* I have not encountered thus far, but almost immediately it sucks me in and under. Before I know it, Jane has endured her abusive childhood and student life, and is on her way to Thornfield House. Plain and poor, Jane is not on the surface a heroine who would appeal to me. But she has pluck, and I find myself wanting her to win the day.

Stiff, I shift my position and realise that I am sitting in the dark. The lamp spills a circle of light onto the page. The corner has been bent before so I reinstate the bookmark and head for the kitchen, switching on lights as I go.

The kitchen is as chilly as the rest of the house. The squally rain lashes the windows in bursts and the air feels damp. I light the gas cooktop and fry off some onions and garlic for a leek and potato soup. While it is cooking, I go to the front room to find a warmer cardigan. As I dig through my bag, I realise that the clothes I packed were for mild April and are not at all suitable for a draughty house in late autumn. I will need to do something about that.

Piled under the overhang of the shed are stacks of rough-cut logs that I will need to bring in to build a fire, but it is too wet to go out tonight. Tomorrow morning is soon enough so that they can spend the day drying in the hearth.

Eyeing my makeshift bed, I know that I will need more than a waffle-weave picnic rug to avoid shivering through the night. Before I go hunting for a quilt, I stir the soup and stick a hunk of garlic bread in the oven, as much to have an excuse to switch it on as anything. Drawing my cotton cardigan tightly around me and hoping I quickly find what I need so I can return to the warm kitchen, I start up the stairs.

As I climb, I can hear the wind shrieking around the eaves. Something is rattling. A loose pane or pipe, perhaps? The stairs creak under my socked feet and I grip the polished bannister. The air feels damper up here and I remember the black stain in the main bedroom. Dreading the thought that the water leak has worsened in the weather and that I may need a bucket, I walk into the master bedroom to check the damage. Just then, the lights flicker and die.

Startled at the sudden darkness, I almost lose my balance and have to brace myself against the wall. My ears are tuned for the sound of drips but all I can hear is the sound of my breathing. Relieved, I turn to head back downstairs. There is no point groping around trying to find bedding until the lights come back on. In any case, I can smell the garlic bread and am suddenly ravenous.

At the top of the stairs, I suddenly hear it and stop dead. My missing phone is ringing.

a a a

Christmas, the year before last ...

Marriage, I quickly discover, changes nothing.

Morocco is an exotic brew of strange sights and scents and stories. By day we wander from landmark to bazaar to café. By night we make heady love. Then we are back in Sydney, and I realise the drama of the wedding has obscured the question of what comes after.

For Marc, work is a given. It has piled up in his absence, whereas I am floundering for direction by noon on the first day back. I call Claire but she is frantically preparing to take on a stall at Paddington Markets and cannot talk for long. Brendan, I know, has left early to return to the family farm for Christmas. Something about coming out of the closet, and admitting he is a photographer, not the chemical engineer they believe him to be. Even around the apartment there is little to do; the unobtrusive and ferociously efficient Rosa Saatchi comes in to take care of housekeeping duties twice a week as she has always done.

Christmas! It is the eighteenth, already, and garish lights are springing up across the city. Even our usually uber-cool inner-city street of terraces and warehouse apartments is suddenly strung with more glitz and glitter than the Las Vegas strip. Out on the balcony, I wince at the large inflatable Santa, half stuffed down the brick chimney of a narrow terrace. When did Christmas get so crass?

I want a tree, I decide, a real one as high as the three-and-a-half-metre ceilings in Marc's apartment. Two hours later I have chosen it and arranged for it to be delivered, and have moved the furniture around to what I feel should be the summer configuration—to face the bank of glass bi-fold doors that open onto the breezy balcony with its expansive city view.

By the time Marc returns home, the tree is in situ just outside the bi-fold doors so that it can be enjoyed by others as well as us. A swathe of gold fabric conceals its pot, tied with an enormous red bow. I am hip-deep in fabric and ribbon when he walks in the door that yesterday he carried me through (over his shoulder, eschewing anything too romantic), having decided to hand-make our decorations—stars, suns and moons—with an invisible line of tiny fairy lights winding through the branches.

'Wow,' he says. 'We have a tree.'

I have been so carried away by the vision I could see in my mind that I have forgotten that this is his apartment. Perhaps I shouldn't have been so rash.

'I wanted one,' I say lamely. 'I've never had a Christmas tree before.'

'No?' He takes off his tie and comes and sits cross-legged next to me. He knows I never speak of my life before Sydney, but from time to time he says something that seems like an offer to listen if I want to share. I don't.

Today, I just shrug. I can't remember ever having a tree growing up. It just wasn't the kind of thing my family did. But that's old news. 'It's kind of big.'

He studies the tree, head cocked to one side. 'It works with the way the room is now. I like the stars.'

We sit there, looking at the tree for a while. I am not sure what he is thinking, and suddenly I have the notion that, on returning to the real world today, he has realised he made a terrible mistake in marrying me. Having been the reluctant one before our wedding, I wonder now if it is now Marc who has had a change of heart and wants out? The lump in my chest is so heavy, I actually put up a hand to it and press hard.

All it has taken is three weeks of concentrated togetherness for him to see through the sham. The only question is why it took him so long. I am desperate, wondering how I can paper over the cracks before they become crevasses. If I promise to take a course, start a career, read the newspapers daily, be a good person, will he stay?

Then he bumps his shoulder companionably to mine. 'You forgot something important.' He waggles his eyebrows suggestively and my panic subsides. 'Mistletoe.'

My anxiety eases but doesn't disappear. Christmas, I discover, is littered with all sorts of meanings and rituals and family politics— mini landmines invisible to the untrained eye but designed to maim at the very least.

My big mistake is to presume to organise cocktails at the apartment for friends and Marc's family two nights before Christmas. However, my beautiful hand-made and mailed invitation to Yvette and Gordon strangely never arrives and it looks as if I am trying to deliberately exclude them. I should have followed up by phone when they didn't respond, but I put it off and when Marc finally calls them, they already have other plans.

I am nervous yet defiant as we drive towards Vaucluse on Christmas morning. On the back seat, artfully wrapped gifts are piled in bags, one for each member of the family. I am particularly pleased with Yvette's, having agonised over what to buy a woman who has everything until I found an old black-and-white photo of Marc and his siblings as small children hanging from what looks like a Hills hoist, screaming with delight as it whirls. I have had it framed. Even Marc has no idea.

'Welcome. Welcome.' Gordon greets us at the door and ushers us inside where Léo waits with a tray of champagne.

Yvette comes out of the kitchen, where she has been hard at work supervising the catering staff. 'Darlings!' Her cheek skims mine and I smell something expensive. 'Goodness, what's all this?'

She's staring at the gifts spilling out of the bags by our feet, dismay written all over her face.

'Just a few little things to say Merry Christmas and thanks for having us.' I brush damp palms on my sleeveless silk pant-suit, one leg sporting an iridescent dragonfly.

'We prefer to donate to charity,' Yvette says. 'This year, we decided that there's something a little … vulgar about gifting ourselves when we have so much to be thankful for. Remember, Emerald? I asked you to tell Marc.'

We both know that she has done nothing of the sort and I have to engage my full protective shell to deflect the fragments of the landmine. It's not easy, but I manage.

'What's Christmas without presents?' I smile, knowing I must not do anything that will force Marc to take sides. In that battle, there would ultimately be no winners.

'A Scotsman never looks a gift horse in the mouth,' Gordon responds, raising a laugh. 'Where's mine?'

It's near the top of the pile so I hand it to him. It's a fishing magazine with a two-year subscription. He looks delighted. Yvette looks appalled. I already know she will not approve. There are four approved McAllister sports: sailing, golf, tennis and horse-riding. Even talk of rugby is greeted with a sniff, though Marc played for the state under-nineteens.

Sylvie's family arrive during the unwrapping and her daughter Adele immediately demands her gift—a large inflatable pink flip-flop for the pool. Her father Brand, a rather pale and insipid man—I have to remember not to address him as Bland—immediately sets to work blowing the thing up. His face quickly turns red, but he perseveres and when he hands the thing to his daughter, I can see the adoration on his face. For that, and because I suspect it takes fortitude to make it as a McAllister-by-marriage, I soften towards him.

By that time, the party is underway and, despite Yvette's invitation to move to the deck, we stand in the foyer, drinking our champagne and laughing over the gifts. The framed photo for Yvette is in a separate bag for fragile items. She unwraps it, the look on her face making it clear she is expecting the worst.

'A photo … how thought … oh no, not this terrible one! Darling, we have so many gorgeous photos of our children, why would you pick this one?' She looks genuinely bewildered.

Léo takes it from her unresisting hand and shows it to Marc. They both burst into laughter.

'Mum was always worried people might think the Hills hoist was ours,' Léo says. 'She tried to destroy every copy of it.'

'That's not true, Léo. I just feel that there are so many charming photos of the three of you taken by professionals.' Gordon flushes, and I realise it must have been his finger on the camera button that day.

One of those childhood photos Yvette does approve of is prominently displayed on the drawing room mantel. In it, Marc and

Sylvie stand stiffly behind Léo, as he gamely attempts to school his mischievous, little-boy grin into a polite smile.

For a second, I feel fury rising and I almost say something but the faint crease in Marc's brow deflates my irritation. And as reason returns, it occurs to me that Yvette is a woman afraid of her own children, and at the limits of her ability to control them. Sad. I reach for Marc's hand and squeeze it, receiving a quizzical smile.

'What's that?' Adele points her little finger at the bag. There is one more gift.

'It's for Marc.'

He looks at me in surprise. We exchanged gifts last night. I managed to secure tickets to Australia's rugby test against New Zealand in Wellington later in the year for Marc, Will and James. He bought me a small original painting by John Olsen of a king-fisher diving. I have never paid much attention to art but there is something about this painting that I love, and I have propped it on the table just inside the door to our apartment. I know now one of Olsen's bigger works is in the art gallery and have made plans to meet Claire there in the New Year.

'Actually, it's for us.'

'It's socks,' suggests Sylvie.

'No, definitely a penguin,' Léo says. Clearly this is a family ritual.

'Wrong, all of you. It's a fridge,' Gordon deadpans as Marc unwraps the box.

Adele looks doubtful. 'I think it's too small to be a fridge, Poppy.'

'Grandad,' Yvette corrects the toddler but her eyes are on me. 'Or Grandpère. We don't say Poppy in this family, darling.'

By now Marc holds the plain shoebox in his hands, curiosity etched on his face as the exterior gives no hint of what it contains.

Then he lifts the lid to find a pair of overalls, a paintbrush and a handful of colour chips.

Understanding dawns and he nods, holding up the paint chips—parchment, sea-green and brilliant white. An eyebrow edges upwards. 'The beach shack?'

'You would do better to knock it down and start from scratch,' Yvette begins. 'I can recommend an architect and interior designer. Anyway, Marc is too busy and important for … manual labour.'

Marc is lifting up the overalls, clearly too small for him. 'I don't think I'm the intended painter.'

'That would be me,' I confirm.

'Thanks, gorgeous girl,' he says, drawing me into a hug. 'It's a great present.'

Yes, it is—and clever, because it means I will begin the New Year with a new sense of purpose.

But as I give myself a metaphorical pat on the back for my morning's work, I catch Yvette's eye over Marc's shoulder. Her fine-boned face is a smiling mask but her dark eyes are narrowed in warning, and I wonder if my cleverness has in fact been a monumental act of stupidity. Her attempt to undermine me has failed and she has learned not to underestimate me, which means she will be better prepared next time.

Eight

Present day

Throughout the evening, the phone rings so faintly that in the end I do not know if I am actually hearing a real sound or the imprint of it on my memory.

Even with the light of the long tapered candles from the drawing room lit on the gas stove-top, I know it would be a hopeless quest to try and find it. I decide to wait until dawn to mount a search. After eating my soup, I take the candles to the living room and place them on the mantelpiece where they belong. As soon as I have changed into my pyjamas, I blow them out.

It is a very long night and not only because of the echo of the ring tone. Even curled into a small ball, I am cold. I do not think I will be able to sleep at all but I must do because, when I wake, it is light, the torrent has stopped and the sky through the shutters is a rain-washed blue.

Pushing back the covers, I go to the light switch. The power is back on. I listen but I can no longer hear my mobile. Now, in the light of day, I curse myself for not paying more attention to where the ringtone had come from. Upstairs definitely, which is

73

odd. I do not remember having been upstairs around the time it went missing.

Nevertheless, I climb the stairs in socked feet. At the top I hesitate, tucking my loose hair behind my ear as I debate where to try first.

As I had been at the door to the master bedroom at the moment the lights went out, I return there. The room is as it was then, except less gloomy. Ignoring the locked room, I head for the little balcony where I look for my phone though I know it cannot be there, and note the blustery wind. The bed linen will air well on the old washing line behind the shed.

Back on the landing, I open the large armoire, not expecting to find my mobile. I am right. There is, however, a quantity of dated but good quality bed linen. It feels and smells of the dampness that seeps into every nook and cranny of the house, but I take a pile of it, with the intention of airing it.

Quick checks of the other rooms and bathroom reveal no signs of my phone, which does not surprise me since I haven't been in them since my first exploration of the house, the day after my arrival. I hurry downstairs with my hoard, dump two blankets in the washing machine and select the wool cycle, hoping they will not end up the size of pillowcases.

After my breakfast muesli, I take my coffee and pad through the ground-floor rooms again, in case I have missed the phone on earlier searches, but it remains absent and I cannot think of any-where I have been but not yet looked. It is exasperating. I know those calls last night must have been Marc, out of patience and prepared to wait no longer for me to contact him. Even though it is not my fault, I feel to blame and decide I must get in touch with him, which means finding a payphone.

I am strangely reluctant to leave the house, finding any num-ber of reasons to delay the expedition. Twice, I change clothes, discarding first the bronze tunic over leggings and then jeans and a shirt. Eventually, I opt for a miniskirt and tights with long boots. Over a long-sleeve tee, I wear a knitted poncho the colour of heather for warmth. As I brush my hair in the powder-room mirror, I see that its chestnut-red lights are brighter. My face has natural colour, too, and the shadows beneath my eyes have disappeared.

As the washing machine has finished its cycle by the time I am ready, I decide it does not make sense to waste the billowy wind. I put on another wash, and take the blankets out to the line. They smell fresh and have not shrunk noticeably, and when I peg them out, they flap so enthusiastically that I stand and watch for a while.

In this small patch of garden, I am starting to make a mark with the blankets waving on the line, and the rescued hydrangeas now basking in the weak sunshine. Though time is ticking on, I find the new hose and, skirting the worst of the mud, attach it to the tap. Though it moans and shudders, it delivers a jet of water. I drench the hydrangeas, scatter some fertiliser and water them once more.

By this time, the sun is about as high as it will get at this time of year. I know that makes it around noon and that therefore the sun must be pretty much at north. Come the summer, the hydrangeas will be in full sun for a good part of the day.

I am pretty sure Harry High-pants had said they needed part shade, which means these plants will need to be moved before spring. Was he doling out general advice? He did not strike me as having green fingers. Certainly the paltry collection of dusty indoor plants with their curled labels did not suggest a man with a passion for plants, and yet his advice had been spoken with the confidence of someone who knew what he was talking about.

As I would rather not bump into anyone I know in Lammermoor, I drive for forty-five minutes in the other direction, making my way to a popular tourist town on the coast. Though quiet at this time of year, its population is large enough that I attract little attention.

Until now, I have not noticed the scarcity of public phones. They are an endangered species. I finally find a pair in a small shopping mall but one has been vandalised, and the other has a couple of people waiting. In any case, it is too public for the conversation that is likely to result between Marc and me. I could buy a cheap mobile, but it seems pointless as mine will turn up any day. In the end, I find an internet café and send an email to his business address, anticipating that he will be in the office at this time of day.

Marc, I am sorry not to have called. I misplaced my phone a couple of days ago and have been looking for it ever since. I know that you will have tried to reach me and worried when I did not respond. I am well, better than I would have imagined a few weeks ago. Believe it or not, I have been gardening! Yes, it's true. Try not to work too hard and take some time out with the boys.

It is winter, I think or close to. I have lost track of the days and weeks. The rugby season is in full swing. I picture Marc, Will and James—beers in hand, rowdy and singing off-key—at a game. Occasionally, I have been with them, enjoying the atmosphere and sense of camaraderie, but mostly when they go it is for a boys' night out from which he staggers in some time around midnight, three sheets to the wind, either full of bonhomie or muttering about one-eyed refs. I smile at the thought.

When you go this week, take the bears we bought for them. They will like the bears. Thank you. Em x

He will know what I mean as he goes to see them at least once a week. I hope he will find the bears and that Sylvie has not removed all traces of the nursery as she suggested. I am not even sure they are bears with their goggle eyes, pot bellies and odd colouring—one purple, the other a mustard-yellow. They may be dogs or aliens or alien-dogs. But they made us laugh when we spotted them in a small shop in a country town that advertised one-of-a-kind toys. They were right about that.

For the next hour, I wait, figuring that Marc is probably in a meeting and will respond as soon as he returns to his office or checks his phone. But no new messages appear in my inbox and most of the older ones seem to be from mailing lists for businesses and products that I have no interest in.

One, though, catches my eye—from a design website I signed up to only because Claire wrote a guest blog last year. Usually, I just skim-read the monthly blog or trash it without reading at all, but right now I have nothing better to do and no wish to dwell on Marc's silence, so I read it and find it surprisingly interesting. The subject is the growing movement against mass-market consumerism, and the rise of cottage industries. *Small Poppies* is the name of the website and it features individuals and mini businesses in the areas of produce, textiles and design, for the most part, with the focus on hand-grown or made, quality and unique products.

I can see why Claire likes the site. She worked as a junior designer for a department-store label until two years ago, but feeling like a small cog in a gargantuan machine, she went solo. Her one-off designs have a vintage feel, often using fabric recycled from older pieces, and she now has a small but growing band of loyal customers, but it's been hard work.

She still has the market stall in Paddington, and a couple of edgy boutiques stock a few items. But her main sales are via the website she set up about a year ago, with Brendan as photographer and me as model. Her line of old-fashioned swimsuits cut from vintage paisleys and checks received particular attention, including a small piece in *Harper's Bazaar*. Even Sylvie, who does not trust anything she can't find in David Jones, was at one point debating about ordering one—until Yvette convinced her they looked as if they'd been cut from old curtains.

What is most interesting about the latest blog is the assertion that the movement has nothing to do with designer labels and thousand-dollar price tickets. It is about applying a less-is-more principle to homes and lives as an antidote to the throwaway retail culture that has taken hold.

My two hours are almost up and I dash off a quick, appreciative response to the website, without giving my name. Then I pull on my poncho and return to the car, still thinking about the blog. Something in it continues to resonate with me, something I can't quite put my finger on. My brain and fingers are almost itching with creativity. Quite what I am supposed to apply them to, I am not sure, but for the first time in a very long time, I wish I could talk to someone about it.

❦ ❦ ❦

January last year ...

'I got them to make up a darker version of the sea-green and it's perfect.' I am prattling away to Mark as I scrub at my face, which seems to bear traces of all the paint colours I used today. Worse, several clumps of hair are stuck together with the gloss white I've used on the doors. I will need to wash my hair before we head out to dinner.

'And the wicker pendant lampshades I found at that auction, you know the ones, they're perfect for over the breakfast bar.'

He is a little distracted but that is usual when he first gets home, before he has shed his wheeler-dealer skin. I am still alert to his moods, though they are rarely extreme, but as we have survived six weeks of marriage, I am no longer anxious that he has imme-diate divorce plans.

In fact, it is he who is particularly anxious to celebrate our six-week anniversary. I am more of the opinion that this is far too soon to claim any sort of success in the marriage stakes. You need to survive a bankruptcy or life-threatening car accident first, surely—some sort of test. My mind flicks to Yvette's intermittently malignant presence, but decide that she is just finding it hard to adjust to her firstborn being taken from her by a woman wicked enough to recently pose wearing only a strawberry.

It's not as bad as it sounds. The ad was for a group of organic farmers who are trying to play hardball with the big supermarket chains. You don't see my face, which is a small blessing in Marc's mother's opinion; but everyone knows it's me, which is not. After it went viral, the 'Eat me!' campaign even attracted the attention of the mass media, but its success is my failure in her eyes.

'You have a position now,' she lectured me last week. 'You are a McAllister and we don't do this sort of thing.'

'Actually I'm not,' I tell her. 'I'm a Reed and I do all sorts of things McAllisters wouldn't approve of.' This is the most direct challenge I have made, but she is a guest on our balcony, sipping our champagne, and I will not be lectured to here.

'Marc?' She looks to him for support, and the moment kind of freezes as everyone waits to see which way he will jump. I have resolved not to feel betrayed if he takes her side.

With a serious look on his face, he nods. 'They're doing bananas next and I can't tell you how worried I am about that!'

Gordon snorts, Sylvie coughs and turns bright red, while Léo spits his drink over everyone. Yvette is mystified at first—and quickly mortified.

I jump in and tell her that there are no bananas, only the possibility of something with artichokes later in the year if they have the money.

I thought it had blown over, but maybe he is worried about it. Or perhaps he is worried about the darker sea-green. Paint colour is so difficult to get right. More likely, though, he is mulling over something that happened at work.

Although the financial markets seem a big yawn, I do try to read the business pages and watch the business news so that we can occasionally have meaningful conversations about his work.

'Is the stock market down?' I ask, knowing that this is the thing most likely to weigh on money managers; that and government meddling.

'Hmm? No, slightly up today. Still the holidays so not much action.'

Vowing I will probe more at dinner if I can do so without dropping a clanger, I drop my towel and get into the shower. I shampoo and scrub at my hair until there is so much lather piled up on my head that I resemble an albino Marge Simpson.

About to rinse off, I turn to find my exit blocked by a very large, very naked male.

'Oh, um.' Desire suddenly swamps me like a tidal wave. The mundane aspects of living together—garbage nights, hangover mornings and a difficult mother-in-law—have not yet tempered our ardour. When I am prepared for his advances, I affect a cool flirtatiousness designed to conceal his effect on me. When I am not, I am quickly out of my depth.

I try to brush past him, trying to feign nonchalance when there is nothing casual about what burns between us.

'Not so fast, gorgeous girl.' His hand loops loosely around my wrist. 'Your hair's still soapy. Lean your head forward and I'll rinse it.'

'I can do it,' I mutter, wondering why these moments of every-day intimacy are so difficult. I stick my head back under the spray before my eyes are closed, with the obvious result.

'Ouch! Damn it.' Eye stinging, I blink myopically at him and wave my hand around trying to splash water on my face.

'Stand still.' One of his hands holds my head steady while the other dabs at my eye with a face cloth. Within seconds, the soap is gone. He flings the cloth aside, and now both hands are cupping my face. His eyes are nearly black with want but all I can think of is that I look like a vampire with stringy hair.

Inwardly, I curse. I should have been home, showered and dressed in the strapless pale green dress I intend to wear before he returned from work, but I'd wanted to finish the skirting board at the beach shack. 'We need to leave in five,' I say. 'You said we had a booking.'

'Em,' he says, almost growling my name. That intense sexuality of his is so focused, I feel almost faint.

'Y … yes.' I am stuttering, incoherent, aroused. How can he cut so easily through defences I've spent a lifetime erecting?

'You're shaking. Are you cold?' He turns the tap to lift the temperature. Warmth is the last thing I need. I feel feverish already.

I make a last-ditch attempt to turn the mood from carnal to flirtatious. 'So … where are we having dinner? Somewhere expensive?' The gold-digger persona is wearing thin, and he does not take the bait.

'Hetty's.'

It's our local bistro—small, dark and private. As well as a wedding anniversary celebration, it's also a pre-birthday thing, just us, as Marc will be overseas for his actual birthday—his thirty-second. His mother is planning something for his return.

He moves closer until we are skin to skin. His breath smells of toothpaste. My insides turn to liquid.

Desperately, I close my eyes. 'Do you know what you want for your birthday?' I manage.

There is a pause. Eventually, I open my eyes to find his sexual urgency overlaid with something else.

'Yes,' he says at last.

'What?'

He shakes his head, shifting back and giving both of us some space. 'I didn't plan to raise it this way. I thought we could talk about it over dinner.'

'Talk about what?' He is usually very direct in expressing his desires. I know he is probably more experienced sexually than I am, but there has been no sign of anything kinky so far. 'Do you want a threesome?' I blurt.

I am not sure where it comes from, only that it is out there and Marc has dropped his hands from me. He looks more startled than I have ever seen, and then he is staggering back against the shower tiles, hands on naked hips, howling with laughter.

Scowling at his mirth and feeling foolish, I stomp out of the shower, grabbing a towel on my way to the bathroom door. I have my hand on the door handle when he says words that stop me in my tracks.

'Em, I want a baby.'

Nine

Present day, evening

Although I rush through the rest of my errands, it is late in the day by the time I return home. Scooping my bags from the front seat, I jog windblown up the steps through the door and am immediately enveloped by its dark familiarity.

Inside, I dump the bags on the hall floor. Right now, I would love a glass of red wine but I have remembered the blankets on the line. They must come in before they are damp again so I unlock the kitchen door, switch on the outdoor light and scoop them up. They smell of fresh air. As I turn to walk inside, I notice the woodpile by the shed. When I have dumped the blankets in the kitchen, I return for three chunks of wood, the driest I can find.

Anyone who has tried to light a fire for the first time will know that it is not as easy as you might think. After several false starts, the motoring pages of the newspaper I bought today have created enough of a blaze to catch the wood alight. I watch it carefully for a few minutes until I am sure it will not expire, and drape the blankets over a chair to warm, before I go to pour my wine and put my takeaway curry into the oven to heat up.

When I have everything I need, I take my boots off and curl in front of the fire half hypnotised by the flames, sipping my wine and enjoying the surprisingly good food. Even when the last of the light disappears, I do not turn on the lamp, not for a long time. I am comfortably drowsy, but not yet ready to leave this cosy room.

Eventually, I stir and reach for the lamp and *Jane Eyre* next to it, but the book is not where I thought it was. I must have put it away or taken it into the living room with the idea of reading it in bed.

Getting up, I go to the bookshelves and there it is, slotted in neatly where I got it from. I must have put it back. As I pull it out, I see that there is another book that has been pushed back out of sight. I reach in and pull out a dated edition of a military encyclopedia. From the scuff marks and dirty fingerprints, it has been read and re-read many times. In my hands, it opens to the fly leaf, which contains one of those old-fashioned book plates.

The writing is fussy and difficult to read, the ink faded, and I return to the chair and the lamp to study it but eventually I think I have worked it out.

For Louis on your 15th birthday.

Wondering what kind of teenager would be interested in a book like this, I shove it back into the bookshelf and find the turned corner in *Jane Eyre*. Within moments, the gothic mystery sweeps me up and away.

Sometime later, a sudden sound awakes me and I realise I have fallen asleep in front of the fire. It is almost out, but for a deep amber glow from its heart. My eyes fly around the room, seeking out potential threats. A sudden pop from the disintegrated logs makes me jump and I realise this is what has awoken me. I am starting to feel cold, so I gather up the remains of my meal and shuffle into the kitchen. When I return, I pull the bronze guard in front of the fire to prevent embers from spilling out onto the thick rug.

Taking Jane and the warm blankets with me, I cross the hall to the living room and the chaise, noticing as I go the bags dumped in the hallway. As I see them, anticipation curls inside me. Tomorrow, I will start to map out my plan.

☙ ☙ ☙

January last year ...

Much of my sense of satisfaction about the way the beach shack is shaping up has evaporated in the face of Marc's pronouncement.

We sit in Hetty's—me in my mint-green dress, he in indigo jeans and a blue shirt with the sleeves rolled up to show off the forearms that make Brendan swoon. We are both trying to act normal and have everyone fooled except ourselves. The lights are low, and in the window I can make out our reflection. We look like the It Couple that one gossip rag has dubbed us. Surreptitious glances are flicked our way by other diners who probably wonder why they can't have it all too while, at the same time, being glad they have no profile to live up to.

Marc shows no awareness. He has commanded attention and admiration from the moment he was born, and simply accepts it as the norm.

We have ordered our favourite dishes and Marc is trying to do his pork belly justice. I move my fork from side to side without making a noticeable difference to the delicate duck pancakes on my plate.

I simply cannot comprehend why he has said such a thing when we have been married just weeks and are still trying to make sense of it. Or at least, I am. Perhaps to him it is just the natural next step in his grand plan, or a strategy to win over his mother. Maybe there is pressure on McAllisters to produce heirs as soon as practicable, to continue the aristocratic bloodlines, so to speak.

'Don't overthink it,' he advises, looking at me. 'I'm just telling you what I want and asking you to consider it. It's not a foregone conclusion.'

'Oh, well that's decent of you,' I mutter.

'I'm going to be thirty-two, Em,' he points out. 'I want a family.'

But you have a family, I nearly protest. *You have me! Am I not enough?*

Clearly not.

'And who is going to care for this progeny?' I ask. 'Will you be the one to deal with the drool and vomit and worse? Get up in the night to do whatever it is babies need done at antisocial hours? Give up your career?' I keep my voice low and a smile on my face so anyone looking at us would think we are deep in intimate conversation, not having our first married row.

'I expect we'll both have to make changes,' he says carefully, not rising to my bait, for we both know that my career is part-time at best. While refurbishing the beach shack has given me some purpose, and I have found it surprisingly absorbing and satisfying to give it new life, it has also allowed me to put off thinking about what I am going to do longer-term, that doesn't involve fruit and vegetables.

Apart from a few ad-hoc modelling commitments, my diary for the next few months is scarily empty. Most of that is my fault; since Brendan's show, I have had several offers of work but, because of Marc, I have been more choosy than perhaps I can afford. At the moment, our lifestyle is funded almost completely by Marc and, despite my gold-digger quips, I feel uneasy about the state of play. Marc has never given the slightest hint that he resents this, or that he expects to be the sole decision-maker because of it, but there is an inherent imbalance of power.

'Tell me more about the shack,' Marc says, dismounting just as I am getting on my high horse. It is typical of him, this ability to parlay a treaty before things can escalate to all-out warfare. We may have known each other only eight months or so but I have seen him in action enough times with business colleagues and his family to recognise why he is so successful at managing both.

'I'm letting you change the subject only because you're going away and it's your birthday,' I tell him, just to make him aware I'm wise to his tricks.

He grins and tops up our wine. 'Are you sure you can't show me a photo?' I have forbidden him to go to the shack before it is finished—hopefully when he returns from overseas.

'Very sure.' I have deliberately not taken photos in case he is tempted to check my phone, even though to do so would probably be against some code of honour I don't share. 'You'll have to wait.' I cock my head to one side. 'It will be a surprise … and give you an incentive to get back as soon as you can.'

He is only away for ten days in Europe and the States but the looming separation is unsettling both of us.

'Em.' He takes my hand. 'I already have all the incentive I need.'

❧   ❧   ❧

Present day, morning

Bright-eyed and bushy-tailed does not begin to describe it. After a night undisturbed by phantom phone calls or wild winds—and tucked warmly under fresh blankets—I feel full of energy when I wake. It is not the restless, directionless energy of recent days. I have some anchor points now that my day can pivot around.

There are clean sheets to hang out, and more bedding to wash. The windows need cleaning, too, the winds having enveloped them in a thin grey shroud. I start with the kitchen and the impact is immediate. What I had thought a gloomy room is actually bright and airy, especially in the mid-morning sun. For good measure, I scrub all the benches and the sink, and wipe down the walls and pantry.

Tucked away in two low cupboards, I find a twelve-piece set of bone china with a white crackled glaze and green trim. It is too good to be tucked away and I pile it onto open shelves. Old copper pots now gleam as they hang from the ceiling rack, adding further warmth, and I have cut some sprigs of rosemary and lavender for scent. There are two new linen drying cloths too, found hiding under piles of tablecloths and serviettes, hanging neatly near the sink.

I consider whether to paint the kitchen. What I suspect was originally a warm yellow is turning brown. A soft white or cream would be a distinct improvement. It wouldn't take long to paint but I do not know if I will be staying long enough to justify it.

By the time I make it back outside, it is late morning and the sheets are dry. I bring them in, hang out the next load and choose some logs for the evening to dry by the hearth. The old ashes from last night, I scrape into the newspaper pages that I won't read. I put aside the news and business pages to tackle over lunch, take the ashes to the bin and spend the next two hours in the garden clearing the herb beds of weeds. I have also used the spade to re-establish the edges of the plot where the line between garden and lawn had become blurred. At the end of it, I am feeling pleasantly fatigued, but keen to get inside to begin the project that has been fermenting in my head since yesterday.

Trying to find a good warm, woollen scarf yesterday in the mall had proved impossible. Everything was of some man-made fabric that looks cheap now and will be abysmal after one wash. Walking from store to store, I couldn't help notice the bland uniformity of everything. Nothing caught my eye because it dared to be different. I know I am lucky that my work—particularly with Claire—gives me access to one-of-a-kind pieces that most people with my budget could never aspire to. I supplement it with occasional finds at vintage and charity stores, and Claire and I used to haunt the Saturday markets. Marc also surprises me with the occasional piece.

My knack, though, is being able to see beyond today's fashion to a timeless style I've made my own. I know instinctively what works together, how to curate a wardrobe, what to recycle and—importantly—pieces I like but cannot find a use for right now I will save as the basis for a new look in the future. Ignore anyone who tells you to discard anything you have not worn in twelve months. If you love it, leave it—that's my advice. Its use may well become apparent over time.

More than an hour of searching yesterday turned up precisely nothing until I happened to venture beyond the mall and main shopping strip along a side street on the shabby side of town. I think it was determination that my quest not be in vain that brought me to the narrow second-hand clothing store called, uninspiringly, Vintage Rose. Inside was a treasure trove of the awful and the awesome, including collectors' items from as far back as the 1920s. It took me only fifteen minutes to fill three bags with scarves, hats, jackets, bolts of fabric and balls of wool.

Now, as the sun drops low on the horizon, I pour everything out onto the long table in the oppressive dining room that I've barely ventured into and stalk around it, pondering as I drink a mug of pumpkin soup. After dumping the empty mug in the kitchen, I go upstairs to the armoire, which yields dozens of old padded hangers. Downstairs again, I grab my own bag of clothes, and return to the dining room

For the next two hours, I mix and match, trying every combi-nation of old and new that I believe has potential, and narrowing it down to the nine strongest. My favourites are an exquisite silk slip from my own wardrobe paired with a mohair cardigan from the shopping expedition, still with its original price tag on, and a black embroidered cape from the shop teamed with singlet and skinny indigo jeans. With the ensembles finalised, I arrange them on hangers and play with hanging them around the house—from the bannister, against a window, from the armoire—in an attempt to find the most evocative backdrops.

I wish desperately for my phone to record them—and think wistfully of Marc's old SLR camera. But, feeling inspired by my creations, I sit and write notes on each outfit, why it works and my feelings when I look at it. Fired up, I then draft ideas for a post about creating an individual wardrobe on a budget, thinking I will submit it to the *Small Poppies* website when I get a chance. I'm still not certain where the career is in all this, but I like the idea of helping women to dress sustainably and uniquely without spending a fortune.

Exhausted but elated, I suddenly realise that it is after eleven. It is time to pack up for the evening. I have resigned myself to the fact that I will need a new phone in order to be able to do anything, and that this will require another shopping expedition sometime soon.

Leaving the outfits where they hang like shrouds in the dark, I get ready for bed. In the bathroom mirror, my reflected face has a flush to it, my eyes a sparkle. I have been here more than a month, and time is slowly doing its job. Something about this house also has healing properties. Day by day, I can feel it— almost like a cushion, adjusting around me, protecting me from the sharp edges of what lies beneath, as I learn to function nor-mally again.

I pad slowly to bed hoping that tomorrow is as good as today has been. As I walk in the door of my makeshift bedroom, I get the sense of someone close by. Even at the moment I feel it, I do not know that I could accurately describe it—a touch of static in the air, perhaps, or the whisper of a human breath. There is nothing in the slightest way malevolent about it, but I quickly switch on the light and glance around and behind. Of course, no one is there.

But sitting on the top of the waffle-weave blanket is my phone, the battery dead.

Ten

March last year ...

Self-preservation can convince even rational human beings to do the most ridiculous things. I know many of my own shortcomings—self-absorption, selfishness and superficiality probably top the list, but you probably have worse to say about me by now. Vacuous, bitchy and insecure, perhaps? No doubt, though, we would agree that I would make the very worst type of parent. Children surely need parents with qualities the precise opposite of these to thrive.

Even knowing all of this, I have stopped taking my birth control pills because I have told myself that a child is the price I must pay for Marc. I knew there would be one, of course. You can't plunge into marriage with someone you have known only a few short months and not discover down the track that there is a cost.

Neither of us raised the topic of children prior to our marriage; it wasn't even on my radar. If I had considered it, I probably would have assumed Marc would want a child at some unspecified point in the future, perhaps in two or three years' time. It was a major oversight. Now I know him and his family better, I am starting to understand that the whole lineage thing is a big deal for the

McAllisters. I suppose when you are successful, you are keen to see it continued.

Me? I can imagine nothing more stifling than a child, nothing more certain to demand attention I don't have to give.

I've tried to allude to this without spelling it out to Marc that he has chosen a lemon if it is child rearing he is after. He should be smart enough to work it out for himself, but about this one thing he seems to be in denial. He is adamant about wanting a child with me, even if he has to wait until I am ready. Doubtless, it will be a pretty thing, especially its ears. I only hope that it has his head for numbers and not mine; his easy charm and not my discomfort in my own skin.

The thing I do have—apart from a certain style—is time. The beach shack has been finished for five weeks and I am back to twiddling my thumbs, or at least working sporadically on short-term projects that could easily make way to manage a squalling newborn. Is this why he has chosen me? Because I do not have a proper career?

For weeks, I find myself analysing every little thing he says to try and uncover his real motive. In the end, though, I decide all the obsessing is irrelevant. The only thing I need know is what the hell am I going to do about it?

Autumn seems endless and balmy, and now that the beach shack is finished, we spend virtually every weekend up here. Marc says he always knew it would be a triumph; I am not so sure of that. It is simple and uncluttered, without being too uncomfortably minimal. Structurally, little has changed bar a deeper verandah; it remains the unassuming weekender he bought shortly before we met. Our bedroom is upstairs in the eaves, small and quiet and cosy, with a tiny bathroom off it. The downstairs is almost all living area, with a kitchen along one wall, and adjacent dining and sitting areas sharing both the cosy winter fireplace and the glass doors that lead to the verandah and the beach.

The natural tones and fabrics bring out the best in it without giving it airs and graces, and any tension between us seems to dissolve the moment we park under the old fig tree outside.

I know the source of my tension but the cause of Marc's eludes me. The subject of our prenup has not been discussed since before the wedding but I think it may continue to dog him because he is often distracted these days. Or perhaps, like me, he is consumed by thoughts of a potential pregnancy? Either way, suspecting I may be the source of his preoccupation spurs me to lead him up to the attic bedroom the moment we arrive, where I knead his shoulders until he groans. Sometimes, one thing leads to another that relaxes both of us still further.

Apart from making love, there is little excitement. We sit on the verandah over breakfast and the papers, wander down to the beach when we feel like a swim, people-watch from one of the local cafés. At some point in the late afternoon, one of us will find sufficient energy to clatter around in the small kitchen, usually Marc wearing an apron that sports an upright finger and the words *Bugger off, Chef!* I think he bought it for his father to wear while barbecuing, but Yvette won't have it in the house.

Sometimes while we are at the shack I notice Marc casting me a glance from the corner of his eye as if unsure whether I am happy. The fact that I am—with the exception of the pregnancy issue—surprises even me. Certainly, a low-key weekend at the beach is not the kind of weekend I enjoyed before meeting him. Then, I would spend my days at bars—assuming someone else was picking up the bill, of course—or at opening events, sleeping in the following day, then shopping and dancing until dawn. In short, I was the ultimate party girl. Even I cannot quite believe how content I am just to be.

The size of the shack discourages visitors, although Sylvie and her family have been for the day, and Léo has slept overnight on the sofa a couple of times. Yvette and Gordon came for lunch one Sunday, and I have to say she was well-behaved for her, merely suggesting that a few family 'treasures' loaned from their Vaucluse home might save the beach shack from blandness. As yet, we haven't taken her up on her offer.

It has been around six weeks since I stopped taking the pill, and nothing has happened yet. I felt Marc's eyes keenly on me when my period was due two weeks ago, and his disappointment when his seed failed to take. I breathed a sigh of relief, though.

My renovation of the beach shack did not miss the attention of the magazine editors. We turned down two offers by magazines to do a photo shoot, but we could not prevent a paparazzo from showing up. Fortunately, we were not in residence at the time. The photos of the closed shutters and the hot yellow pigface on the verandah have done some good, however.

Since then, I have done a style consultation for a friend of Claire's who has bought her first apartment and seems to have taken my suggestions on board with some enthusiasm and success. Given my fortunate circumstances, I felt I couldn't charge a fee, but now Gordon, of all people, has referred me to someone with deep pockets who will be prepared to pay for the privilege of my style wisdom.

There has been a smattering of modelling jobs, too, enough to keep me from feeling like an utter freeloader. But nothing has really gelled yet. All around me, people who once were happy to drift—opening themselves to opportunity, as they called it—seem to be discovering their niche. Mine, though, remains maddeningly elusive. One thing I do know is that I must find my life before I bring another person into it.

ð   ð   ð

Present day, night

I don't know what to make of my phone's return. There is nothing surreptitious about it. The mobile has been left where I would be sure to see it, almost like an offering. I grab it and rush from the room. The battery is so flat that it needs to be charged up before I can do anything with it, and once it has enough juice to restore the usual display, I realise my twenty-sixth birthday has been and gone without me noticing.

How can my phone disappear and reappear this way? It's just not possible, unless …

As I stand in the kitchen, phone in hand, a shiver ripples through me at the implications. With so many of the house's nooks and crannies unexplored, maybe it is not impossible that I am not alone. Perhaps my mind was not playing tricks a few minutes ago when I sensed a presence nearby.

The thought is enough to put all of my senses on high alert. Every shadow holds a threat; every tiny sound screams terror. My heart beats like a drum and I'm so paralysed with fear that if a knife-wielding stranger suddenly materialised in the kitchen doorway, I don't think I could run to save myself.

When my phone is partially recharged, I unplug it and steel myself finally to re-enter the drawing room. My hand shakes on the handle. But the room is as I last saw it; nothing has been moved or removed.

In bed, I leave the light on and remain stiffly on guard, fingers curled tight around the sheet, until tiredness begins to overtake me. Even then, the only thing that eases my mind is to think of the house as a hotel. You don't know every other guest in a hotel, do you? It does not mean they harbour ill intentions towards other guests.

It takes a while to get to sleep, despite my fatigue, yet oddly, I have another dreamless, restful night. While still on the chaise staring at the ceiling the following morning, I force myself to acknowledge there must be an attic level to Lammermoor House. When I picture the house in my mind's eye, I can see the little pointed windows right under the roof. What I haven't seen is access to the attic.

If I am not alone—and I am only acknowledging the possibility—whoever I am sharing the house with could have been living up there since before I moved in. The only other possible hiding place is the locked room but it's not feasible for them to have been closeted in there all this time, is it? I surely would have seen them come and go.

In the cool light of day, it is easier to admit that perhaps I have sensed someone from time to time. Perhaps it is not so surprising that they might have wanted to observe the person invading their territory. In fact, I might consider myself lucky that they have not apparently objected to my presence and have only availed themselves of my phone for a short period. This suggests to me that they do not wish me ill. Once I have had the thought, it feels suddenly right. Whether it is logical or not I cannot be entirely sure, but I believe I am in no danger.

But who am I sharing the house with? Why are they here?

As I stand under the shower washing my hair, I consider how I feel about the house. It has been my sanctuary. Would that continue once I make the acquaintance of my housemate, and they make mine? Somehow, I don't think so. At the moment, we can still maintain some pretence of being alone. If the status quo changed, one of us—or even both—might feel obliged to leave.

Certainly, a change to our current arrangement is not something to be approached lightly. Panic pinches at my gut as I envisage having to leave Lammermoor House. Although I feel stronger, the thought of slinking back to Sydney or having to find a new home fills me with disquiet. I am not yet ready to leave this comfortable womb. Equally, I am loathe to precipitate another's departure. There is something comforting about the arrangement, about an unseen companion who asks nothing of me.

Dressed in a brushed cotton shirtdress and tights, I go into the kitchen to make pancakes, feeling ravenous. I know I must phone Marc as soon as possible and I try to anticipate the conversation in my head, but it is impossible. I know it will not go the way I want it to, even though I have no clear idea of what that is.

When my belly is filled with pancake, banana and Greek yogurt, I can put it off no longer. It is past nine, and Marc will have been in the office for an hour, responding to emails and preparing for the day's meetings. I think of him, reading glasses on and a faint frown between his brows, and steel myself for the confrontation. To prepare, I finally scroll through the text messages on my phone. There are several, mostly from Brendan, Claire and a few friends who have been avoiding me since … well, before I left Sydney. I ignore them and check my emails.

To my surprise, there is just one from Marc in response to the one I sent days ago: *Please call me.* There is no endearment, which may indicate anger or frustration.

I feel momentarily light-headed, fearing something terrible has happened, but quickly discount it. Claire or Brendan or one of the rugby boys would have alerted me. It occurs to me that a mystery housemate snooping through my phone might have deleted some calls, texts or emails. The thought makes me queasy but when I look more closely at my text and call history, it does not appear to be the case. Neither do they seem to have initiated calls or texts of their own. The web browser, though, suggests an interest in French royalty. It surprises me until I realise it was probably me browsing European fashion.

In any case, all I can think of is Marc's silence. The devil in my head taunts me with the thought that he has lost patience with me, but I push it aside. Yesterday's paper lies unread on the table, and I pull it across to me, flicking the pages to find the finance section. I have no idea what the stock market and money markets have been—

My hand stills in the action of turning the social page. A photo of Marc and a former girlfriend, Daisy Davis, who is known as Double D for more than one reason, hogs the centre of the page. Her breast is snuggled very close to Marc's side and to be fair he looks less than delighted by it.

This may explain the relative silence. Feeling not so intimidated, I call his number and he answers almost immediately.

'Em. You found your phone.'

'Yes.'

'I did … as you asked.' His voice falters and he clears his throat.

I had expected Marc to leap into an explanation of the photo; his words catch me off-guard.

'Those freaky bear things we bought at Blackheath,' he adds, alluding to the last request I made of him.

'Yes, thank you.'

'Flowers, too. Pansies in pots.'

'Okay. Good.'

'Can I see you?'

On the verge of saying yes, I stop myself and counter with a question of my own. 'How will Double D take that?'

'Ah.'

'Yes. Ah. Did you think I would miss it?'

'Not for long. In any case, I wouldn't have kept it from you.'

He seems in no rush to justify himself, a good sign in my opinion. And hell will freeze over before I lower myself by demanding an explanation like some pathetic clinging vine.

'If you see her again, you could tell her that she needs a stronger hammock … bra, I mean.'

He barks out a laugh. 'You sound more like my snarky Em.'

'I'm getting there.'

'Thank God. And I won't be seeing her again if there's any mercy in the world. Claire will explain if you need to know more.'

'I don't.' Much.

'I'm only interested in us.'

I released a breath. 'How have you been?'

'James and Will dragged me to the rugby. It got ugly.'

It is my turn to laugh. 'Good.'

'Em.' A note of urgency invades his casual tone. 'I've given you the time you wanted.'

'I know.' I squeeze my eyes shut. 'Soon. I just … another few weeks.'

'And then we'll talk? Do you promise?'

'Yes.'

'Okay,' he says but he must be wondering how he can trust this vow when I've broken all the others.

I am too.

Eleven

April last year ...

'Well?'

Marc's voice is muffled by the closed bathroom door but his impatience easily breaches the timber.

'I don't know yet. Just wait.'

'I don't understand why I can't come in.'

Marc has no problems peeing in front of me. I, however, have always preferred privacy—and especially now when I am crouched awkwardly over the toilet bowl, trying to aim at a skinny stick.

At the bathroom sink, having shaken the living daylights out of the thing, I stare hard at it for a full minute. I can hear Marc breathing on the other side of the door. I give it two minutes longer but the line indicating a positive result remains absent.

Relief and guilt war within me as I open the door. I shake my head and watch Marc's eager expression dim.

'Sorry. I'm probably just a little late.' I try not to let my relief show.

Almost fiercely, he pulls me into his body. 'Don't,' he says tightly. 'It's not something to apologise for.'

But it is, isn't it? When you are happy about something that hurts the person you are supposed to love most in the world?

'We haven't been trying long,' I say.

'I guess.'

'There's no rush.'

He nods but I can see he is not mollified, and a few days later while he is out playing squash with James, I log in to his email account and see that he has made an appointment with a fertility clinic.

I feel truly frightened in that moment, in a way I have not felt since my post-honeymoon panic when I feared he would realise just what a big mistake he had made. For several long months, I have managed to push it back into the dark recesses of my consciousness, but now it has broken its leash and is snarling viciously, threatening to rip and tear.

Realising my fingers are clenching the edge of the desk so tightly they are turning white, I deliberately relax them. Yet my mind is not so biddable. It is a frenzy of possibilities and certainties. I know that as soon as tests prove Marc's sperm to be in excellent shape—as I am certain they are—the attention will fall on me. And once I am proven to be at fault—as I am certain I will—what then?

Marc, of course, will be supportive and loving. He will remind us of all the reasons—timing, our lifestyle and so on—that having a child is a not the best idea right now, as though he was the one to point this out originally, not me. But over time, he will begin to think quite differently. I know that some of Marc's friends already have children; his younger sister is about to have her second. Will Marc not begin to think of what life might be like with a woman who isn't barren? While, behind the scenes, Yvette will be plotting and planning, and in the background, the spectre of the curvaceous Double D lingers, her ripe body purpose-designed for producing children.

Stop it! Pulse racing, needing some physical release for my anxiety, I log out of his email account and shove up from the desk. I have not come this far just to give in without a fight. I am a survivor; I will feel my way through this situation as I have everything else.

When Marc returns from squash and a post-game beer, I am ready for him. As he comes into the apartment, calling my name, I waft by him dressed only in his navy robe. He loves it when I wear his clothes, even more so when I remove them as I do now on my way to the bedroom. His blood is up, the sex is spectacular, and my strategy works wonders. We are lying face to face on the pillow, satiated almost to the point of stupefaction, when he tells me what he's done.

I thought he would; he's always been one for pillow talk. I listen and nod, and that afternoon he phones the fertility clinic and tells the specialist that we will be attending the appointment as a couple.

&a &a &a

Present day

I spend a full day photographing the outfits I have created, against different backdrops, from alternative angles and at various times of the day. They look as good as I hoped, but as I scan them, I realise that the house has inserted itself more compellingly into the frame than I had realised.

In the back of my mind, I always thought the house would add an element of drama to the shots. But it is as though, in the absence of a model, the house itself has breathed life into the clothes. In one image of the silk slip, a draught has caused the hem to lift, almost as though someone has just walked by. In another, of a beaded yellowish-green evening gown draped over an armchair in the library, it is almost as if an invisible partygoer sits waiting to go out for the evening. A third is of heavy corduroy pants and the lightest of angora sweaters hanging from a hook on the outside wall of the shed, half in shadow and half lit by the glowing sunset, above the muddy wellington boots.

Excitement fills me afresh and I return to the draft web post, adding some further points that have occurred to me about style being not just the clothes you wear but the way you wear them. *Dare to be different*, I write. *Dare to be you.*

When I've finished, I am keen to send it to the *Small Poppies* website but am reluctant to use my own name or email address. In the end, I create a new email account and a byline inspired by the dress—Chartreuse—and submit the post and three of the images.

Even when I am done, I feel so fired by energy that I wander the house as I have done since arriving here, laying fingers here, my cheek there, feeling its heartbeat as my own. If it were mine, I think, I would retain the slightly scuffed hardwood floors in the reception rooms but repaint the somewhat sombre walls in ivory or pale grey. The heavy drapes would be replaced by something lighter that blows in the breeze, but the old brass light fittings would be retained, except for in the drawing room where scale demands a chandelier.

The peach-and-black bathroom dates from the Art Deco era and simply cannot go. I would, however, need a larger master en suite bathroom. The natural place for that would be the locked room if it is big enough. In the bedroom itself, I would opt for a magnificent bed with a padded French headboard and a couch large enough to make love on, comfortably. The ceiling stain would have to be dealt with, of course, and the walls finished in a soft grey with vintage-style wallpaper similar to the remnants of the old paper that has survived.

Of the other bedrooms, each would have its own character—perhaps one echoing the verdant garden, with freshly cut hydrangeas arranged by the bedside in summer, another masculine and austere in stripes and the third guest room decked out in sumptuous jewel tones. The smallest bedroom, I don't know. In other circumstances, it might have been a nursery in white and aquamarine, and filled with half-chewed books and odd-shaped soft toys in purple and orange.

And a train set?

The question is so clear, so immediate, that at first I think I have said the words aloud although I could have sworn my mind was on soft toys that look like alien-dogs.

And then a small, slightly sticky hand slips into mine, and I know that the words were someone else's.

ⵣ ⵣ ⵣ

May last year …

Our doctor wears half-moon glasses on a chain around her neck. They make her appear more severe than she probably realises. Or maybe it is just because she goes to such great pains to emphasise that fertility is a no-fault zone that I imagine she is accusing me of being to blame.

Marc has had to supply a fresh sperm sample—something I had fun helping him with just this morning, following two days without making love—which has been duly handed over in its special cup. My starring role in today's proceedings is just as undignified but far less enjoyable. Marc does not get to share it but is ushered outside to wait while the doctor checks everything is where it should be, takes a blood sample and asks a range of searching questions that I stammer and stumble over.

We go away with a date for another appointment the following week and when we return, it is to find that, in fact, I am not at fault and neither is Marc. It is no surprise to me that his little swimmers are Olympic standard—not the doctor's words but my interpretation. We go away with a prescription for folate, some dietary advice and Doctor Macpherson's exhortation to keep trying.

As we drive home, I envisage Dr Macpherson peering around our bedroom door, half-moon glasses firmly on, as we are having sex, urging us to try harder. I tell Marc and he laughs so much he only just brakes in time to avoid hitting the car in front that has stopped for the traffic lights. When he is back in control, he tells me he finds that mental image rather arousing. I tell him he's disturbed.

We drive to Marc's office, which is in Castlereagh Street, in a low-rise, mid-century, serious-looking building that Marc says gives clients the confidence that he and his colleagues know what they're talking about. His firm, McAllister & Co, is cautious when the competition is throwing caution to the wind, and takes risks when all others are sitting on their hands. It has paid off for the business in the eight or nine years of its existence so I guess he and his colleagues do know what they are doing.

The financial crisis a few years ago that brought many of his competitors undone brought Marc to national and then international attention in financial circles, proving that there was far more to him than being one of Sydney's most eligible young men. From the way people talk about him, he was some kind of wunderkind, not that long out of uni but with a phenomenal knowledge of economics and the confidence to go his own way. Claire describes him as a sexy Warren Buffett. That didn't mean much to me until I realised she wasn't talking about that plastic-y actor from *The Bold and the Beautiful* but some American squillionaire. Anyway, the point is that the clients in Marc's fledgling firm came through the crisis well and smashed it in the aftermath. So Marc has a reputation.

As a result, he's often in demand by the media when they want to know what's going on in the world of economics and high finance. Marc doesn't often agree to interviews because of the time it means away from poring over spreadsheets and other nerdy tasks that would send most people cross-eyed. But today he is filming a short segment for the evening business news about interest rates, which is why he's wearing his newest suit and a fabulous dark red tie that I bought him.

'Wear your glasses,' I tell him as he gets out and I hop into the driver's seat. 'They draw attention to your ears.'

'My ears?' Marc leans in the open driver's side window.

'Your best feature.'

'Is that right?'

I nod, the wattage of those mesmerising eyes and brilliant smile having taken my breath away.

'You've never told me that before.' He seems oddly delighted.

'Your head's already big enough.'

'Did you say *head*? Or something else?'

As I flush, he grins and ducks his head for a quick kiss. There's a camera flash and a smattering of applause, and I realise we're attracting attention—not only from a few onlookers. Marc's car is stopped in a no-stopping zone and now a police car is drawing up behind us.

'Look what you've done,' I hiss.

As usual, he's unfazed, giving a brief bow to the crowd and me another kiss.

The police officer approaches, sees me and says something about how his girlfriend loves my show but unfortunately he still has to give me a ticket. Then he notices Marc, does a double-take, shakes his hand enthusiastically and forgets all about the ticket and me in the haste to ask him some question about superannuation. I take my chance to make a ticket-less escape.

I'm not sure if I am more amused or annoyed—both that the police officer mistook me for someone else and that—among some people, anyway—my husband is better known than I am.

Today, I am inclined to feel gracious towards Marc as I also have work—a real paying job. Gordon has come up trumps and I am taking a brief to restyle the house of an old friend of his. All I know is that her husband recently died and she needs a bit of a shake-up. I'm not quite sure how we will get along given the age gap, but Ina Johnson turns out to be a sprightly sixty-year-old, fond of dropping four-letter words and whose interior design style looks like a crime scene. When I find two Jackson Pollock prints in her study, I understand her reference points.

We have a blast and when I get home late, I am so full of myself I almost forget to ask Marc about the interview. We watch it later, and he nails it with absolutely the right mix of fact, opinion and sincerity. I tell him that when Ina pays me I'll invest it with him.

It's a good day, a great day. That night, we make love on a high, joyously oblivious to the long fall that awaits us.

🙖 🙖 🙖

Present day, evening

The touch is there—a child's hand in mine, a soft weight against my leg—and then it's gone. I almost think I'm imagining it, except that I can still feel the stickiness of their palm in mine.

'Who are you?' I whisper at the foot of the stairs, staring upwards into the dark. I'm not sure why as I've heard no footsteps in any direction. 'Come back. I won't hurt you.'

Of course, there is nothing except the grumbles of an old house settling in for the night, the creak of timber boards and the clank of the loose gutter, or whatever it is, in the wind.

I do not know what to think; that is to say, I know which way my thoughts are veering but I am trying to push back. True, I have been through a devastating experience, but this is not the first time I have faced difficulties, and I have somehow fumbled my way through without losing my mind. The oddest thing is that I don't feel I've lost it, not at all. Since those first awful days of overwhelming grief, I have improved. I am sleeping and eating. I have had exercise and fresh air. I have spoken to people in the village, even had a constructive conversation with Marc. I have kept myself busy and, in fact, just before the little hand wormed its way into mine, I felt fired by creativity.

Alive, that's what I feel. After weeks and weeks of simply existing, first in a fog of disbelief and then in a maelstrom of unassuaged grief, I feel alive. Or is it all a mirage? That's what madness is, isn't it? A disconnection from reality when it becomes too much to bear? Perhaps none of this is real.

I have a sudden and desperate urge to call Marc, to tell him everything and let him take over and make it all right. He would know what to do, the best doctor to see. I could so easily let my burden rest on his shoulders. But I can't do that. I took that option away from both of us by running. The loss of his dependability and sure-footedness pierces me suddenly. Nature is remarkably clever, pairing us off in a way that offsets one person's inadequacies with the other partner's strengths. And how quickly we come to take it for granted! Now I have to somehow work this out alone. It is up to me but I have no idea where to begin. The sense of paralysis is overwhelming, and I have a sudden insight that this may be what madness is, a trap from which there seems no way out.

Instead of eating, I turn in because it is cold and too late to light a fire. Huddled under the blankets and with the lamp from the library on a table beside me spilling light onto my phone, I make a listless attempt to find my answers online. But it is next to impossible to find authoritative or more than superficial information, and what there is seems to be targeted not at the person experiencing strange symptoms but at their nearest and dearest.

The only pages that strike some sort of chord are those that deal with schizoid conditions. It is common in many of these cases to hear strange voices exhorting the victim to perform unusual acts, even violence. I suppose an urge to acquire a train set could be deemed a strange act—for me at least. But it doesn't seem consistent with the cases referenced online. I'm reassured by that, and at the same time feel utterly alone. If even Google has no answers, what hope do I have?

On the verge of catastrophising, I find the strength to resist. I have never before seen things that aren't there. Maybe *seen* isn't the right word. Whatever the thing is my mind has conjured, it has engaged just about every other sense. I have felt its touch, heard its whisper and sensed its proximity. But there has been nothing to see, except …

Except, once or twice, there has been a shadow where there really shouldn't have been, which made it easy to pretend it wasn't there. My memory rewinds to that day in the garden, the movement captured in the corner of my eye that I thought was the dart and swoop of a playful bird. Except that it wasn't. I think I've always known that.

My hand curls around the rug and I feel the stickiness of my palm against the wool. When I raise my hand in the dark, it still smells faintly of oranges, sugar and salt.

Just as I drift off, a thought flits through my mind, that perhaps there is another way to approach this. But before I can grasp hold of it, the thought is gone and sleep is upon me.

Twelve

Isn't there a saying about idle hands doing the devil's work? If there's not, then there should be. I make a resolution not to dwell on the subject of madness, and over the next few days keep occupied with physical tasks and simple decision-making that requires a minimum of imagination.

In reality, the garden at Lammermoor House requires all three. But the imaginative bit can wait until later. For the moment, there is plenty of hard graft to do. From shortly after eight each morning for the next few days, I am out there doing something somewhere in the garden.

At first I am less than strategic and organised, flitting from one disaster zone to another, not always finishing one job before I begin another. Today, my priority is to move the hydrangeas to a shadier position. I have them dug out before I have decided where to move them, and spend the next half hour carting them from place to place, trying to decide. But finally I decide on a spot on the southeast corner of the house. It is shady, and provided the

113

plants respond positively, I envisage a spectacular mauve display next summer, even though I will not see it.

The spot I choose is already occupied by something straggly that I remove and dump in a wheelbarrow. Carefully, I dig large holes for each of the three hydrangeas, grouping them together for impact. After scattering slow-release fertiliser, I spray with the hose and then place a plant in each hole. The next stage is to reapply the displaced earth around the plants. I give them another shower with the hose for good measure; this is called watering in, according to Google.

At that point, I realise how overgrown the front garden has become. The rain over the past few days has flattened trees and shrubs so that they spread themselves across the drive. Unlike the back garden where the structure is just about visible beneath the overgrowth, it is almost impossible to see the garden's original bones.

One of the first things I must do is cut back the shrubbery along the driveway. It is not exactly exciting work but I roll up the sleeves of my shirt and hack away with saw and secateurs. It is slow, dirty, miserable work—especially when the sky begins to spit cold rain—but by early afternoon I have made solid progress.

After a short break for a tuna salad sandwich and hot chocolate, I return outside. The rain has stopped but there is a real bite to the air. As the day lengthens, every breath puffs out a mist of warm air into the cold. It is while taking a brief rest, leaning against a tree, that I realise May has ticked over into June. That explains the falling temperature, and the short days. By half-past four it is too dim to work on, and I pack up for the day, feeling good that the drive is substantially clear of foliage, but annoyed that I haven't quite finished.

All I want to do now is get inside, build a fire, take a warm bath and snuggle up with Jane Eyre and Mr Rochester. The last few days, I have not read much, partly because I have been too distracted but also because once it ends I will be even more alone. I am tempted to leave everything in the garden where it is; after all I will be back out here tomorrow. But with the likelihood of more rain, I trudge back and forth until all the gardening equipment is returned to the shed. I return for a final time in the gloom to return the wheelbarrow to the shed, when a flicker of light catches my eye in the direction of the gates.

My pulse quickens as it comes again, and I am thankful for the new padlock on the gate. Sheltered by the trees, I feel certain I cannot be seen. Cautiously, I inch towards the gates until I can see that the flicker is coming from car lights on low beam; presumably it's Val.

Someone is there, waving tentatively. It takes me a second. It is not Val, but her offsider, Sally.

'Hi!' I call. 'Hang on a minute, I'll get the key for the padlock and let you in.'

She shakes her blonde mop, made even wilder by the humidity. 'No! I can't come in. I just have a message from my uncle.'

Bemused, I approach the gate. 'Sally, we've already had this conversation. I'm not going anywhere.'

'I'm serious!' She is really upset and I am completely at a loss to understand it. 'My uncle says you're in danger.'

'If your uncle has something to say, why doesn't he speak to me himself?'

'He wanted to. He tried, but he finds it difficult to talk about it.'

'Tried? When?'

'At the hardware store. And he came out to the house.'

'Oh.' Evidently, he hadn't simply been bushwalking that day I'd seen him where his niece is standing right now. 'He helped me with my hydrangeas. I don't understand why he didn't say something.'

'If you knew what he'd been through you'd understand,' she says, her eyes flicking around uneasily.

'Look, why don't you come in? I'm ready for a glass of wine. You're welcome to join me.'

I don't really want company, apart from Jane, but neither do I want to linger out here.

Sally backs away from the gates. 'No! No way. My uncle would kill me.'

I shrug. 'All right.'

'He didn't want me to come out here. But I've been trying your phone and couldn't reach you.'

'It's inside. I've been working out here all day.'

'He says there are things you don't know about this place. Things—' Her face closes in and abruptly she stops.

'What things?'

'I don't know. Stuff. You should talk to him.' She turns away. 'I'm not supposed to be here.'

'What can he say now that he couldn't say when I went into his shop?'

But she is leaving, heading for a small, older model car.

'Wait! Sally!'

She does not stop, hurrying away almost as though she believes I can pursue her through the padlocked gates. Seconds later her car takes off, the small engine pushed to its limit. And I am left here, on my side of the gate, thinking that if I am not mad then perhaps the world is.

ï»¿ðŸ•® ðŸ•® ðŸ•®

May last year …

'Keep them closed,' Marc says.

Not averse to a little cheating, I've been attempting to surreptitiously open my right eye a crack, but he is wise to me. So I squeeze my eyes shut, grip his hand tighter and follow his directions as he walks me across the uneven ground. We are high on the cliffs near South Head on the morning of my twenty-fifth birthday. From the smug and sneaky smile that has played around his face for the past couple of weeks, I know he has something up his sleeve. Despite regular inspections of his phone and email, I have no idea what it is.

My best guess is a champagne breakfast at this scenic spot over-looking the ocean. He knows it is one of my favourite places in Sydney with panoramic views of the sparkling harbour and ocean. I just hope James and Will aren't going to leap naked out of the bushes and perform one of their ritual celebratory dances.

'Okay, open!' Marc says, standing back.

The autumn sunshine is bright this Sunday morning and I blink for a moment. I recognise our picnic rug, with a silver ice bucket, crystal glasses and bottle of French champagne. A vintage platter and bowl that I bought last month at a market hold crois-sants and berries.

'We'll go to a café for coffee later.' He gestures across the road, knowing I can't make it past ten o'clock without an espresso.

'It's lovely. Thank you.' I blink again, nothing to do with the sunshine this time. It is beautifully styled, and although Marc has good taste, I suspect Claire's hand in this, or possibly Brendan's. 'No one has ever ... ' I falter, not wanting to bring up unhappy times when I am happy. And I have had a couple of good birthdays since arriving in Sydney. Just last year, Claire organised someone to come and give us home facials and massages before we went out for cocktails. I think it is the surprise element, the fact that Marc has planned it in secret, that touches me so. He waits for me to continue but when I silently hand him the champagne bottle, he doesn't push me to continue.

A second or two later, the cork has been popped and we are clinking glasses. I sip and glance around. The view is sweeping and dramatic, of cliffs and sky and pounding surf.

'Maybe we should move away a little.' I nod towards the dark grey car parked nearby, wondering why they have stopped so close to our picnic. Then the large red bow around the wing mirror captures my attention and I lower my glass and stare at Marc.

He has the biggest, soppiest grin on his face.

'But it's a car,' I say stupidly, walking forward. 'You can't give me a car … an Audi.'

He follows and clinks his glass to mine again. 'Happy birthday, gorgeous girl.'

I try again. 'It's a car.'

'A small one.'

'With four hoops.' I know nothing about cars except the ones with hefty price tags, and this is in that group. It's also seriously good-looking.

'You need a car.'

I do. I've been borrowing his for my client meetings when I need to transport samples, magazine and books. Yet there is nothing on Marc's face to suggest that this is about him not wishing to share. All I can see is pleasure on his face and I can hear it in his voice. Nevertheless, a spark of resentment leaps to life. Doesn't he see what position this puts me in? How it makes me even more beholden?

Marc's delight dims a little as I don't react quite with the delight he expects, and my guilt increases. What is it in me that will turn a gift freely given into something faintly grubby?

Desperate for anything that will save the moment, I take another sip of champagne to steady myself and saunter up to him. Careful not to tip bubbly down his neck, I loop my hands around his neck and smile into his eyes.

'I do confess this charming picnic is not what I expected,' I murmur, 'after your birthday surprise.'

'Ah that.' He nods. 'I thought you'd prefer something classier than Will and James dressed as can-can dancers.'

Yvette had organised the French-themed *soirée* (her word), after Marc had returned from Europe, as a belated birthday celebration, even though I'd suggested a family day at the cricket. Everything was oh-so-chic—on the terrace surrounded by French lavender, with salmon to start, followed by *beouf* and Crêpes Suzette. And Will and James in drag.

She still doesn't believe I had nothing to do with it.

'I do.' Dropping my arms from his neck, I walk to the car and run my hand over its curvaceous lines. I see the slightest of dents down low, and glance at the number-plate. I realise then that the car's not new, and feel the immediate release of pressure. I look away as tears sting my eyes. How can he know that a pre-loved car would be easier for me to accept than something right out of the showroom?

'It's nearly four years old but it has relatively low mileage and it's in good condition,' he says from behind me. There is the faintest note of uncertainty in his voice. 'I thought a new car might make you uncomfortable.'

'You're right.' Stupidly, the tears are running unchecked now.

'I didn't notice that ding. I'll get it fixed up.' Now he sounds worried.

'No. No.' Turning to him, I smile through my tears and shake my head. 'No, it's just right as it is. Perfectly imperfect.'

'Sure?' He doesn't sound certain.

'Absolutely.' I nod and swallow a mix of champagne and tears.

He takes my glass and places it and his on the ground. I walk into his arms and push my damp face into his neck. We stand there for a few moments, swaying a little. There's this enormous beast clutching at my entrails. You always think love should feel like butterfly wings or sunshine inside you, something sappy. In fact, it feels like a Rottweiler has a grip on your throat.

There's so much I want to say it's overwhelming and I haven't a clue where to begin.

'You're a good husband,' I mutter, knowing that my words are woefully inadequate.

Below his breath, he laughs.

'I'm a terrible wife so maybe that evens us out,' I add.

Drawing back a little, he studies my face, which I'm sure is a disaster zone. I'm just glad I opted against mascara. 'You're not a terrible wife. What on earth gave you that idea?'

I shrug. My inadequacies are so legion, where do I start?

Fortunately at that moment, there is a shout from the beach below, and up, into our line of sight, rises a bright red kite in the form of a Chinese dragon. Marc refills our glasses and we settle down on the rug to eat our breakfast picnic and watch the kite rise and fall with the wind current.

When we are done, I take the Audi for a brief circuit, enjoying the way she hugs the road and takes the corners. The wheel feels right in my hands, and the manual gearstick puts me back in control. When I return, I am steadier and Marc is holding two steaming takeaway cups of coffee.

The roller-coaster has hit a straight stretch.

Thirteen

Present day, afternoon

The driveway is clear and I have been busy pruning the rest of the front garden. It seems like a never-ending task. This afternoon, though, the rain has intensified and I have been forced indoors. Over a lunch of chicken and vegetable soup, I doodle landscaping ideas in a dog-eared exercise book found in the library. It is turning yellowish with age and the ruled lines are so faint they are almost invisible.

The centrepiece will be the spring-flowering *Magnolia x sou-langeana*, with large white and mauve teacups for flowers. Even on my phone, it looks magnificent. When I next go into town, I will buy some gardening books and study up on the conditions it needs to thrive. Around it will be strappy Brazilian walking iris and a new lawn of soft green. The perimeter will be camellias in whites and soft pinks and—

My phone beeps to announce an incoming email, interrupting my train of thought. It is just as well. Despite my vow to rein in my creative spirit, my imagination was starting to run away with me as I planned how the garden would look.

When I check my email, it's from the *Small Poppies* website. Since the night I'd submitted the blog and photos—and felt the small sticky hand clasp mine—I'd put it out of my mind. If I was deluded enough to be feeling things that weren't there, I was also deluded to think that my creative ideas might be interesting to others.

Feeling more than a little nervous, I scan the email. It's from someone named Alicia Vere, who informs me that she and her colleagues love my blog and plan to publish it in late July. She adds that she thinks I have utterly captured the zeitgeist, contextually and visually. Everyone, she says, is looking for ways to reduce their imprint while expressing their individuality. Furthermore, she would love my piece to become a regular feature if I am interested and have time. There is even a fee attached—small, but a fee nonetheless.

My pride is a warm glow inside, it really is. Working and thinking alone is freeing—you can let your imagination soar without anyone to bring you down to earth. But it is a double-edged sword. When your doubts are crushing, there is no one there to raise you back up. When you are beginning to suspect you might be going mad, there is no one to reassure you that you are not.

Now, the knowledge that someone else sees what I do signals that I am not utterly delusional. The relief is immense, as is the realisation that I have no reason to continue keeping my creativity in check.

After re-reading the email several times simply to draw out the pleasure, I write back to confirm that I am happy for Alicia to publish the blog and photos for the fee proposed, providing the copyright is cited as belonging to Chartreuse. I am reluctant to commit to a regular column—what if my confidence deserts me?—but promise I will work on another idea that has been fermenting and send her something in a couple of weeks.

There are plenty of ideas, although I don't tell her that, but I am thinking about my brief career as an interior style consultant and the lessons I learned from those experiences. I even have before-and-after photos stored somewhere on my phone that Ina Johnson and Claire's friend have already cleared me to use. I think they thought that with my profile they would see their homes in *Vogue Living*, which of course was never going to happen.

Forgetting my mantra about controlling my imagination, I now throw caution to the wind. As the rain splatters ceaselessly against the windows, I fill page upon page of the exercise book with jottings and notes, ideas and sketches. I pull out a dove-grey cropped jacket with a mandarin collar from the vintage store that I hadn't known what to do with a few days ago. Now I pair it with my skinny indigo jeans and a second-hand peaked cap in amethyst, and the result is cool Oliver Twist.

Liking the idea of giving each look a name, I glance at the other outfit I've pulled together—a bright floral skirt with striped shirt—and call it The Odd Couple. Those two should not go together, but together they are. The third of the ensembles consists of slouchy tweed pants and a silk camisole, both from my own wardrobe. This is a look I have worn before many times because the combination of sober and sexy drives Marc crazy. I add a lacy alpaca shrug to the ensemble and call it Siren.

Sitting back in my chair in the dining room, which seems to have become my default studio, I let out a breath. My brain is still whirring with half-formed ideas.

While they ferment, I light the fire in the study and then move around the house, drawing the drapes and enjoying the feeling of shutting myself away from the dark. Tonight, I am hungry for more than soup and decide to roast the hunk of lamb I bought the other day.

Roast lamb is a favourite of Marc's and I have learned to cook it with some success since we began living together. We used to eat out a lot and initially Marc would often cook on weekends as my skills were limited to toast and salad. But by trial and error, I gradually became competent in the kitchen.

The first time I bought a leg to roast, I thought it was outrageously expensive—and a waste, considering there were just two of us. I remember Marc and I standing in the kitchen after dinner, staring at the huge pile of leftover meat. It ended up feeding us for days after in warm lamb salad and delicious meaty sandwiches. We even made a rather odd-looking but tasty pie for a midweek supper with Léo, who described it as 'rustic'. In the end it worked out to be very economical, although working out how to use all the meat took some effort.

Now, in the midst of rubbing the beast with oil and rosemary from the garden, I stand stock still, my mind ticking over. There's a young woman in my mind—and for once she's not me. Her features are a bit fuzzy but she's in her early twenties, just starting her career and living in a shared house. She has some money but not much once rent, bills and fun are paid for. She loves clothes and is developing her own style. She's learning to cook and make a home and planting a few herbs or pots of colour on her windowsill or out on the balcony.

Ten years on, like Claire's friend, Anna, she has her own place or shares with her boyfriend. She is either paying off a mortgage or saving for one. Her tastes are a little more sophisticated, but the purse-strings are still tight. Then, in another decade or so, she has a bigger home—a house this time—a demanding job and perhaps a couple of kids running rampant. There's a bigger mortgage, childcare or schooling to pay for, and dental fees. There's a bit more money but spare time has vanished. Fifteen or twenty years later, there's Ina, still yearning for that beautiful home and lifestyle. She has more time and more money but is finding it difficult to break free of the past.

All women, I think. All women want to dress well, eat well and live well. They just need a little inspiration and sound advice that doesn't involve rushing out to buy designer fashion or expensive clothes, or hiring stylists, cooks and landscapers.

They don't have the time to work it all out for themselves, but I do.

Throwing garlic, onions, potatoes, carrots and parsnips into the roasting tray, I shove it all into the oven. I rush to wash my hands and then race back to my 'studio' to flick through my exercise book and the garden sketches and notes. Most of what I've done requires a lengthy visit to a nursery and a hefty credit card bill for new plants. But if I simply re-use many of the existing plants and invest in just one or two new trees, I could keep costs to a bare minimum. If I can reimagine the garden from what is already in front of me, others could too—particularly if they have just a small inner-city courtyard or suburban backyard to work with.

The room is quite dark, only a lamp spilling a circle of light onto the paper in front of me. Apt, then, that this is my light-bulb moment. A lifestyle website—down to earth and achievable yet gorgeous, with not a celebrity endorsement in sight—for what women of all ages want, in their wardrobes, interiors, kitchens and even gardens. I can make it work. I feel it. I know it. I have already started.

The big question is how to make it pay. I've not made a cent for months now and my cheque account is dwindling fast even though my outgoings have been modest. There is, of course, the account that Marc set up for me but things will have to be dire before I access it.

I need to make a proper, steady living—I make myself say it—whether or not my marriage can be salvaged. For my own self-respect, I need to know I can make my own way, live more than the hand-to-mouth existence I led before Marc. I need to be able to make a life on my own terms if I must.

Many of the lifestyle sites I've visited either take advertising or have an associated online shop, or they are cyber-egos of overseas celebrities who have largely lost touch with the real world. On my website, there will be no chia seeds or six-hundred-dollar bags. It has to be real. It has to be for Australian women. But how can it pay for itself and earn me at least a small salary?

I'd love to discuss it with Marc. He has a passion for entrepreneurship, and since I've known him, he has been mentoring the mother of one of his staff who has set up a floristry business.

Claire and Brendan would be great to brainstorm with, too. Claire's wardrobe and studio would be thrown wide open and she'd know just the right person to design the website. Brendan would be trying to take over the photography, calling me an amateur when I refuse and then giving me tips on lighting and mood.

All of a sudden I have an urgent longing for my old life.

Abruptly, the dining room door slams and sweeps my notes from the table. Sighing, I realise it's time to put work away. Across the hallway, the fire in the study is crackling merrily but it will need another log soon, and the scent of roasting meat from the kitchen reminds me to baste the lamb.

I pour a glass of wine and take it through to the study where I stoke the fire, watching the yellow flames reach higher. Half an hour later, I am tucking hungrily into my dinner, hoping that tomorrow morning will bring enough of a break in the weather to allow me to work it off.

The day after tomorrow, I plan to go to Lammermoor. It will be market day, and I hope the crowd will mean I can shop without attracting attention. I plan to pick up some fashion and interiors magazines to feed my own creativity, along with a gardening book. I need to know what I'm doing before I inflict my wisdom on anyone else.

The garden of Lammermoor house will be my lab, a place to experiment and a source of ideas and images for gardening tips, just as the house has provided a backdrop for my fashion photographs.

It will need more than a few months to get this off the ground, though. I will have to see Val to see if my lease can be extended. Given the low rent I am paying, the owner probably has plans to develop it.

I am not hopeful that the new owner will agree for me to stay on but I will ask, nonetheless.

As a nebulous future takes form in my mind, I latch on to it. It is so easy to grab at the new and the shiny, to let it consume me so I do not have to think of the failures of my past. But even as I am snatching at it, I fear that this time is different because this time I have not simply left behind a mess but my heart.

Can I simply skip off towards a new dawn, leaving Marc broken, and myself still incomplete? Once upon a time, I'm sure I would not have looked back. Now I'm not so certain.

❧   ❧   ❧

June last year ...

We sit in the car, frozen in silence after our appointment with Dr Macpherson. I have rarely seen Marc look as grave even though Dr Macpherson has been her usual matter-of-fact, upbeat self.

Her view is that there is still every chance that we will be able to conceive a child, although she concedes we may need a little 'assistance'. Marc and I both know this is code for artificial insemination at best and IVF at worst.

Both of us flinched when she said it. We spoke of it months ago when it wasn't a possibility. *Thank God that won't be us*, we said. Hormones, needles, scheduled sex, intrusive questions. It sounds laughable but I think we thought a couple who have as much sex as we have—and are pretty good at it, I have to say—would never experience these problems.

But we do.

Not long ago, I was happy enough with the delay in proceedings, as you know, but things have changed. Now, I will do anything to erase that look from Marc's face, even if it means getting a lumpy look and waddling gait, and putting the needs of some squalling, squash-faced infant above my own.

He has that look now. It is more than grave; it is as though he is about to lose the one thing he treasures above all else. I don't understand it, really. After all, you can't lose something you've never had, can you?

Or perhaps you can. What is more soul-destroying than crushed dreams?

I wish so badly that I was enough for him. But I am not, and that is a fact, so one way or another I must get the child he wants so desperately.

'Let's do it,' I say into the silence that stretches the air between us so tautly it feels as though something is about to snap. 'The doctor said most couples are pregnant within a few cycles. Once we've had a baby, we'll forget all about what we went through to get it.' I try to inject a touch of levity. 'Just so long as you don't plan on having six.'

Silence.

Sighing, I reach out and place my hand on his where it rests on the steering wheel. The moment I touch him, he comes out of his trance.

'Sorry, what did you say?'

'We should do it. We've spent months trying to do it the old-fashioned way. I know Macpherson thinks we should wait a little longer because we have youth on our side but I don't see the point.'

Marc shakes his head. 'No, I don't want to put you, either of us, through that. I've heard of too many couples who've let it take over their lives. It becomes an obsession, their entire relationship pivoting on the outcome of something utterly uncertain. I don't want that for us.'

I ponder that, and start to suggest adoption as an alternative, but almost immediately shut it down. For Yvette, already riled by my presence in her family, bringing some poor child of an uncertain background into the picture would be a red rag to a charging bull. I couldn't do that to Marc or the child. In any case, I am pretty certain that he would agree with Yvette that his progeny should be a McAllister in every way.

'So, we keep trying.' I muster a smile. 'We're very good at the trying bit.'

He tries to say something but has to stop and clear his throat. His hand turns to grip mine. 'We are,' he says huskily.

'Alternatively, we could get a turtle.'

'What?' He looks startled, then half-smiles, which is good.

'I really don't take to cats. We're too much alike. And the apartment's no place for a dog.'

He's a trouper and joins in, even though I know it is an effort for him to make light of what weighs so heavily. 'There are other possibilities, you know. A ferret, for example.'

'Penguin.'

'Meerkat.'

'Sloth.'

'Centipede.'

So it goes on for a few moments longer as we drive towards home, but I can think of no way to segue into less sensitive territory, and before long silence is upon us again.

It is nearly six in the evening, dark, and the streets are busy, making it reasonable that Marc concentrates on the road, but I do not like this silence filled with thoughts unsaid.

Rarely is it like this between us. We are often silent for periods, both in the car and at home, often listening to music. But it is comfortable, not this atmosphere of drumming tension.

'Two months,' I say suddenly as we turn into our street.

I know that in his work, particularly when his firm invests in high-risk shares, Marc will impose a finite period to give the shares a chance to move in a positive direction. At the end of the period, he will reassess. I figure he will respond to a deadline, and I am right.

'Two months? All right.'

I have given both of us some breathing space. We don't have to make a cataclysmic decision this minute—or perhaps ever if our bodies decide to do the right thing. Yet, even as I suggest it and Marc agrees, I know this scenario pivots on *if*.

Although the two-month timeline has, on the surface, returned the matter to our control, as time goes on we both know it is just delaying the inevitable. And as June passes and another period begins, the pendulous silence returns. It feels as though we are in a game of Russian roulette. Will the next tug on the trigger be the bullet?

Evenings that had once passed in conversations about our respective days, or snuggled up peaceably on the sofa reading or listening to music, are now spent largely apart. Once we have eaten dinner, Marc holes up in his study, and I am left to flick through magazines, my mind taking in little. Winter has temporarily interrupted our weekly migration to Palm Beach so even that respite has abandoned us, and barbecues with family and friends that characterised the warmer months are likewise on hold until spring.

We try, both of us. I initiate a romantic weekend in Melbourne, where we are delayed for four hours at the airport and end up abandoning the trip. Marc books dinner at Hetty's, after which I spend the night vomiting.

Even our lovemaking, which so far has largely remained untouched by our trials, begins to change. Where once it was an all-you-can-eat smorgasbord of touches, kisses, laughter and passion, now there is only one dish on the menu—driving intensity. The passion is still there. Sexually, we want each other as much as ever, but the desire to please is slowly being strangled by desperation and fear.

This week, Marc has worked late at the office several nights. Last night, he came home when I was asleep, and woke me with his insistent kisses and caresses. Our lovemaking was desperate, savage, seeking. Afterwards, we both lay there awake, saying nothing. Eventually, I went out onto the balcony, despite the wintry night, to cry. When I came back, he was asleep.

Today I am home, preparing for a final session at Ina Johnson's. The painters finished last week, new carpet is down and the new furniture is being delivered. She has some extraordinary pieces—too many, really—most of which I am retaining. But my strategy is to combine them with some more practical but still beautifully made items so that the one-of-a-kind pieces stand out rather than being lost in the chaos.

The Pollocks, although only prints, are good ones. They have been mounted and will come out of seclusion and into the main living area as the flagships for Ina's eclectic style. They will be set off by a lot of white paintwork and a tomato-red sofa. I realise it will take me a good part of the day to arrange everything for Ina's arrival this evening.

She has taken the opportunity to do a short tour of the Australian west coast, visiting friends in Perth and travelling north to Broome and inland to Kings Canyon and the Bungle Bungles. I imagine the dramatic raven stripe through her hair and her scarlet lipstick will have made quite an impression in the desert.

Collecting my folder and the plans I've drawn up, I am making
for the door when the phone rings. I duck into the study, and tuck
it under my ear.

'Reed–McAllister residence. Emerald speaking.'

'Oh hi.' The voice is female, unfamiliar and surprised. 'I'm
after Marc.'

'He's not at home at present. Can I take a message?' I'd rather
not as my arms are full and it is almost ten already.

The woman on the other end gives a sultry laugh. 'Oops, I
meant to call his mobile. Sorry. Don't worry about the message.'

Whoever she is she doesn't sound sorry at all. In fact, she sounds
rather satisfied. And then I catch on. 'Is this Daisy?'

I've never met Daisy Davis before, although she's a regular on
the social circuit and I've seen her photo in the paper. Marc dated
her for a while, casually he says. I do believe him as she's too obvious to really be his type—enormous bosoms squeezed into tiny
tops and dramatic eye make-up night and day.

'Yes. And you must be the wife.'

The wife. The way she says it is both a put-down and a challenge, and I'm caught on the hop. It's one of those moments when
you really want an excellent retort to spring to your lips, but I find
nothing to say that wouldn't sound defensive or childish.

'I'm surprised he's told you about me,' she continues and I am
even more certain this is no accidental call.

'Look, Daisy. I'm sorry but I'm running late for an appointment. You should be able to reach Marc on his mobile or on his
work number. I think he's in the office all day.'

Before she can respond, I put the phone down and take a couple of deep breaths. Okay, so I didn't rock the world with a witty
comeback line, but I kept my cool. Even Yvette would have been
proud of me.

The drive to Ina's apartment in the Audi is, as always, a delight, and I feel almost calm by the time I reach there. Then I am caught up with the removalists and directing the placement of furniture, art and *objets*, but Daisy Davis's voice, smooth and sure, nags there at the back of my mind.

Her phone call was designed to provoke trouble; she made no attempt to make it seem otherwise. *I'm after Marc.* But why now?

My inner voice answers. *Because somehow she knows you're vulnerable.* The question is: how does she know and has Marc told her?

Fourteen

Present day, late morning

Deserted by the few tourists it attracts at other times of year, who presumably flee to warmer climes during the winter or stay rugged up in front of the fire, the fortnightly Lammermoor market today seems to rely on locals to supply both sellers and buyers. I am wearing the Oliver Twist outfit with my hair bundled under the cap and the chunky mohair scarf around my ears. In a sea of jeans and windbreakers, it attracts several stares, which makes me both happy and self-conscious.

I spend longer shopping than I intended. As I wander through the throng, trying to find the woman I usually buy my fruit and veg from, I notice that a couple of stalls carry second-hand clothing, and several more sell bric-a-brac ranging from teapots to trunks. One even has some sizeable furniture pieces. My nostrils have caught the scent of the hunt and, before I can think better of it, I am flicking through racks and bins of clothing and accessories, looking for gems.

Most of the clothing consists of inexpensive high-street brands, but I find a couple of good pieces—a felt beret in wine with a

French label and a pair of black velvet evening pants. The bric-a-brac stalls yield an old woven tray, a pair of vintage brass candlesticks and a huge, four-seat sofa that looks as if it is from the thirties or forties. The upholstery could do with replacing but the structure is sound, and I know it is exactly what the house's grand drawing room needs in front of the fireplace. In just about any other house it would dwarf the space, but in Lammermoor House its proportions will be perfect.

Before I even speak to Val about extending my lease, I am paying for the sofa. The stall owner promises to have it delivered to a local upholsterer on Monday, and gives me their card.

Fortunately, all my purchases are bargains and I have spent only a little more than four hundred dollars, but as soon as I have handed over the money I think of my dwindling funds and wish I hadn't been quite so foolhardy.

When I have lugged the smaller purchases back to the car, I retrace my steps and hurry through my grocery shopping, conscious that the real estate agency closes early on a Saturday. It is nearing lunchtime when I walk in. Sally is fortunately nowhere in sight, and Val is wrapping up a conversation with a young couple.

'Ms Reed,' she says, when they head for the door clutching a handful of brochures. 'What can I do for you today?'

'It's about my lease.' I smile at her, my fingers crossed for a positive response. 'I'd like to stay on longer if that's a possibility.'

She frowns a little but doesn't immediately discount the idea. What she does look is uncertain, which surprises me. Val has never struck me as someone who finds decisions tricky.

'I'll have to consult the owner,' she says.

I recall she said it was some kind of corporation. Presumably then there's no chance of an owner wanting to move in, but they probably have plans for a boutique hotel or something similar.

Inspiration strikes me. 'If it makes a difference, I'm looking to make some small improvements to the house—nothing structural, just painting. I'm also maintaining the garden.'

'Well, I'll find out for you.' She calls up my mobile number on the computer and I confirm that it is still current.

'I should be able to get an answer for you today,' she says.

'Great, although next week is fine if you have problems reaching people over the weekend.'

'How much more time are you looking for?' Val asks.

'Three months, possibly six.'

'Well I'll let you know.' She pauses. 'Everything is all right then?'

'Yes. The house is perfect for me right now.'

I wonder if I should tell her that the house and garden is likely to play a starring role in my new enterprise, but decide I've pushed my luck enough today. Investors might be happy enough for me to make improvements, but using the house for business reasons is likely to trigger an increase in rent that I simply cannot afford right now.

Instead, I say goodbye, glad to have got away without another uncomfortable conversation with the impressionable Sally. My luck doesn't last, however. I have just stocked up on cheese at the deli—where I actually had to wait to be served by people buying pork in order to try out the sticky ribs recipe in the window—when Sally comes out of her uncle's hardware store. She can't help but see me.

'I'm just buying cheese,' I tell her. 'Not old wives' tales.'

'Please, Ms Reed. Uncle Bobby apologises for not saying anything before. He thought you'd go of your own accord.'

I stare at her, flabbergasted. 'What are you saying? That when I stuck around, he decided to put the pressure on? You know what? It's not the house that's creepy, it's your uncle.'

A low voice sounds behind us. 'I'm sorry if I've unnerved you, Ms Reed.'

Sally's uncle has emerged from his shop and is standing on the step, observing us. How he has managed that without me noticing when I am standing just two metres away, I'm not sure. His beanie is pulled down low and his shoulders sag as though under a weighty burden. The prominent brow and sallow skin add to his brooding presence, quite the opposite of his open, freckled-faced niece.

'My name is Robert Sanders. Sally's stepfather is my younger brother.'

The way he seemed to know what I was thinking unnerves me even more, and I take a step back.

'Tell her, Uncle Bobby,' Sally says urgently. 'You have to tell her.'

We are attracting more than a few glances from passers-by, our body language announcing that this is more than locals passing the time of day.

'You'd better come in,' Sanders says, opening the door.

'Talk to him,' Sally says. 'Please. I have to go. Val will kill me if I'm not back at work in the next two minutes.'

I hesitate. The stooping, sallow figure and his dusty, dreary shop are not enticing. But neither do I wish to become the subject of gossip. I nod to Sally and step past him into the shop. As he closes the door, the bell rings and then all I can hear is the steady ticking of the old clock behind the counter.

Neither of us seem sure of where to start and I, for one, have no idea where this is about to go. What is clear is that if I wait for Sanders to get it underway, I could be here all day. I wonder for a moment if I should hit him with my theory that he and Sally are contriving to drive me away for nefarious reasons of their own, but decide on a softer approach.

'You'll be pleased to know I've moved the hydrangeas,' I say—I think startling him that I am not on the attack.

'About time. Never should have been there in the first place, but the miss, she wanted to see them from the kitchen.'

Sanders has stepped so neatly into my trap that I can hardly believe it. He realises immediately that he has admitted some sort of connection with the house and his face takes on a rueful look.

'*She*. Who was she?'

'Evelyn St John was her name.' His mouth moves in what I suspect is his version of a smile. It isn't directed at me but at his subject. 'Prettiest girl in Lammermoor and she knew it. Bit like you. Not that you look alike. She was blonde, with a proper figure. People used to say she looked a bit like Marilyn. Norma Jean was all the rage then. Everyone wanted to look like her but Evelyn really did.'

'When was this?'

'Oh, this is way back in the late fifties.'

I am taken aback that he recalls so vividly events more than half a century ago. 'Oh … you must have been just a boy.'

'Six or seven, I think, when my father first took me to the house with my older brother Michael. Dad was the gardener there, and to keep me out of Mum's hair, he'd take me with him to fetch and carry when I wasn't in school. Probably more trouble than help. But I liked it up at the house, although Michael said it was boring and soon stopped coming.

'Miss Evelyn always had lemonade and biscuits for me, even though the Brigadier and Mrs St John didn't much approve. They were her parents.'

I am confused. 'Approve of what?'

'Fraternising with the child of the hired help, I suppose.' Sanders shrugs. 'It was a different time. Things were changing in other places but Lammermoor was the same as it had always been.'

'How old was Evelyn when you knew her?'

'A few months after I started going up there with my father, she had her nineteenth birthday. Big bash. I remember all the flowers Dad had to cut for the house. He wasn't happy about it, claimed it ruined the garden.' Sanders voice had taken on a dreamy quality as though he had time-travelled back fifty-plus years. 'Miss Evelyn let me have a glimpse of the house the day before the party. I'd never seen anything like it—it was all sparkling glass and gleaming floors, streamers and so many flowers it smelt like a meadow.'

'It's a little different now,' I remind him, intrigued, although it does not explain his eagerness to see me leave. 'What happened?'

He shakes his head. 'This was early fifty-eight, I think. All I knew at the time was that the house was full of lights and flowers and glamour one day, and then suddenly Evelyn was gone—like a fairy tale had ended with no happily ever after.'

'You never saw her again?' I asked.

'At first, I thought it was my fault. That I'd done something but my father wouldn't explain.'

'What did her parents do after that?'

'The St Johns stayed on a few years before moving to the Blue Mountains. We heard he died soon after and I don't think she outlived him by much. They seemed very old to me when my dad worked for them, but I think Evelyn had come late to them in their forties, so they would have been in their sixties I suppose.'

'But what happened to Evelyn?' I ask. 'There must have been talk.'

'No one in the town spoke about anything else for weeks,' Robert Sanders says, looking at the floor. 'Had she married against her parents' wishes? Had she died? I didn't understand it all, but I remember that everyone thought it must have been something shocking to pitch the house into such despair. Then word spread that Evelyn had gone to college in England and that was that.'

'Your father must have known something. Was he still working there?'

Sanders nods. 'He was kept on to do the gardens almost until the St Johns left but he was always tight-lipped.'

I wait for him to continue but he seems to have forgotten I am there, caught up in the past. There is nothing creepy about Robert Sanders now, just weary and faintly maudlin.

'Does this have something to do with the house?' I prompt.

'What?' He jumps as if startled.

'You were going to tell me about the house.'

He shrugs. 'It was never the same afterwards, as though Evelyn's departure ripped all the life from it.'

'But people must have lived there since the St Johns moved out.'

'Not really. People have taken on the place. No one's lasted for more than a few weeks that I know of, and there's been no one at all for the best part of thirty years now.'

'But why?' Frustrated at his vague conclusion to the story, I am not prepared to settle for anything less than a real answer.

'Last couple took it on with big plans to turn it into a boutique hotel. First day in there, one tradesman trips and falls from a first-floor window. Everyone else walks off the job and the couple can't get anyone else to work there. Next thing I heard they had financial trouble, then she had a breakdown, and they cleared out. The bank foreclosed and that was that.'

'Wow!' I'd asked for an answer and I'd got it. 'Maybe they were just unlucky. Accidents and illness happen.'

'It wasn't the only unfortunate incident at that place, believe me.' He glances at his watch and I realise it is almost dark outside.

'Well, thank you for explaining.' I pull open the door. 'But I've been there for months now without anything … any harm.'

'All that means is that it hasn't happened yet.' He shrugs and turns the door sign to CLOSED. 'You take my word for it, miss.

There's something wrong with that house. You need to get out while you can.'

I am thinking of his last eight words as I step through the door. He is closing it behind me and I put out a hand to stop him for one final question.

'The workman, the one who fell. What happened to him?'

Sanders' mouth turns grim. 'He never walked again.'

I stare at him, and am still in shock long after he has closed the door in my face.

Fifteen

July last year ...

I am alone at the beach shack on a grey afternoon. The wind is up and large breakers are smashing into the ocean beach. Above, seagulls wheel and cry.

Marc doesn't know I'm here today, a mohair blanket wrapped around me as I stand out on the deck. The beach is deserted; even walkers and paddlers are in short supply on a day as bleak as this. On the drive up here it rained fitfully, and the dark, heavy clouds threaten more before the day is done.

Not that Marc knows it yet—as my period is not officially due for another couple of days—but our two months reprieve before we decide what to do next is over. In truth, it has been more punishment than reprieve, made worse by the fact that we haven't spoken of it since we made the agreement. I assume he is waiting for me to let him know when our situation changes or perhaps he simply does not know how to raise such a charged topic. I have some sympathy there.

The spotting I have had today at least puts an end to the charade our marriage is becoming. If you've ever wondered about the married-five-minutes couples whose dream wedding is really the beginning of the end, then wonder no more. It can happen all too easily when your bond is made of velcro, fast to seal and just as fast to break.

My bag sits in the room behind me. I'm not sure where to go, only that I am going. Although I am not certain how Marc will react—he may be glad to wash his hands of the whole disaster our marriage has become—I fear that he will take this badly. McAllisters don't fail (and they definitely don't do something as tacky as divorce) and, even though the blame largely rests at my door, Marc cannot escape all responsibility.

Why did he have to want a baby so much?

Sylvie, two years younger than Marc, has had her second—a boy. I suspect that Marc went to see his new nephew without me. At least, I found an order for a large stuffed bear on his tablet when I was snooping. What excuse would he have made for my non-appearance, I wonder.

Busy with my glamorous career—that seems to have ground to a halt since I finished Ina's apartment—or with glamorous friends, I suppose. But it can't have escaped anyone's notice that we have not been seen together for weeks now. I know there must be talk, but I cannot find the energy to care.

Actually, that's not true. I *wish* I didn't care because it is exhausting and confusing and, yes, sometimes downright scary. I'm not sure what Marc is thinking anymore. For all I know, he thinks he is protecting me from unnecessary pressure by keeping me away from mothers and babies. But secrets other than my own are what I most fear.

Rather than abating as evening approaches, the wind becomes more frenzied and a frond is torn from the Canary Island palm next door. Despite its porous wood, it comes crashing to the ground, and I jump. It is the signal for me to go. I can't stay here all day prevaricating and staring at a windswept beach. The only reason I am here at all is that I sometimes think better up here than in the city.

A note, short and sweet, lies on the kitchen bench in Marc's apartment. It just says that I am taking some time to myself, but he can read between the lines well enough. Any legal action I will leave up to him to put in train given that I have nothing except the car. If I were a better person I would leave it behind, but I am not.

I had thought to stay with Claire for a while but her apartment is mostly given over to studio space; the living area is tiny. In any case, I know what she will think of my decision to call time on my relationship with Marc, whom she really likes. Brendan will just curse the fact that he will no longer be able to gaze on Marc's biceps at will.

So, this is it. I leave my key in the kitchen drawer for Marc to find, and when the door shuts I am locked out of the house I slaved and sweated over.

After all, it is easy enough. I have done this before, although the last time I left my life was not in an Audi but on the six twenty-five train from Bathurst. There is some comfort in the familiarity of the leaving ritual, though—the planning, the packing, the writing of the note, and most of all in leaving failure behind like a snake shedding its skin.

That last time, after I left Bathurst, I slept rough outside Central Station on a sultry, thundery night, and then found a cheap share-house the day after. My options are broader this time. I could afford a good hotel, but not for long, so instead I find a bland motel room and take it for a discounted weekly rate. My first act when inside the room is to chop off my long hair. With my ragged crop and watery, pink eyes, no one will recognise me as Sydney's It Girl now.

The motel in Frenchs Forest is a strangely utilitarian, characterless place to ride out the emotional collapse that comes with a relationship breakdown. It has a pool, where in the first few days I swim despite the weather, sometimes twice a day, until my muscles ache and my head is empty. Then, I can't even swim as fatigue envelopes me like a fog, muting the outside world. Day might as well be night. Even when the motel manager insists my room be cleaned, I sit by the pool in my pyjamas until the maid is finished.

My phone has been switched off all this time, but I know from overhearing a TV talk show when I was paying for my third week, that my absence has provided rich pickings for the gossip vultures.

Rumours are growing that It Girl Emerald Reed-McAllister has abandoned her husband, the investment guru Marc McAllister, and is currently in LA hunting for an agent to help launch her Hollywood movie career. Did you see that coming, Tory?

As Tory responds with a laugh that her celebrity crystal ball is in for repair, the clerk swipes my card with no idea the bedraggled creature in front of him is the subject of the on-screen speculation.

I shuffle back to my room, leaving the TV experts to agree that even La La Land would certify me for leaving a husband as gorgeous, talented, connected and wealthy as Marc.

Days and weeks blur into more days and weeks. I survive on little more than what the mini-bar holds until my stomach begins to rebel at the unrelenting diet of salt, sugar and alcohol. I throw up two days in a row and have to go to the vending machine in reception for orange juice. While I am there, the clerk asks me to pay another week's rent. It's then that I notice the date and realise I have been here almost six weeks. I will have to move on soon.

Back in the room, I have had only a few mouthfuls of juice before I vomit again. While I am heaving over the toilet, the significance of the date blindsides me. My period is almost two weeks late. I cannot understand how this could be until I remember that my last one as I was leaving Marc never amounted to much more than a bit of spotting.

Despite my misery, I am tempted to howl with ironic laughter at the suspicion that the very thing that drove me to leave when I did was actually the only reason I would have stayed.

❧ ❧ ❧

Present day, early morning

I am dreaming, a fragment of fact giving birth to a tangled fantasy. Marc is there, in a tie I never would have chosen, telling a TV interviewer he can't have a baby because he's about launch a Hollywood career. At the news, the Australian stock market crashes, causing pandemonium.

Can you laugh in your sleep? I think I do at first. It is ridiculous, and I am laughing and trying to untwist the truth and tell everyone what is really happening. No one pays any attention and I realise I am just a poster on the wall—me and a giant strawberry. I cry out, trying to escape but I am held back from reaching Marc by Yvette in a jaunty security officer's cap, saying, 'But we don't know where you've been!'

Something soft is against my face, dabbing at my eyes. A voice says 'blow'. I do as told, blowing loudly into the tissue, and realise I'm awake and the night is pitch black.

They say what the dark takes from your sight it adds to your other senses. Mine are on full alert. My own breath is deep and ragged, as it is when you've had a good crying jag. But there's another breath, light, its rhythm a counterpoint to my own. My mysterious housemate is here again, and I can see nothing. The hairs on my neck stand on end, and fear tangles with my grief. But there is no sense of malice or evil intentions, so I reach out.

'What's your name?' I murmur, not wanting to scare it away. 'Mine's Em.'

There is nothing but the breath, yet I get the sense it is listening.

'I won't hurt you,' I add, in case the stranger is scared.

As I wait for an answer, I feel the soggy mess of a paper tissue in my right hand. It is the first time I have dreamed and cried in weeks. Perhaps I disturbed the unseen one.

'I'm sorry if I woke you up. I had a bad dream.' I squeeze the tissue. 'Did you bring this to me?'

Silence.

'Are you … are you Evelyn?' It's a stab in the dark, and there's a gusty out-breath in response.

'I mean no harm. Did something happen to you? You can tell me if you want.'

I tune my ears to catch the next breath, but it doesn't come. I hear the door handle move and the click of the door closing.

'Wait! Evelyn!' Bolting up, I reach for the lamp and almost send it crashing. By the time I right it and switch it on, the room is empty except for me.

Well, not quite empty. The stuffed bear from the library is sitting at the end of my bed. He has a note pinned to him, the corner of a yellowing exercise book page.

Dunt be sad. I can be yure frend.

Tentatively, I reach for the bear and detach the note, hold it as though it might disappear after its author. Now I know for certain that the apparition is a child, but I am none the clearer as to his or her identity.

Is it Evelyn the child reaching out? Had she died a beautiful, unhappy teen and then reverted to her happier childhood?

Someone has to know. Robert Sanders for one. He might have been unexpectedly forthcoming at the hardware store but there is something he isn't telling me, I am sure of it. Local newspapers and local records, too, might yield something. There is no town hall in Lammermoor, but I've passed a tiny library, which may have microfiche or digitised newspapers from past decades.

And, most of all, there is the house. I suspect that the house has not yet given up even a fraction of the secrets it keeps.

Even though I don't expect to sleep any more tonight with plans and possibilities flying through my mind, eventually I start to drift off. A sound makes me jump. It is my phone. Before I can stop myself, I am reading Marc's text.

Hi, gorgeous girl. Woke up dreaming of you.

I write back: *A night for dreams. In mine, you were exchanging the ASX for Hollywood. The stock market crashed.*

Not going anywhere, Em. I'm right here.

Calm, steady Marc. He will always stand his ground, and he deserves a woman with the same kind of strength. She is not me and probably never will be.

The tears threaten again but I ruthlessly push them back as I try to formulate a reply that captures the emotional war going on inside me. After six attempts, I give up, unable to find the right words although my feelings are so overwhelming it does not seem impossible that he might be able to sense them from Sydney. Perhaps he will try again with something that leads us out of the minefield. I wait for a time but there is no text message.

A little later, because I cannot stand the thought that our tenuous reconnection was no sooner forged than lost, I text: *You're far more than I deserve.*

Throughout the day, while I am at the upholsterer's to choose fabric for the couch and agree a price for the job, and then in the garden, I check my texts for new messages. But my phone remains silent.

❧   ❧   ❧

August last year …

Hetty's opens for coffee during the day before it transforms into a bar-bistro at night. It has lots of slender palms in large pots and ceiling fans, still today, that make me think of somewhere more exotic than Surry Hills. Marc waits for me at our usual window table, a long black already in front of him. When our eyes meet through the window, he raises a hand to the barista to order my espresso.

'Hi.' I manage a brief smile. My mouth feels tight and I realise I haven't smiled in a while.

'Hi.' He reaches over as I sit and tugs the blunt ends of my hair. 'Interesting.'

'You can say it. I look like crap.' I don't intend to be antagonistic. I think it's a defensive thing.

'That's impossible. Thank you for … contacting me.'

'Don't be polite, Marc. And by the way you look like shit too.'

He does, comparatively, although you have to look closely. As usual, he's dressed immaculately for the office, although his tie is a little loose around his neck, but there are lines around his eyes and mouth that weren't there a few months ago. Tellingly, the devil in his dark eyes is missing. He looks deadly serious.

'I'll fight you,' he says, dropping his voice but its quiet intensity is enough for the barista to hesitate before delivering my coffee.

Of course he will and I don't blame him. He has worked hard for everything he has. Why would he just let some fly-by-nighter take a sizeable chunk of his assets? But even though I have sometimes taunted him with the idea I might be a gold-digger, the thought that he might actually believe it makes me feel a little sick.

I wait until the barista has departed before replying. 'Believe it or not, I'm not after your money.'

'I'm not talking about money. I mean divorce, assuming that's what this little meeting is all about. I can't stop you but I'll fight you every fucking inch of the way.'

From behind the coffee machine, the barista's head jerks our way in the quiet space. It's probably only the fact that we are regular customers that prevents her from coming over to see what's up.

'I don't want a divorce.' It's not what I'm here to say, but it is said now and it stops him in his tracks.

'Well, too bloody bad ... what did you say?'

'I don't want a divorce—not unless you do.'

'Of course I don't want a bloody divorce. I love you.'

'Don't say that!'

'It's the truth, Em. I love you. Trusting is another matter.'

In his expression, love and hate are difficult to tell apart at this moment. But my priority right now is not to know how he feels about me, but to memorise every feature in case it is the last time.

'Things weren't good between us those last two months,' I tell him baldly. 'I thought you'd had enough, that you wanted out.'

'God damn it to hell!' Even hissed low, his fury is palpable across the room. The barista heads towards us.

'Is everything all right here?' She is holding a phone, clearly preparing to call for assistance, and I don't blame her. Marc looks as though he might tear someone apart limb from limb. I've never seen him this way.

'Sorry,' Marc mutters.

'It's okay,' I tell her. 'We've finished. I'll come and pay.'

At the counter, the barista asks me if I'm all right and if I want her to call the cops.

'I don't know yet.' I answer her first question with wry smile and wave my card at the machine. 'But it's nothing the police can help with.'

'Okay.' She shrugs. 'Love the hair, by the way.' She's serious, I think.

Marc is leaning against my car when I come out. I unlock the doors and we get in. He turns to me and in the close confines, his emotions are palpable.

'Let me get this straight. You thought I wanted out so you left?'

'I couldn't give you what you wanted, so I thought I should give you the chance to go and get it with someone else. Daisy, perhaps.'

'Daisy? Davis?' He is genuinely perplexed. 'Em, for God's sake, we're married. You don't just walk out because things are a bit rocky. Why didn't you talk to me about it?'

'We were barely talking if you remember. You worked late every night and I … I thought you blamed me.'

'I didn't blame you! I blamed me, for ever raising the topic in the first place—for putting so much pressure on our marriage when we'd known each other for such a short time. I just didn't know how to admit I'd been a bloody idiot.'

'I panicked,' I blurt, hope blossoming, even though he has not quite told me everything, I suspect. But in this situation, who in their right mind would spread their entrails on the ground to be picked over when there is still a significant possibility of things not ending well. I share something that I have already discarded as irrelevant. 'She phoned one day when you were at the office. Daisy. At least, I think it was her. She never actually said.'

Marc nods. 'I spoke to her on the phone. She wanted to tell me rumours were flying around that you were seeing someone else, and hinted that her shoulder was available should I need one to cry on.'

'What?' My eyes open wide in surprise.

'I laughed and told her thanks but no thanks.'

'I didn't—'

'I know that. There were no rumours, except ones Daisy started herself.'

'I guess I was just feeling low when she called. It wasn't her, just everything else.'

He is shaking his head. 'What a fucking mess. I'm so sorry, Em, for taking my eye off what's really important. You're not enough—you're everything. If you come back, no more talk of babies, I promise.'

'Ah,' I say. 'That could be a problem.' That's when I tell him.

Sixteen

Present day, afternoon

My palms are a little damp as I rub them together at the door to the locked room, and my stomach is doing cartwheels, but there is excitement as well as fear. Will I be admitted this time, now that we have acknowledged each other? As I put my ear to the door, I can hear a rhythmic creak-creak-creak. Something inside is moving.

Instead of trying the handle, I raise my hand and knock. The creaking slows and stops.

'Hello? Evelyn, is that you?'

Nothing.

'I realise I didn't introduce myself properly the other morning. My full name is Em Reed, well McAllister-Reed, actually. I hope you don't mind me sharing your house.'

Silence reigns.

'I'd like to meet you again sometime.'

I retreat halfway to the bedroom door, not wanting to push things too far too fast. I have not forgotten Robert Sanders' story of the man who fell from the window, which I have not yet had the

155

opportunity to confirm or disprove. The weather has not relented enough for me to venture any further than the woodshed these last days. Even now the rain lashes the long windows, rattling the old panes and cascading in showers from the ancient guttering.

Glancing back towards the door before I leave the room, something catches my attention. I'm not sure what it is but it is enough to keep me there, watching and waiting. There it is again, but still I cannot identify what it is. The third time it happens, I lower my line of sight. I think I know. Something is glinting through the old-fashioned keyhole. It vanishes and returns at random intervals. I am certain it is the blinking of an eye.

I am being watched.

I am this close to calling out, to pleading with Evelyn or whatever is behind that door to reveal itself, but some instinct keeps me silent. It has already offered the hand of friendship, and will most likely do so again. Forcing the issue may be counterproductive.

This does not mean I will not look for other ways to satisfy my curiosity. I have not even begun to hunt for a way into the attic that must be there. Now, I slowly move through the first-floor rooms, my neck craned, staring at the ceiling, looking for a hatch. I am sure it must be here but though I carefully scan every inch, even in the bathroom, no manhole is visible.

Back on the landing, I stand uncertainly, looking this way and that. Yet another mystery. There is a ladder in the shed and I consider propping it against the outside wall, once the weather is better, and inspecting the attic through a window. But I am pretty certain the ladder will not reach the twelve metres or more necessary to reach the top floor. Even if it does, I am not enthusiastic about making the climb while I am alone—for all practical purposes—at the house.

I do have an idea, though, but not one I can put into action yet. In fact, there is nothing I can really do this afternoon. The garden is off limits. More than that, it is a bog after the rain we've had. Even when the rain finally stops, the garden may take days to dry out enough for me to continue working.

Downstairs, I wander into the dining room and aimlessly flick through my sketchbook. I have finished a second blog for *Small Poppies* on the topic of quality versus quantity. If there's one thing I hate, it is cheap throwaway fashion designed to be cast out after a season. Cheap is never cheerful, in my experience; it is always depressing and looks ready for the bin after one wear. It is also wasteful, and unnecessarily so when it just takes a little creativity to have any number of looks available. Clothes swapping is one option; Claire and I do it all the time. Well, did. *Fashion is seasonal, style is eternal* is the title of the piece.

Today, I am not in my style mindset, though. The eye in the keyhole is all I can think of. I turn to the torn page where I have placed the scrap used for the note pinned to the bear, and re-read it. Without doubt it was written by a child—or someone the age of a child.

My mind conjures a vision of nineteen-year-old Evelyn falling from a window, fifties skirt flipping over her head as she plummets. Perhaps her life was saved, but brain injuries cast her mind back into childhood and ... what then? Did she die sometime later, condemned to remain forever a child? Did her parents hide her here in shame until they moved away? If so, what happened to her then?

A shiver runs through me. I want to know—and I don't want to know. I still believe Robert Sanders was being overly dramatic. This ghost, if that's what it is, has shown no aggressive tendencies, quite the opposite. From what I know of ghosts, they may be prevented from passing on, either by their own incapacity to acknowledge their death or the need to pass on a message before they pass. But that is about all I know. Until very recently, I had not even known I believed in them.

Frustrated at my impotence, I do another Google search, but without turning up anything new. Lammermoor is too small and insignificant to even warrant a Wikipedia entry, and all I find are advertisements about market days, four-year-old news about a neighbourhood dispute that ended in the decapitation of twelve garden gnomes and a couple of dated alerts about the River Lam, which is known to break its banks in heavy weather.

Of Lammermoor House, there is nothing at all. I expect to find something, real estate advertisements at the very least. But just as the house has retreated from the physical world behind its forest veil, it seems also to have disconnected from the digital realm.

I remind myself that Val is a businesswoman. She had probably seen no reason to waste money advertising a house she thought she had no chance of leasing. And if the last event of any note was the tragedy of the man falling from the upstairs window years ago when the internet was in its infancy, why would there be anything about the house online?

With nothing else to do, I head into the library to find *Jane Eyre*. It is definitely the kind of afternoon to curl up inside with a book. But even that I cannot settle into, my eye drifting to the gap in the bookshelves where it used to sit, and the military history encyclopedia now resting diagonally across the gap. On an impulse, I grab it and open the cover.

For Louis on your 15th birthday.

I squint at the inscription as I reread it. The more I look at it, the less sure I am that the *15* is a 15. The writing is so loopy that the *1* could almost be an embellishment of the *5*. I flick through the book. It's not something I would imagine a parent giving a teenager for a birthday present, let alone a five-year-old. It is a rather dry account of the battles of the ancient world, with only few pictures, obviously intended for a much older person. I wonder if it once belonged to the Brigadier, Evelyn's father.

Robert Sanders would surely know the Brigadier's first name. I will ask him when I am in town. I want to go now, to find some answers to the questions raging inside.

Going to the window of the study, I stare out down the drive. But the rain is so torrential, it looks as if it may never stop.

November last year ...

'Someone with your build needs to be especially careful.'

Yvette makes me sound like a Ukrainian shot-putter, even though I've put on just three kilos and am barely showing although I'm nearly at the four-month mark. My face is rounder, though, and my breasts—well, Marc is the expert on those.

Marc opens his mouth to respond but I shake my head. As the recipient of a mega-dose of super-happy pregnancy hormones, which have also brought some sort of dewy sheen to my skin, I am inclined to go easy on Yvette. Less than a year ago, she lost top spot in her firstborn's affections—to a hussy!—and next year she'll lose her runner-up spot, too.

I smile benevolently, placing my hand over Marc's, which rests over my belly. 'We're both enjoying my womanly curves.'

The reference to sex, however obscure, hits the mark. Yvette's face turns pinched and sour. Quite frankly, I'm not sure how she came to have three children. 'In polite circles, one doesn't embarrass one's hosts, dear.'

Léo interjects cheerfully. 'I'm not embarrassed. In fact, I'm dying to know more.'

Gordon joins in the banter and before long the matter that provoked it is long forgotten, and we are assembling on the terrace for the first barbecue of the season. It is cool still and I am wearing one of Claire's designs—a short crocheted wool dress in black and white—and high black boots.

Marc hovers, putting his jacket over my shoulders before the breeze can touch me, and keeping the champagne out of sight. I do miss champagne and soft cheese. Sylvie and Brand's son, Rainier—Yvette, of course, is beside herself at the royal connotation—will be christened this afternoon, hence the gathering. I would much rather be on the couch at the apartment, my head on Marc's lap and him playing with my hair as we watch some crummy old movie on TV, but family comes with duty.

'How's Peanut?' Marc murmurs for about the sixth time that day. He has been almost overbearingly attentive since the moment outside Hetty's when I told him he was going to be a father, despite all the evidence against it. It was only when I threw up all over his shoes—ones he'd bought against my advice—in the lift up to our apartment later that day that it became real to him, I think.

He had been horrified when I told him I had not yet visited a doctor, and we went to see Macpherson that afternoon. She calmly confirmed my diagnosis and showed not a trace of smugness that her advocacy of patience had been proven right. Since then, we have gained an obstetrician of some renown and an album full of scans that show nothing even vaguely human in my opinion, although one of the early ones depicts a shadow resembling a large peanut if you hold the picture upside down, hence the nickname.

The next time we go, I am hoping to see a hand or foot—even a tail would be a relief. The obstetrician, too, has been frustrated at not being able to get a clear shot of the fetus's development. He says we have a wriggly one on our hands, although I have yet to feel more than a fluttering inside.

'Fine.' I take the plate of well-cooked steak and carefully washed salad he offers me. 'Everything's fine.'

'I suppose you'll have to move,' Yvette says. 'An inner-city apartment isn't really suitable for a child. The Vaughans at number eight are about to relocate and would prefer to sell off-market. I could put in a word.'

'No!' Both Marc and I almost shout in horrified unison.

There is a strained silence.

'We're quite happy where we are,' Marc says. 'And we have the shack if we need to get away.'

'It has no garden, Marc. Be practical. Children need space to run around. Something like Sylvie and Brand's lovely place at Rose Bay would be perfect.'

Yvette talks as though Rose Bay was Sylvie and Brand's idea but everyone knows it was hers. Heat rushes into Brand's face at her words; not only was he bullied into his choice of home, he had to accept a handout from his in-laws to pay for it. That, too, is common knowledge.

'Unless our child is unusually advanced, it won't be running for a while,' I say. 'And there are parks.'

Yvette screws up her nose. 'But there are all sorts of people there.'

'Exactly.'

She is done for the moment, but it drives home that the next few months will not be the cruise I have experienced since returning home from my self-imposed exile. Marc has done everything possible to make sure that this time we succeed. He has pared back his work hours to attend prenatal appointments, watched unflinchingly a film designed to prepare new parents for labour—in which three other fathers fainted and two left the room just in time—and has thrown himself enthusiastically into baby shopping. When Claire dropped over last weekend to brainstorm the nursery interior, he willingly lobbed up creative ideas for us to shoot down.

He even grinned when Brendan welcomed him to a spontaneous up-the-duff party with a cry of 'come here, you fertile bull of a man', and nodded with due respect when warned of the dangers of over-tight underpants. James and Will, also invited to the party, have since presented Marc with a pair of tighty-whities featuring a snorting, stamping bull.

My only gripe is the fact that he treats me as though I am a fragile eighty-six instead of a healthy, pregnant twenty-five. Now the morning sickness has stopped, I feel fantastic. Everything glows the way it is supposed to and I am bursting with energy, especially in bed, where I have had to take control in the face of Marc's caution. It is a reversal of roles and one I have embraced.

My brief disappearance is not questioned by the media once my pregnancy is announced; I suppose everyone thinks I was just keeping a low profile. But interest in my life seems to be greater than ever. Even casual comments to strangers or acquaintances turn up a couple of weeks later in some gossip rag, twisted in order to make them more portentous. Sometimes no one says anything. 'It's a boy!' declares one magazine cover after I was snapped walking past a sports shop with a cricket bat placed prominently in the window.

It is amusing in its way, and I am in demand at a time— ironically—when my focus on building a career seems to have blurred. Despite this, I have done another tongue-in-cheek fruit advertisement—melons this time, much to Yvette's continuing horror—and have been collaborating with Claire on a range of children's wear made from recycled forties fabrics.

Most significantly, my pregnancy has inspired the concept for Brendan's next show—*Elemental*. He says he wants to capture a woman coming to terms with her own power. I don't think I am the right person to achieve what he has in mind but he is adamant. There will be some nudity, although I think it will be impressionistic, but I have not told Marc yet. I need the right moment.

I will not be asking permission, don't get me wrong. Part of me thinks it does not require discussion at all. But the new more adult me recognises the sensitivities. He has never before been anything other than supportive of whatever I want to do, or pushed me— even when perhaps I wish he had. Now though, a part of him grows inside of me, yet he has few rights and no control.

The other matter we need to discuss is the imbalance in success, wealth and maturity that has dogged our relationship. It is not his fault and the solution is not with him, but it is what I feel and I must try to tell him before too long. Since my return, it has been too easy to wallow in our re-found happiness. Neither of us is willing to rock a boat we suspect still has a hidden leak.

Perhaps I will say something after the next scan, late at night after we are gorged on sex and drowsy. I know he is excited at the prospect that it will show a peanut transformed into a fetus. Maybe we will even know the gender. Marc wants to know; I am undecided. Either way, he will be on a high and, if I can get the words right, I am hopeful we can talk about some of the big issues.

The day of the scan arrives and, as usual when Dr Chan prods my belly and the image appears on the monitor, it is a pulsating, writhing soup of shadows and light. I do see a couple of hands. At one point I think I see three, but the angle is constantly changing so I am not particularly worried about the prospect of a tri-armed child.

All of a sudden there's a distinct face—two eyes, a nose and mouth. Marc and I see it at the same time, crying out. Dr Chan offers a professional smile before the usual small frown creases his deceptively youthful face as he checks the heartbeat.

'So,' he says a few minutes later as we sit at his desk. 'Did you see what I did?'

Marc's eyes are so fixed on the latest printout, clutched tightly as though someone will try to rip it from him, that he doesn't pick up on Dr Chan's tone of voice.

'Is it a boy? I think I can see a penis.'

'I certainly hope not,' the doctor says.

My eyes widen. 'You mean—?'

'You're having girls,' Dr Chan says. 'Two of them.'

Seventeen

Present day, late morning

The library is tucked away in a narrow side street, around the corner from the main shopping strip in Lammermoor. It is nothing like the architect-designed ultra-contemporary Surry Hills library that my Sydney neighbourhood enjoys; it is an old shopfront that seems to have its origins in the Victorian era, with an uninspired 1960s makeover that hasn't been updated since. I am not even sure it is open; the inside appears shrouded in gloom, but the opening hours suggest that I have come at the right time, and when I twist the handle the door opens.

No wonder it looks dark. The shelving has been positioned to prevent as much light as possible from reaching deep inside, and the light bulbs are those eco-friendly ones from about eight years ago shaped like a goat's innards that had everyone blundering around in a sickly green light inspired by a zombie movie. I thought everyone had instantly realised these were truly appalling and had dispensed with them, but clearly not here.

'Hello?' I call out. 'Is the library open? I'm looking for information on Lammermoor House and wondered if you had a local history section?'

No voice replies, but now my ears are attuned to the atmosphere I believe I hear a vibration from the far reaches of the room. Making my way past towering shelves, and stacks of books where the shelves run out, I reach what appears to be a vast heap of books and paper, but a closer inspection suggests a desk is hidden beneath the pile. A tiny wrinkled prune of a lady with fluffy white curly hair and papery skin sits behind it fast asleep. At least I hope she is asleep.

She makes no sound for long seconds before her chest rises and a soft snuffle emerges from her open mouth. I back off, not wanting to startle her for fear of what might happen.

As I am here I decide to make the most of it, though I despair of finding anything in this jumbled heap. As I move down the crooked aisles, I see the remnants of an old cataloguing system that appears to have been swamped by the sheer volume of books, most of which seem to have been donated as they bear no serial number or barcode. Nothing I come across seems to have been published more recently than the 1990s, and there is a complete absence of digital information.

This library seems to be an informal community relic rather than something the council actively manages.

I am in the third of three aisles and thinking I have just wasted forty-five minutes when my foot shifts a pile of books on the floor. As I reach down to right the stack, I see a narrow-spined hardback entitled *Lammermoor: A Century in Pictures*. I lift it and take it to the front of the shop closest to daylight and open it up.

Published in 1986, it is divided into ten decade-specific chapters. I am intending to head straight for the 1950s, but before I reach it—at the start of chapter two—is a black-and-white photo of Lammermoor House, imposing, stark and slightly forbidding without the softening effects of colour. There is scant information; just that the house was completed in 1892 as a country retreat for a Sydney merchant. It is disappointing until I notice the minute fine-print below referring to the Curse of Lammermoor House and directions to turn to page 142.

There in a panel is another smaller picture of the rear of the house, taken across the backyard with its fruit trees and vegetable plot, dated 1958. I suppose it is as Robert Sanders must have seen it in its heyday.

CURSE OF LAMMERMOOR HOUSE
**Occupied for most of its history by textile merchant
Walter Jenkins and his descendants—
by most accounts happily—Lammermoor's only grand
home has been bedevilled by a series
of unfortunate incidents in more recent years. Most serious of these involved the house's
gardener, who in 1965 lost a foot in a gardening mishap.
In 1971, a woman
was knocked unconscious when she stepped on a carriage from a train set in the attic, and three years
later, another woman suffered an almost fatal asthma
attack in the library. Perhaps Lammermoor
House's anticipated transformation into a conference
centre will put to rest its dark past.**

It is an overly dramatic way to describe three events years apart but two things jump out at me. Assuming the gardener was Robert's father, this is confirmation Robert has not revealed all he knows. It is also proof that in the early seventies there had been access to the attic.

I glance through the rest of the book but I can see nothing else of interest. Returning to the desk, I see that the wizened little lady is still deeply asleep so I cannot even check the book out, although to be honest I doubt if anyone would notice if it went missing for a few days. Eventually, I return it to its position in the shelves, make a mental note of its location in case I need to find it again, and head outside.

The wind has whipped some of the cloud away, and I turn my face to where the sun is making some attempt to break free as I consider whether to confront Mr Sanders. In the end, I go to the hardware shop only to find it is closed for a full hour for lunch. I consider whether to drive on to Saddler's Bend and the council library there but the couch is being delivered later and I need to get home. In any case, having been cooped up inside for days, I decide to take advantage of the break in the weather and work in the garden this afternoon.

Before heading home, I stock up on groceries in case more bad weather is due. The newsagent makes colour prints of my photos and I buy two new interiors magazines and a gardening book by a well-known author, which I'd completely forgotten to do last time I was in town. It seems comprehensive, and in any case as it is the only one the general store offers, it will have to do for the time being.

Determined to make the most of the afternoon outside once the couch has been safely delivered, I set to with purpose, yanking weeds, deadheading, pruning and turning earth until my boots are caked with mud and my hands are tingling with heat. When I stand back to take stock, the front garden is looking cropped and bare, and I realise I am at the point when I can stop removing and begin the plantings that will shape the garden.

Before that can happen, I need to refine my plan—currently still at draft stage—and confirm what I can and cannot recycle.

This is the difficult part as many of the plants are difficult to identify at this time of year. In a stroke of inspiration, I decide to invite Robert Sanders to the house to advise me on the plantings. Almost certainly, he will not accept but it will give me an opportunity to speak with him again and turn the conversation to the matter of his father's accident.

The wind has died and the rain has held off, but the last of the daylight is about to be extinguished when I walk inside, cold and exhausted. I think of the old roll-top tub in the bathroom that serves the master bedroom, next to the locked room, and decide that this will be the night to christen it. I usually prefer showers to baths, but today a long relaxing soak is an appealing prospect.

Although the plumbing protests when the hot tap is turned on full, the tub is soon two-thirds deep in steaming water, fragrant with some crumbled lavender brought in from the garden. With the overhead light off and only a candle for company, it is easy to close my eyes and ease down until the water is up to my chin.

Having flicked through the gardening tome, I know I still want a grand spring-flowering magnolia for the front garden, and wonder what Sanders will have to say about that. I can recycle some of the arum lilies from the back garden—where there are big clumps of them—in the shadier corners of the front. From glancing at the book I know there is a new creamy-white clivia cultivar that I can interject as a connection to the fiery orange variety in the back.

One thing that will need to be replaced is the turf in the front garden, which is patchy with age and lack of care, and the recent rain has turned it to mud. Perhaps Sanders—

My daydreams are broken by the creak of the door as it opens a little wider. The wind must be picking up again. Or maybe not. As I open my eyes, the candle sputters out, plunging the room into shadow, illuminated only by a sliver of light from the landing. The matches are naturally out of reach. In any case, time is getting on and while the fire is laid in the library, I have soup to prepare with the last of the leftover lamb.

Cold air brushes my skin, raising goosebumps. Nervously, I reach for the towel draped over the edge of the bath, and wrap it around me as I step out onto the mat. When I have re-lit the candle, the bathroom is empty except for me. I dry off, carefully moisturise my face and slick body lotion onto every piece of skin I can reach.

I turn and that is when I see the words clumsily drawn in the condensation of the full-length mirror on the inside of the door.

I AM LOUIS

My breath catches and I stare at the words. Even as I do so, they are disappearing before my eyes in the rain of condensation. Already, they are almost illegible and a moment or two later the racing droplets have swallowed them.

It all happened so fast that my mind is scrambling to keep up, but I know I have not imagined it.

Louis. I breathe his name twice, first pronouncing the *s* and then not, wondering which is right. Rather than fear, I am filled with a feeling of immense triumph at this latest approach. My little friend has shared his name. I try his name louder, but even before I open my mouth I know I am alone. Still it is enough, it is more than enough! Perhaps, in time, he will share his identity and I will understand his relationship to the St Johns.

Swinging into my robe, I belt it tightly around my waist and ensure my hair is still securely pinned in its topknot. Through the cascade of droplets on the mirror all I can see is me. My face is rosy and shiny, my eyes the emerald-green they turn when I am excited and happy.

When I have hung the towel and bathmat up to dry, I pick up the candle and matches, and run down the stairs. I am almost down when I look towards the door and see a broad, square-shouldered silhouette of a man outlined through the decorative glass panes.

❧ ❧ ❧

December last year ...

Brendan has spent six exhausting hours shooting me for his latest collection, and now it seems as if most of the portraits for his show will come from the final fifty minutes of that session, the period during which my husband has been in the studio looking on.

Apparently, my sensual power is laid bare when Marc and I lock eyes, Brendan tells us matter-of-factly as I duck behind the screen to unwrap the gauzy, flame-coloured layers he has asked me to wear for the shoot, and dress for dinner.

We had agreed that Marc would pick me up as my belly is starting to make it difficult to get behind the wheel of the Audi. However, as he arrived forty-five minutes prior to the agreed time, I am certain he was also motivated by a wish to see the images.

When I told him about the shoot several weeks ago, he was still so buoyed by the surprise announcement of twins that I think he would have let me cavort naked around the city had I wished. In the last few days, however, he has been asking subtle questions, trying—I think—to ascertain exactly how much of his wife will be on display.

In the end, I think he is beguiled and not just a little turned on by what he sees. When I come out from behind the screen in an empire-waisted maxi dress that leaves my shoulders bare, I can see the dark line of colour that slashes across his cheeks—a sure sign of arousal. Despite this I am determined to get my pizza tonight before any funny business.

I have also had a glance at some of the images Brendan shot earlier and recognise the 'elemental' nature that he has conjured and captured, particularly in the images where the shadow of my belly and breasts are visible. The images are dark, the light turning me to flame in some. In the most arresting, I am whirling, blurred, my face raised to the sky, eyes closed.

'What do you think?' I ask Marc, en route to Upper Crust in Waterloo.

His eyes are steady on the road. 'Breathtaking.'

'But you're okay with them?'

'They're beautiful.'

'You can't buy them all this time.' When I first moved into his apartment, the shots he'd bought from the previous exhibition lined the corridor between living areas and bedroom. One has been moved to his study, the others are in storage. Staring at myself day after day became too weird and narcissistic; it is the reason I never take selfies anymore unless it's a group thing. I see no reason why Marc would want to stare at photographs of me, either, given that he now has the real thing. But he insists the one in the study stays.

'I doubt I can afford them,' he admits of the new shots. 'Brendan's stocks have risen considerably in the last year. But he's promised me one of the out-of-exhibition ones.'

I think I know which one—it's the simplest, of my hands on my belly. I like it too.

Marc has been preoccupied recently, rather like he was just prior to, and after, our marriage. I am no longer worried that he regrets tying himself to me, but it occurs to me that the time he is taking away from work because of my pregnancy is having repercussions at the firm. He is the boss, but that just means he has to work harder than anyone else.

A couple of times, I have woken in the night and found him in his study, working to make up for hours lost during the day. He has already advised his staff that he will be away from the office for a minimum of two months when the babies are born, and even though he will be available by phone and for the occasional meeting, I gather from Will that this caused some uproar. Furthermore, he plans to cut back on his responsibilities in the longer term in order to take a major role in rearing the girls.

I am hugely relieved. The announcement of twins knocked both of us for six, and for me it has been terrifying. I'd barely got my head around one kid and suddenly there are going to be two. Since the initial shock, Marc, though, is taking the whole thing in his stride. Night feeds and nappy changes will be accomplished with his usual calm efficiency I'm sure, and he'll be fun too and occasionally tough. I suspect I will come into my own when they are older and need fashion guidance.

'We will need help,' I say now as we wait at the Anzac Parade lights. 'It's not realistic to think we can do it all, and you may change your mind about the amount of time you can be out of the office.'

He gives me a brief look of surprise, then turns his attention back to the road as the traffic begins to move. 'No I won't. Other people can take over at work. No one else can look after our kids as well as us. Don't worry, I'll do most of the messy stuff.'

'The two of them mean double the work.'

'We'll get help if we need it, but I'd rather not have anyone living in. I think I'd find it ... restrictive.'

So it wasn't work he was worried about, then. Perhaps his mother's comments about the apartment had hit the mark.

'If you want to move to a house with a yard, we can talk about it.'

'Do you want to move?'

'Well, no.' I would hate to be shunted out to Double Bay or Vaucluse. 'Not unless you do.'

'No.'

'Okay then.' I am at a loss so I push the boat out a bit. 'If it's your terminal brain tumour you're worried about, now's the time to tell me.'

Marc brakes a little harder than strictly necessary, gives me a look and reverses into a tight parking space.

'What's that supposed to mean?'

Oh God. 'You don't do you?'

'Have a brain tumour? No, of course not.'

'Or anything else vaguely fatal?'

He starts to smile. 'That's got to be a contradiction in terms.'

Exasperated, I roll my eyes. 'So what's going on when you look like this?' I pull a face meant to replicate his preoccupied expression but feel myself going cross-eyed so it may not come across as intended.

'If that's accurate, I'd say constipation.' He snorts with laughter.

'Stop it, I'm serious.'

'So am—what the hell?'

His grin falls away as his eyes drop to my belly which has taken on a life of its own. Abruptly, I'm reminded of that scene from *Alien.*

Tentatively, I touch the rippling mound. In response, something foot-shaped juts out on the right-hand side. Marc brushes it with a gentle finger and after a second it retracts. This goes on for another couple of minutes before the activity slows and stops.

'They've gone back to sleep,' Marc murmurs.

'Good,' I reply. 'That was seriously creepy.'

'Em.'

'It was. Anyway, can we get something to eat now? Your children are starving me to death.'

Eighteen

Present day, evening

Time falls away. Moments, seconds, minutes are meaningless. Is it two minutes or twenty we have been standing here, me on the step, he in the shadows of the porch? It might even have been two hours.

I want to stay here like that, drinking him in, though I cannot see his features clearly. There is no light on the porch. Only the faint glow from the foyer provides illumination. His overcoat is open, and beneath I can see he is wearing a crumpled cotton jersey and jeans that look a little loose. He should have a scarf, I think. On a cold night in mid-winter, he should have a scarf. But his neck is bare; his hair brushes his collar, a little longer than I remember.

'Can I come in?' Marc asks hoarsely.

I take a breath—perhaps my first since I saw him standing here—and my hand curls around the edge of the door. Abruptly, I do not want him in the house. It is mine, I think. If I let him in, I will have to share its secrets. If I let him in, something bad will happen. If I let him in, I am relinquishing control. It is like the feeling I had all those weeks ago when Val came to the door. Does the house have more power over me than I realised?

'What?' he asks, reading my face. 'What is it?'

His hands are on my shoulders, manoeuvring both of us inside. I want to shout *no*, but it is too late. Before I can react, a breath of wind catches the door and shuts it with a soft click behind us.

Under the hall light, I can see him and am shocked at the changes the past months have wrought. It is grief, but not just grief. The edges of him are harder, skin stretched tighter across bone, and where his mouth turned up, now it is a flat line. Loss is etched not just into his skin but his core. It is carved deep, and in his eyes burns a dark furious kind of fire.

It is as if he has suddenly figured out that life can be cruel as well as kind. The confidence he has always had in things working out well, just because they always have, has vanished.

Not too long ago, I started to believe that his charmed life would become mine. Instead, my train wreck has become his. This is power of sorts, I realise, but not the kind I want.

'You look good, Em,' he says. He lifts a hand to my face but drops it before he touches me.

I back away. 'This is a mistake, Marc. You shouldn't have come here.'

Marc throws back his head and a bitter laugh emerges. 'What's one more mistake?'

As his chest moves, I can see he's lost weight ... too much.

'Mrs Saatchi didn't do a good job with that shirt.' I nod at the crumpled garment. He looks nothing like the slick executive I am used too.

'She doesn't come anymore. She abandoned me too.' His tone is self-deprecating. 'Sylvie stole her.'

'I would have come back,' I tell him. 'Soon. I just need time. I told you. You shouldn't have come.'

'I gave you fucking time!' he grates. 'I don't have more time to give.'

'But I need—'

He cries out then; a howl of agony that seems to have boiled up from deep inside, ragged and terrible.

'I don't give a fuck about what you need, Em! I'm over trying to work out what it is. What about what I need? What about that? Does it ever cross your mind to think about what it is like to be me right now?'

In the face of this barrage—the like of which I've never heard from Marc—I take a step back. I am shaken, and then in denial, and then horrified by the truth of it.

How wrong I have been for so long. I have always thought the scales swung in his favour because of his affluence, but it has been the antithesis of the truth. I have always known he would move heaven and earth for me, had he the power to do so. That time, I think, has now ended.

'You have your family,' I start. 'You could have gone to them.'

'My family is you, Em. And ... them.' The roar drops to a whisper as it always does when he refers to those two little lost ones.

The reference to them scalds as it always does but perhaps not as fatally. The box I placed my grief in all those weeks ago for safekeeping, and tucked into the locked room, is back in my arms, but I am not ready to untie the ribbon and face what lies inside.

'I'm sorry, Marc,' I say and take his hand, for even I—with all my inadequacies—cannot remain untouched by his pain. 'I'm sorry for all of it.'

He is compliant, as shaken by the past few minutes as I am. He does not resist as I lead him into the kitchen and make him sit at the table. When I pour two glasses of rich red wine and press one into his hands, he obediently sips from it.

Neither of us say anything as I prepare the lamb and rosemary
soup. I remember that I had been thinking of him as I had roasted
the meat that day. It was just days ago, yet seems an age. Even this
evening seems to have lasted eons. Was it less than an hour ago
that I read the message in the steamed-up mirror?

Louis, I think. Marc mustn't know about you. He mustn't know
my secret. I stop stirring the soup and listen to the house but I can
hear nothing except for the hiss of the gas flame, and the steady
rain that has begun to fall again outside.

Marc glances up from his wine. 'I didn't think it would be like
this,' he says.

I nod, understanding. Those days after we met were so overwhelming, you think you will be forever carried along on the
crest of that bubbling, frothing wave, forgetting what is at the end
of the peak.

'I don't think I thought of it at all,' I admit. 'I wanted you irre-
sistibly.' That is true, even if there was an element of opportunism.

'I mean the house,' he says as I ladle soup into two deep bowls
and bring them to the table.

It is then I realise I have no idea how he has found me—or
even how he got through the padlocked gate.

❧   ❧   ❧

January this year ...

How rapidly things change. I never think too far ahead, but if I
had I never would have seen this.

Standing in the newly decorated nursery, my arms looped
under the vast mountain of belly, I am swaying as if to the twin
heartbeats in my womb. I think of them, clinging to each other—
to life—fragile yet strong, gathering to make the journey into this
world.

Since Christmas, it has seemed like a time of gathering to me. This period before something else, immensely powerful in its own right, has proved mighty enough to have pushed all my other concerns to the fringes. I have not worked since the day at Brendan's, more absorbed by what is happening inside than out.

I never thought it would be so, or that I could feel so content about it. I know it must be those nesting hormones. Marc has read about them, but I don't need to. I am feeling it all—the sense that I am the protector of a tiny world of my own making, and I will defend its borders come what may.

Its capital is the nursery, created in the smaller of our spare bedrooms. It is still a decent size and on the quieter side of the building away from the street. Claire and I designed it together to replicate the feeling of being inside an egg, or what we thought that would be like. The walls are on the yolkier side of eggshell and billowing canopies curve the ceiling and corners. Pale stain is on the floorboards, and the accoutrements of nurseries—a change table, rocking chair, bookshelves and storage—match the boards.

Atop a cushiony rug, a modern double-cot takes centre stage. Marc has also read that twins should sleep together when they are small, and sometimes I can already see them there, heads close together, hand in hand.

A big mobile of bright yellow chicks dangles above the cot, still in the thick, sultry air. It is the height of a crushing summer now, but soon autumn's fresh breezes will arrive, bringing with them new life. With the window open, the mobile will swing and sway, and the girls will watch it move with big, astonished dark eyes.

Last weekend, we went away, Marc and I, into the mountains where it was cooler. We wandered (in my case, waddled) through Leura and, later, Blackheath. I made myself look at the sign to Lithgow as though it was just a place that meant nothing. Marc insisted on buying a couple of ugly stuffed toys. We joke that they look like aliens. They are kind of funny, I suppose. But they are still ugly and I have tucked them away in a drawer. When he comes in tonight, he will release them from captivity. It is a game we play.

Since the nursery was completed and despite Marc's frequent protestations, I have been so busy around the apartment that poor Mrs Saatchi has started to think of herself as quite unnecessary. I have had enough energy for ten, and have reorganised every drawer, shelf and cupboard in the place. The ironing is done almost before the dryer has finished. The floor shines and the windows sparkle.

Marc yelled at me when he found me up a ladder the other day, cleaning the lights above the kitchen bench. He scooped me off and dumped me on the couch.

'Don't even think of doing it again,' he says, wagging his finger. But what can he do to stop me? Nothing can touch me in this bubble. Why did I ever worry about work and our relationship and who I was supposed to be? About Yvette's dislike of me? Now, I simply don't care about anything beyond my tiny world. Without any effort, everything has worked out the way it was meant to be. Weirdly, I have never been happier. It's a little bizarre considering how I fought this, but I have found a calling of sorts, a purpose. I can't believe it's just hormones.

The phone rings in the study, pricking my bubble. I do not really want to speak with anyone, and it will probably be for Marc. I walk down the hallway and across the living area where two great fans rotate slowly. The breeze feels wonderful on my warm skin.

In the study, I pick up the phone but whoever it was has already given up. Marc's laptop is open. I have not snooped or spied for weeks; there has been no urge or reason to. But today, the lid is flipped up and it pings to announce a new email.

And there it is, in Marc's inbox—the one thing I thought I had left far behind has found its way to my door.

☙ ☙ ☙

Present day, night

'Did you really think I didn't know where you were?' Marc tastes his soup. He seems a little surprised it is so rich and tasty. He goes back for more. I have not touched mine.

'But for how long?' I ask him, dumbfounded.

'Weeks, longer.' He shrugs.

'Val,' I say, trying to remember her surname. I give up. 'The real estate agent in Lammermoor, the nearest village to here.'

'I know who she is, but I contacted her, not the other way around.'

His eyes are on me and a small smile plays around his mouth as if he is daring me to erupt. Maybe I should. Perhaps it is what we need and what we have never had—a full-blown fight.

'Then who?' I think of Sally's freckled open face, her uncle's closed one. Maybe. I am still suspicious there is a plan afoot to extract money. The deli owner? Unlikely. The upholsterer? I had to give my name and address, but he seemed more interested in fabrics and buttons than me.

Marc taps my mobile, which is on the kitchen table.

'It's been on the whole time.'

'You had me traced? Seriously?'

'You're my wife,' he spits out. 'You were upset. I didn't know what you might do. I needed to know where you were and if you were all right, and I'd promised not to call in the cops, remember?'

'You shouldn't have done it.'

'We've both done things we shouldn't have.'

My growing anger is halted. I remember all those times I scrolled through his tablet and computer. Not because I was looking for anything in particular, but just because I felt a lack of control. Because I felt there was something I didn't know and if I knew it, it would help me to survive.

Marc gets up and pours us both a hefty slug of wine, perhaps his way of telling me that we are in for a long night. We may yet have that fight.

'If you've known where I am ...' I don't finish the question but I don't need to.

'I promised you some time,' he says simply, his black eyes on mine. 'I kept my word.'

'We never said how long,' I mutter defensively.

'Not in words but we both know that the deal was you would come back when you felt stronger. And you didn't.'

I stare at the table. 'I would have. Soon.'

The old fridge rattles and hums for a couple of minutes and then subsides into silence.

'Em, I can be a patient man, but you would try the patience of a saint.'

'You knew life with me wouldn't be easy.'

His lips part to let out a mirthless laugh. 'Is that your only excuse? That you're high-maintenance?'

I look around the room, hunting for words that will capture my inadequacy and hopelessness and uneasiness in my own skin. My eyes alight on the small bundles of herbs stuffed into glass jars along the window ledge.

'They're from the garden,' I tell him in a voice that sounds rather rusty. He swivels around to face where my finger points. 'The rosemary and thyme and stuff. I've spent time in the garden, and in the house. I needed to be on my own here to find ... something.'

I sound rambling and incoherent, but perhaps some of what I've said has made sense because this time he doesn't snort with disbelief.

'Find what? Peace?'

'Yes. Maybe more than that. I don't know.' I shift uneasily, unused to having these kinds of conversations. 'You said the house surprised you.'

'It's not your natural habitat.'

You're wrong! I want to say, disappointed at the inference that I don't belong here. For most of our time together he has been very astute in judging what lies beneath.

'Although I could be wrong.' His chair scrapes the floor as he pushes it back and stands. Without consulting me, he wanders through the kitchen, looking up at the burnished copper pots and around at the unruly garden cuttings stuffed into bottles and vases.

'Did you cut the chain on the gate?' I ask.

He shakes his head, and looks down ruefully at his scuffed shoes. 'I came over the wall. The car is parked out in the lane.'

Before I can guess his next move, he is moving through the double doors into the adjoining dining room where my sketches of the garden and notes are spread all over with the photographs I've had printed.

It's too late to stop him but I follow and lurk near the door, watching as he stops at the table and begins to look through the mess.

'Is this yours?' He holds up the plan of the front garden, probably the most finished.

I nod and fold my arms around my waist.

Next he picks up the prints of the vintage outfits.

'I'm writing a blog,' I say. 'About fashion … and stuff. I'm thinking about starting my own website.' I take a breath. 'I *am* starting my own website to help women with their wardrobes and interior design, perhaps cooking and gardening too.'

I know he won't laugh at me but I'm not expecting his complete confidence in my partly formed plans, either. He surprises me. 'Good. You have incredible instincts when it comes to style.' He looks around. 'The real estate woman says you plan to make some changes to the house.'

'Oh, nothing much. I don't have the money. Maybe some paint and there are some repairs to be done if I can get tradesmen out here. When did you speak to Val?'

He glances up at me but doesn't say anything. That smile, the not-so-nice one, is playing around his lips again. It only takes me a second to connect Marc and the superannuation fund that owns the house.

'It's you, isn't it? Lammermoor House belongs to you.'

He is about to answer when from upstairs comes an ominous creaking sound, a second or two of portentous silence and then a crash that shakes the house and has the dining room chandelier quivering wildly.

I rush from the room, ignoring Marc's call to wait, and fly up the stairs through a cloud of dust to find that the old armoire along the landing wall has come toppling down in a mess of shattered wood and glass.

And behind it, leading upwards towards the attic, is a set of steps.

Nineteen

February this year ...

Do you know what I did? Nothing, apart from delete the email I'd found in Marc's inbox. I did not open it. I pretended I did not know that name. I told myself I had not seen it, that it had never happened.

It is a more extreme version of a child closing her eyes and believing no one can see her. Don't acknowledge it and it doesn't exist. And as time goes on and nothing happens you can almost believe it is true. Almost.

In any case I have more immediate concerns, namely Yvette's offer to stay with us for a month after the girls are born to 'help out', which she makes following a casual lunch at the apartment to celebrate Marc's thirty-third birthday.

Despite my blithe outlook, a threat like this is not to be ignored and, as Marc is currently outside on the balcony talking about the new rugby season with his father, I will have to nip this in the bud myself.

'You don't have anyone, Emerald,' Yvette points out, an expression of kindly concern on her face. 'And I'm worried you're not coping.'

I am sprawled on the couch in the apartment, my belly rising up like Mount Vesuvius between us, eating dark chocolate. For the last few weeks, I have had a craving for the stuff. Dr Chan is pleased I have put on a few kilos in the last couple of months. I am glad to be carrying most of it out front and not on my bum.

'I have Marc,' I point out. *Your firstborn. Ha!*

Yvette waves her hand impatiently as she would at a mosquito. 'You can't expect him to drop everything to deal with this. Do you know how important he is? How much they rely on him? You will have to pull your weight, dear.'

As she says 'weight', she frowns at my belly. I want to tell her it is their fault, not mine.

'I think Marc plans to become a househusband,' I say airily, feeling the urge to stir the pot. 'I may have to become the breadwinner.'

'With what?' The faux concern is forgotten and her voice drips acid. 'Your melons?'

As goofy as it was, I knew she wouldn't approve of the melon ad. Fortunately, the sharpness of her tone cuts through the rugby rumble and Marc is immediately there beside me. I give him a square of chocolate and a beatific smile, happy to hand off his mother for him to deal with now that I am pretty sure she has dropped the idea of being an unwanted house guest.

'Have you decided on names yet?' Gordon interjects into the silence, a hint of desperation in his smile.

Since Peanut became Pea and Nut, Marc and I have had numerous conversations on this topic, conversations that usually become more hilarious with each outrageous suggestion. But with just a month to go, no decisions have been made.

'Something classic,' Yvette says in that throaty way. 'French, to honour Marc's heritage.'

Marc's eyes meet mine and we both hold back a laugh.

'Champagne and Merlot! What a wonderful idea,' I exclaim. 'My favourite wines.'

Gordon starts to cough, his usual reaction to impending conflict. Marc just looks amused.

'I didn't—' Yvette starts, looking appalled.

'Inspired, Yvette.' I heave myself up and give her a warm hug. 'I'll think of you every time I look at the girls.'

'But that's not—'

'No, no.' Settling back on the couch, I wave my finger at her. 'You're too modest. It was all your work and everyone will know it. I'll make sure of it.'

'Well, in that case … time we went home,' she replies—a clear admission of defeat in my eyes. 'Gordon?'

I can't say she runs out the door, more of a gentle jog, dragging Marc's father behind her, and we are finally alone again.

'Sometimes you are positively wicked, Mrs Reed-McAllister,' Marc says. He lifts my feet, settles down beside me and props my feet in his lap.

'You're no help.'

'Do you need any?'

I shrug. 'It is kind of fun, now she doesn't scare me.'

He shakes his head. 'I think you always had her measure. The issue is, what the hell are we going to call them? We can't use Pea and Nut forever.'

I break off another piece of chocolate, munching slowly. 'Don't worry about it. We'll think of something.'

'Nothing too … affected.'

'Like Emerald, you mean? You don't want to add Ruby and Sapphire to your collection?'

'I prefer Em to Emerald,' Marc replies, his eyes steady on mine. For the first time I wonder if he knows. Maybe I should say something. It's my chance to get it out in the open. I may never get another opportunity, another time when I feel so completely that I have shed the lost, damaged girl who arrived in Sydney on the six twenty-five train from Bathurst all those years ago. Marc will understand, won't he? He'll understand none of it was my fault, and agree that it has nothing to do with who I am now? It can't touch us now, can it?

But then I remember the email, and what is likely to happen if past and present collide. If I do nothing else, I must protect him from that wretchedness.

He is still watching me. 'Do you?' I ask.

'You're everyone's Emerald, my Em.'

'That's kind of … pathetic,' I tell him to hide the fact that my heart has just turned over. Either that or I am having a dark chocolate overdose.

In retaliation, he begins to tickle my feet, which is not fair as I am pretty much a beached whale and can do no more than kick and scream. To prove he's not as pathetic as he pretends, he carefully rolls us until he is lying on the couch and I am sprawled across him, the babies between us.

'A month to go and they'll be here,' he whispers in this kind of awed voice. 'Can you believe it?'

I shake my head.

'No doubts?' His eyes search mine.

An ocean full of them. I shake my head.

'Liar, liar, pants on fire,' he murmurs, pulling the tie from my hair. It is back to the length it was before I hacked at it, although in this humid weather I have considered chopping it off again. When he combs his fingers through it, from nape to end, my neck arches back with pleasure.

By the time I have a measure of control back, my dress is scrunched around my hips and my underwear is adorning a lamp. I feel his knuckles against me as he opens the button fly of his jeans and I bite back a moan. He presses forward, his eyes on mine as he joins us.

ॐ ॐ ॐ

Present day, night

'Bloody hell.' Marc surveys the scene of destruction. 'Just as well nobody was walking past when that thing came down.'

'Yes.' My eyes are fixed on the small door but he is focused on the splintered wood and broken glass. The atmosphere is thick with more than dust.

'Don't go too close in those bare feet. I wonder how it happened.' He picks his way through the debris, heads to the end of the landing outside the master bedroom and looks back. 'Everything's out of square from the looks of it. Walls, ceiling, floor. Not unusual in an old place like this, but still. I guess the weight of that thing ...' He shrugs.

'I'll clear it up in the morning,' I say, anxious to get him downstairs.

'What's up here?' he asks, looking around.

'Worried you've made a bad investment?'

He looks at me. 'It's not an investment. You were here.'

'How much did you pay?'

'A touch over one point five.'

While he is glancing into the master bedroom, I move so I am in front of the small door.

'Five bedrooms and two bathrooms,' I tell him as he passes by me, sticking his head briefly through each doorway. I say nothing of the locked room.

'It's on about fifteen hundred square metres, according to Val, and includes a small parcel of woodland and a river frontage.' He cocks his head to one side, calculating. 'It has heritage features, easy access to Sydney. Despite the fact it needs plenty of work, I think I got a bargain.'

Clearly he is not aware of the house's history, but when I glance at him, his eyes are on me and I wonder if the last sentence is a reference to the house at all.

'Anyway, it won't be mine for long,' he adds.

My throat closes. 'What?'

'As soon as it settles, the deeds will be transferred to you.'

I am confounded. 'But why? Why would you do that? After everything ...'

'Because I think you feel safe here.'

Why can't he hate me? Just tell me I am a heartless bitch, a hopeless fake, and just walk away?

'But I must be a disappointment to you.' There, I've said it, even though my lips feel stiff and my insides shaky. 'This can't be what you imagined your marriage, your life would be.'

'Maybe not, but I've learnt that expectations have very little to do with reality.' He sounds calmer than I think he is. 'It is what it is.'

'It doesn't have to be. We could end it.'

We stare at each other across the wreckage of the armoire.

'Is that what you want?' His eyes boil with emotion that somehow he is holding in check after his earlier explosion.

'I ... no. I don't know. What do you want?'

He smiles and it's bittersweet. 'I want my wife to be able to face what has happened.'

❧   ❧   ❧

March this year ...

In the dark, I wake. Something has changed, though I am not sure what. I turn my head towards Marc's, close to mine on the pillow. He breathes deeply and easily.

I have been waking a lot at night recently. It is hard to get comfortable when you're the size of a hot air balloon, and it seems the babies are always ready to play when I am ready to sleep.

Tonight, though, they are still. I groan under my breath, wishing I could take advantage of their quiet mood to get a good night's rest.

When I shift a little, Marc mutters under his breath for a moment, his arm tightens above the rise of my belly. I know he is awake, that he too has sensed it.

The softest of March breezes sighs through the bedroom and vanishes through the open window. Summer has fled, and it is autumn.

I press a hand to my belly. Marc's hand covers mine.

Tonight, the babies are still.

❧ ❧ ❧

Present day, night

'I know what happened.' I fold my arms tight around my middle.

'Do you?'

'Yes.'

This is not the firefight I had imagined, but a war of stealth, which is irritating beyond belief because it gives him a distinct advantage.

'So how do you feel about it?'

'Don't!' I put up a hand as though it has the power to repel his words.

'Do you want to know how I feel?'

'No. No!' In my mind I can see a little girl, hands over her eyes.

'Em, denying feelings doesn't mean they don't exist.' His voice is soft but exasperated.

'I know that.' Rationally, I do know it but there is a long way between knowing and accepting.

'I don't think you do, Em.'

I step back, feeling the bannister behind me. My hand reaches back to grip its smooth surface. 'This is stupid.'

'You don't want to know how I feel but I'm going to tell you because I have to. I felt ... I still feel as though the best of us has been stolen. And I want to get it back, so desperately. And I can't.' There is that rasp in his voice that makes me fearful. 'I'm scared I will never be happy again.'

'Marc ...'

'I still see them ...'

I squeeze my eyes shut to ward off an image that I cannot bear to see.

'I miss them, Em.'

'Stop it, Marc.' I can feel the fluttering of panic at my throat. 'I don't want to talk about it.'

'You need to. You can't just push it away forever. Push me away.'

I feel like I can't breathe. I need to get away. Blindly, I turn to head for the stairs, but he is there, pulling me around to face him.

'Em, you need to face this. You need to—'

You don't know what I need! I want to yell. *You don't know who I am!* The sound echoes around us and I realise that I haven't only said the words in my head but in fact.

Marc's hands drop to his sides. 'I've always known her. The person who doesn't know her is you.'

'That's ridiculous. I know who I am. What I am! I know I'm vain, self-serving, bitchy, flaky, sneaky. I'm a coward. I let people down. I don't keep promises.'

Marc counts off against his fingers as though he has a mental list. 'You make me laugh. You're a good friend, most of the time. You're sweet, when I least expect it. Passionate.'

'More crosses than ticks.'

'It's not all black and white, positives and negatives. I love your bad bits, Em, even though they drive me insane, because they're *your* bad bits. It doesn't make any sense but it just is.'

What do you do when the man you love disarms a hand-grenade without turning a hair? I don't know about you, but pushed to the edge, I pick up the rocket launcher.

'I'm a liar,' I tell him baldly. 'I've lied since the very start. You don't know me! How can you? You don't even know my name!'

Twenty

March this year ...

The one saving grace, for me, is that most of what happens is a blur. I am locked inside my head, and the physical ordeal is nothing. I'm aware that people are there, telling me things and asking me questions. I think I answer lucidly enough because they seem satisfied. Then there is nothing for a while.

When I wake up in a hospital bed, Marc is beside me—in shock, I think. His shirt is inside out, I notice, and his hair is sticking up on one side. His eyes are fixed on my face.

'Em,' he says, clutching my hand. 'Em.'

'Good drugs,' I manage through a throat as dry as dust. 'You should take some. You look terrible.'

'Love, our girls—'

I turn my head and close my eyes, finding oblivion in sleep.

It seems only moments later that I wake again, but it is broad daylight. He is still there. I am desperately thirsty and he pours water for me.

'Em, you know—'

I drink thirstily. 'Yes.'

'They're beautiful, Em. Perfect, except … when you're ready, I'll bring them in so you can hold them for a bit.'

'No.'

'Just let me bring them in and see how you feel. Please.' The hand not holding mine shakes as it tunnels through his mussed hair. His voice is unsteady. 'I can take them straight out again if …'

Strangely calm, I say again 'no'.

There are voices at the door and Marc is telling them to give us a minute. When they insist, he tells them to fuck off.

It makes me smile. 'Thank you,' I tell him when the voices are gone.

He is crying and I reach out to wipe a tear from his face. 'It's okay,' I tell him because it's what you do when your husband is sad and nothing will comfort him except a lie.

'Sweetie, you need to see them before they take them away. It's important. Please. If not for you, for me.'

But even for him I won't look at those still, still faces. After a while, he leaves for some time. And when he comes back, I know from the look on his face that he has done what has to be done, and it is over.

❧   ❧   ❧

Present day, night

At midnight, we sit on opposite sides of the kitchen table. Marc has topped up our wine glasses but neither of us has touched them.

'Why don't you tell me who you are,' Marc starts.

When I say nothing, he sighs. 'Very well. I'll tell you. You are Emma Ashley Reed.'

I am frozen, unable to say anything to stop him. All I can think is that he knows. *He knows!* Of course he knows! How could I be so stupid? People like the McAllisters don't marry without doing a background check.

'You were born the second child of Jaclyn Hobbs and her de facto, Wesley Reed, in Orange. After your father was sentenced to prison for armed robbery, when you were four years old, your mother moved with you and your elder sister, Vanessa, to Lithgow to be with Darryl Marlon, a known drug manufacturer. Your mother and Marlon had three children, two boys and a girl.' He paused. 'How am I doing so far?'

When I am mute, he shrugs.

'It was a chaotic, dysfunctional household. You and your half-siblings often missed school, and when you attended, teachers noted that you were always hungry, dirty and poorly dressed. Despite obvious signs of neglect, and regular reports by teachers to welfare authorities, you were not removed. Other cases were deemed a higher priority.' He seems to have memorised a report.

I feel numb. Everything I'd put behind me—the grubby history I'd tried to keep from my new life and shiny, perfect husband—has returned to smother me. 'Enough, Marc,' I say faintly.

'We need to finish this,' he says. 'Finally, the authorities act when one of your younger half-siblings finds the heroin your stepfather has left lying around. He is left brain-damaged and removed, aged eight, and shortly afterwards Vanessa is also taken into care, for underage prostitution.'

'Stop it! I don't want to hear it!' I have the urge to cover my ears with my hands to block out his voice, but that will not protect me from the memory he has restored—of coming home to find Jacki and Darryl off their faces, oblivious to Ryder's violent fitting and the little ones' screams.

'At age seventeen, you leave in the middle of the night and take a train to Bathurst. Two days later, authorities receive emailed photos of you trying to protect your youngest half-siblings from

assault by their vicious father, while your mother looks on, drunk.'
His voice is thick with disgust. I can't take it. I just can't.

'Stop now, Marc. Please. Just stop.'

'No.'

'Please.'

He shakes his head. 'Did he hurt you?'

I don't want to remember the raised fist, the mad eyes and spitting mouth, or the whimpers of terrified children. I don't want to remember my terror that he would wrench the broom I picked up to defend myself, and use it against me.

'No.' Not that time.

'In Bathurst, you call yourself Erica and work in cafés and do other cash-in-hand work for more than eighteen months before leaving for Sydney.'

'What is the point of this?'

'Your half-siblings all have good homes now, if you're interested. Vanessa works in a bar at Port Stephens and is studying beauty therapy.'

'I'm not interested.'

'All right. Back to you. You change your name to Emerald, drift from share house to squat to share house, working in casual hospitality and retail jobs. You have friends and boyfriends, but don't allow anyone to get too close. Your unusual looks, style and don't-give-a-damn attitude are starting to attract some attention. You do some modelling work, become the face of rising fashion designer Claire Vincent and the muse of photographer Brendan Hughes.'

'How dare you have me investigated?' My voice is low but without heat. I should be incandescent with rage but I just feel drained.

'I haven't finished. Age twenty-four, you marry wealthy funds manager Marc Lucien McAllister, thirty-one, after a whirlwind romance. You leave him briefly, a few months later, and reconcile shortly after.'

'Stop it. Stop it now.' I lift my wine glass and drain it, then slam it down again so hard it is surprising it does not break. 'Why are you doing this? Because you hate me?'

He shakes his head. 'Because I love you.'

'Loving someone doesn't give you the right to invade their privacy.'

'You're right and I didn't. My mother did when you returned after leaving me the first time. I shouldn't have read the report, but I did. And I told her if she wanted to maintain a relationship with me, she would not breathe a word. As far as I know she hasn't.'

Why doesn't it surprise me that Yvette was involved?

'That was my old life.' I am surprised to hear the words emerge through my stiff lips. 'I didn't want it to touch us.' I think of the email, glad I deleted it. 'You don't know what they're like, my mother and stepfather.'

He utters an abrupt, brief laugh, laced with bitterness. When his dark eyes meet mine I know then that I have been fooling myself to think I could keep the old poison from spreading.

'I know exactly what they're like,' Marc says. 'I received their first blackmail letter two weeks before our wedding day.'

❧ ❧ ❧

March this year ...

There is a thin film of high drifting cloud above a pale blue sky. I sit on the balcony and drift with it, weightless, thoughtless, empty. A mug of coffee sits next to me, going cold.

A hand touches my shoulder and I look up into Marc's red-rimmed eyes. I feel remote, helpless to do anything for him, as though we are on different planes, he and I. Will and James, for all their ridiculousness, seem to know to listen when he wants to talk, to distract when he doesn't. I have no idea how to help him, let alone myself.

'I'm going for a run, sweetie. I won't be long.' I see he is dressed in his running gear and know he is trying to find the threads of his old life and hang on to them until the world stabilises. 'Do you want anything?'

I shake my head and turn my gaze back to the clouds. Thinking he has gone, I drift again. Then I realise he hasn't gone after all and is sitting opposite, hands clasped loosely between his knees, head bowed. Or perhaps he has been and returned. Don't know, don't care.

'This is hell on earth isn't it?' His voice shakes. 'Having to organise a funeral for ...' He can't go on. After a minute or two, he wipes his eyes. 'I didn't know ... burial or cremation. Both seem inconceivable. But I need somewhere to go ... to be with them. So it's a burial. One coffin. Friday. I have to be there and so do you.'

The final sentence is uttered in a firmer voice than the rest, as though he is shoring up both of us, and offering no alternative.

But when Friday comes, I exit the shower dressed in leggings and long T-shirt, my feet bare and hair loose. And I return to my spot on the balcony to stare at the sky and not think and not feel.

Marc emerges in a dark suit I've never seen, and an orange-and-purple tie that reminds me of those two stupid stuffed toys we bought. I suppose he thinks there should be colour as well as dark. Where are they now, those alien-dogs? Still in the nursery, I suppose. When Sylvie was here the other day, she hesitantly proposed 'restoring the spare room'—that was the way she put it. I didn't much care but Marc refused. I suppose he wants to do it himself and tear himself up just a little more. His choice.

'Em, I've put out a dress that Claire chose for you. We need to leave in ten minutes.'

From the look in his eyes, I know he is already defeated. I will not be there. I feel a brief surge of something like gratitude for my background, my lack of exposure to doing the right thing. I have no compunction to even try, whereas Marc has no option and it is killing him.

'Okay, Em,' he says a few minutes later. 'I'll tell them how much we were looking forward to meeting them. How much we love them.' He picks up something from the table, two small but perfectly formed arrangements of orange roses, purple iris and white lilies. They match his tie.

He can say what he likes. *They won't hear you*, I want to say. *They are dead and no sweet words, no pretty flowers, no doing the right thing will change that.*

As he walks away, he glances back and our eyes briefly meet and I can see in them that he already knows that nothing he can do will change any of it. But he does it anyway. It makes no sense to me.

The door clicks quietly shut and I am left alone to drift with the big sky. The humidity has returned, and bilious grey clouds are threatening a cataclysmic storm. I imagine it reaching into the depths of the balcony and lifting me up, up and whirling me away. At one point, I stand at the rail—it is the only thing separating me and the storm. I drag the coffee table close to the rail and climb up on it. My arms are raised. Come and take me, storm. Carry me away!

I close my eyes and step onto the rail. It would be so easy to let go. I like easy. Hard is too hard.

Something reaches through the wind and rain and thunder. I open my eyes and look down three floors to the ground where

Marc is staring up and screaming at me, his mouth a dark O of horror. And then I can't see him anymore.

≈ ≈ ≈

Present day, night

The clock in the foyer chimes midnight.

I think that between twelve and one there is a no man's land of time—a period that belongs not to the day just gone or the day to come, but to the dark. The natural time for all that we most dread to emerge from the shadows, whether that is the monster under the bed or the monster in our minds.

I bring the waxy candles in their tall brass sticks into the kitchen where I light them and place them on the table, between us. With the overhead light off, and the flames flickering, everything we are is here in the pool of light cast over the table.

'What are you thinking?' Marc asks softly.

'That candlelight is probably our best friend right now.' Marc looks pretty ragged and my hair is coming loose from its knot.

'Are you cold?' he asks, and I realise I am still in my light robe and the night is freezing. He comes around to where I sit and lays his warm coat over my shoulders.

'I thought it was the prenup,' I tell him when he is back in his seat.

He frowns slightly. 'Thought what was the prenup? We didn't get one.'

'I know. I thought that was the problem, that in the final days before our wedding you were regretting we hadn't gone ahead with one. But it wasn't that at all, was it? It was him, Marlon.'

Marc nods.

'What did he want? Money, I suppose.' I feel tainted by association.

'One hundred thousand or he'd sell the story of your background to the media.'

'You didn't pay him, I hope.'

'I met him and convinced him his plan would be most unwise.' There is an edge of menace in his tone that is most un-Marc-like.

'You met him?' In what world did the Marc McAllisters and Darryl Marlons ever meet? 'When? Where? Don't tell me you invited him to the apartment.'

'No. I went to Lithgow, to the house you grew up in. He and Jaclyn still live there. They have very little.'

I think they are lucky to have that.

'And after that—after he sent you that letter—why didn't you have me investigated?'

'I still hoped you would confide in me once we were married and you felt more secure. And I didn't need a private investigator to tell me what Marlon was.'

'You kept that very quiet.' I think of the strain on his face in those days before our wedding, and feel a queasy combination of guilt and gratitude that he didn't tell me.

'As did you,' Marc fires back. 'Tell me, if you'd known your stepfather had tried to blackmail me, would you have gone ahead with the wedding?'

'No, of course not.' I'm not sure but I hope I would have had the guts to walk away. 'I just don't understand why you did.'

He looks at me. 'Don't you know, Em?'

I look down at the table. 'Yes.'

'I wanted to marry you, desperately. And to stay married to you. Marlon terrified me—not him but what he could do to us. I think it was partly why I wanted a baby so soon, to tie you to me.'

When I look up into his eyes, I can see the truth in them, yet I haven't the heart to blame him when my actions are mostly at fault for bringing us to this point. Any questions about my background earlier in our relationship, I had deflected with a practised wave or casual comment, giving the impression there was nothing to say on the subject, all the time suspecting that it was only a matter of time before its ugly influence began to spread.

I do not want to think of my stepfather's narrow, weasel face and my mother's bloated one but I can't help a decades-old image forming in my mind of slurred words, unfocused eyes and manic laughter, of slaps, pinches and bizarre threats. A hard-edged warning from someone like Marc might have stalled them for a while, but not forever.

'I know it didn't stop them,' I admit miserably. 'I saw an email from him on your laptop in January but I tried to put it out of my mind, to pretend it wasn't happening.'

'Your pregnancy was public by then and I think Marlon thought it would make me more vulnerable, that it would be enough to make me pay up to keep him quiet. So he tried again.' A grim smile flits across Marc's face. 'I had the company's lawyers draw up something to the effect that if he and Jaclyn wanted to get clean, they should approach a facility that I sponsor, but that we were fully aware of his criminal history and that further attempts at blackmail would be referred to police.'

'Oh God, no wonder Yvette hates me,' I groan.

'She doesn't know about the blackmail. No one does, apart from me and my legal people. Unless Marlon or your mother told anyone.'

'Don't call her that.'

Marc nods. 'Jaclyn.'

'Anything since?'

'No. I guess ...' He shakes his head but I already know what he is thinking.

'I suppose after ... after we separated, they thought there was no point.'

'I'm guessing so.' Marc nods.

'You must be glad about that.'

'Em, I'd rather deal with Marlon every week than for us to have gone through what we did.'

'You're a good man,' I tell him.

'Do you love me?' he asks.

There it is, the heart of the matter. The candlelight flickers as he poses the question in the simplest of terms. The box of painful secrets has somehow extricated itself from the locked room and sits unopened in my hands. I don't want this conversation but he deserves no less than the truth.

'I don't think I'm capable of loving someone else. Not the way you love me.'

'I think you loved the girls with everything in you.'

Wildly, I shake my head. 'No, no. It's not true. I didn't want them.'

Marc smiles. 'You didn't want to want them, and I can understand why. But that's not quite the same thing as not wanting them. If you hadn't loved them, I don't think you would have reacted the way you have to their deaths.'

Even though my head screams *no*, my fingers are untying the ribbons that secure the box. I can't stop them. I can't stop my secrets spilling out. In my mind I am back on the balcony, stepping off ...

'I thought they died because I didn't want them enough, didn't love them enough.'

The words hang between us. I can see the shock on Marc's face. Everything I am, the bit of me that is missing, is laid bare. 'I thought they died because of me.'

Twenty-one

March this year ...

The storm has me in its embrace. I am being lifted up, whirled away from the nightmare, free at last.

But suddenly, at the last moment, hard arms are around me, wrenching me back. Marc's voice is screaming incoherently, his face a pale mask, and we are huddled on the ground, soaked, the wind whipping us as though angry at being thwarted.

Will and James stand at the door to the balcony, asking panicked questions. Will is on the phone to emergency services until Marc tells him I am all right. The boys are hesitant to go, but eventually they are convinced and leave us alone. With them gone, there is only the sound of the storm and our shallow, urgent breathing.

Marc pulls us into the corner of the balcony where we are protected from the wind if not the rain. I turn my face into his shoulder and hear his heart beating near my ear, still too fast.

'I didn't mean—' I stutter.

'I won't let you go.' It is a warning and a promise.

The shock of it has shaken me from the stupor I have inhabited these last days, and I have to try to explain. 'Marc, I'm sorry. It wasn't … I wasn't thinking.'

'It's okay, sweetie.'

It's clearly not. I think of him, of what an appalling day it has been for him—two dead babies to bury and a wife driven to jump from the third floor.

'How bad was it?'

He knows what I mean and his hand tightens in my hair. 'Worse than anything I imagined. James and Will had to hold me up.'

'I'm sorry.'

'There's nothing to be sorry for.'

But there is. I should have been there, not for them but for him. 'Yes. Marc—'

He interrupts, speaking quickly as though speed will get us through this faster. 'Listen, now that it's over, I was thinking we could go away for a few weeks. The States, maybe. New York. Claire says she needs someone to research emerging fashion trends. Could be a job for you. Or perhaps the Seychelles. We can just swim and lie on the beach.'

'Not yet. In a few weeks, perhaps.' I can't imagine getting on a plane with all those staring, wondering faces.

'Whenever you're ready. I need to make arrangements at work, in any case.'

It occurs to me he hasn't been in the office for days, not since it happened. He has been with me every second, until today. It's true he was preparing to loosen the reins, but I imagine not quite this abruptly.

'You should go back to work on Monday, Marc.'

'No rush.' Our fingers entwine. 'It's only been eight days.'

As he speaks, I know that we are both thinking the same thing, that while our world has spun tragically off course, the wider world is unchanged, still turning on its axis.

Marc, though, can get back. It will be a struggle, but he has his work and his family and, most of all, his will. He will make it back to the real world. I may not.

❧   ❧   ❧

Present day, early morning

The words hang there between us, still trembling in the air for long moments after they have been spoken.

I thought they died because of me.

I am expecting Marc to react with astonishment followed quickly by denial; his fury catches me by surprise. He stands up suddenly, hands on the table, and leans in, eyes flashing dangerously.

'That's just fucking stupid, Em. The most fucking self-indulgent, fucking stupid thing I ever heard. It was nothing to do with you or me, or the doctors or anyone. They were wrigglers and the cord got trapped around their necks. Their oxygen supply was cut and they died. It was as simple as that.'

It is true, brutal but true. And effective as nothing else could be at snapping me out of my self-pity. And he's not finished yet.

'I love you, Em, but I hate the way you make everything about you—even something like this. It was a terrible, terrible thing and it still is. If we'd been able to share it, talk about it, it might have been just that bit more bearable. But you decided to make a martyr of yourself, and turned a tragedy into our own private hell.'

'I said I'm sorry.' I give him a wounded look.

'Fuck sorry!' He throws his arms up in the air before planting them back on the table. 'You know what? I'm sick of apologies, of excuses. It's time to grow up, Em, and think about the people who love you. Or you can keep living life on the surface, never delving too deep, never digging in. Run when it all gets too tough. But if you do … shit!'

'No, go on,' I tell him. 'If I do, what?'

He backs off a little but stays standing, his arms folded across his chest. 'I'm not about to make ultimatums.'

'Sounded like it to me.' I'm standing too and we are facing off, the fight we should have had all along. 'You knew what I was and you thought you could change me from a silly, shallow girl into what? Someone like you? Smart and clever and thoughtful and charming? A high achiever with impeccable connections? Someone your mother would approve of?'

'Don't be fucking ridiculous.'

'So it's fine for you to tell me what you think, but when I speak my mind I'm ridiculous?'

'No, of course not!' His hands are back on the table, as are mine, our faces centimetres apart, glaring at each other. 'I just want a partnership of equals, not to feel like I'm having to be the grown-up for us both.'

'Is that right?' I smile coldly at him. 'You know what? I don't believe you. I think you like being the boss in our relationship. You enjoy the ego boost of being the one to look after helpless, incompetent little Em!'

His eyes narrow. 'Maybe you see yourself as helpless and incompetent. I don't. I think it suits you to think that.'

'What's that supposed to mean?'

'It means that you don't ever have to commit to making things work. To work at making things work. You can just throw up your hands when it gets hard and say "sorry, but I told you I was a lost cause".'

'Like our marriage, you mean?' I throw back at him. 'Stupid to commit to something that was obviously a mistake from the very start.'

'If you felt that, why did you go ahead with it?' he asks.

'Because you—' I stop, aware I'm venturing onto thin ice. Marc's gentlemanly side has been throttled by his anger.

'Because I made you? Convinced you? Cajoled you? Did I drag you down the aisle?'

'No, although you can be pretty pushy when you want something. But that's not why I married you.'

'So why did you marry me?'

'Because I wanted to, even though I knew it was a bad idea.'

'So you married me knowing it would fail.' He presses fingers to the bridge of his nose.

'Well I was right, wasn't I? Look at us now. Not exactly glowing with married bliss, are we?'

'Sounds like an "I told you so" in there.'

'Well, I did. I warned you it was a mistake.'

'Which conveniently excuses you from all responsibility for making our marriage work.'

'You're saying it's a self-fulfilling prophecy?' I am enraged. 'That I deliberately sabotaged our marriage just to prove myself right?'

'Well, didn't you?'

I am mute with anger, but also with the dawning realisation that there is some truth to what he says, maybe more than some. But there are two sides to this, and neither is innocent.

'Yes. You're probably right. But instead of calling me out on it, you just worked even harder to prop it up. Because you thought you were so invincible you could make our marriage work on your own.'

'That's not … shit!' Marc sits down suddenly, and drops his head wearily into his hands. 'I don't know what we're doing.'

A few months ago, the concept of Marc being unsure of anything would have scared me almost more than anything. If he didn't know, who was left to steer the ship? But, now, somehow, it is heartening that he can be as uncertain as anyone.

'We're having a fight. We should have had one a long time ago.' I don't say it, but I think that when I am cornered and can't run I am more of a scrapper than Marc, whose charm has worked so well, he's never had to fight dirty for anything.

He looks up and gives a tired smile. 'Maybe, but can we call a truce for now? I'm too tired to go another round. And it's bloody cold.'

I glance at the oven clock. It is after one. We have been fighting for more than an hour. Even though my blood is up, my nerves are humming and I want to slug it out until we have a resolution, I too am shattered.

'You can have the couch,' I tell him. 'I'll take the chaise.'

I can't imagine I will sleep, not after everything that has happened tonight—not just Marc's arrival and our explosive confrontation, but the words written in steam and the discovery of the door to the attic. How can so much have happened in the space of six hours when so many days have drifted past almost unnoticed while I've been in this house?

It is only as I rise from the table and return his jacket to him that I realise how utterly dog-tired I am. I direct Marc to the powder room and, when he has finished, give my teeth a cursory brush.

'Goodnight,' Marc says when we are in our respective beds and the lamp is out. Even now, after months apart and revelations we may never recover from, it seems unnatural to sleep apart, but it would be too easy to let sex heal our cuts and grazes, while the real wound festers untreated.

'Night,' I reply, my eyes wide open though my brain is fried.

It will be a long night, and what tomorrow will bring I cannot imagine.

☙ ☙ ☙

April this year ...

Marc is working from home with occasional trips into the office for meetings, usually when he knows that Claire or Brendan will be dropping by. Each time I suggest that he returns to his usual routine, he makes some excuse. The truth, that he dares not leave me alone, remains unspoken.

After a while, I stop suggesting he go back to the office full-time, and accept that I am a child, to be watched and supervised. I get up at seven each day, and shower and dress, not because I feel like it but because Marc will worry less if I have a routine. I have done such great harm and feel such immense guilt, it is the least I can do.

I still cannot explain what happened the day I almost went over the edge. Haltingly, I have tried to tell Marc this once or twice. He says he believes me, but still he watches me for any further signs of a death wish.

We are both trying in the only way we know to get through each day, but the longer-term future seems hazy, impossible to gauge. And the half-truths that it requires to get through the days are taking their toll. They simmer under the surface, pushed to boiling point by the fact that we are with each other almost constantly with no escape valve. When we socialise with Marc's family or friends it is worse, as we are forced to lie to them as well as ourselves. We have even convinced them that the worst is over, and the fraud we are perpetuating makes us feel unbearably isolated.

I go along with it all, even though every instinct in me rebels against it, because it seems to be what Marc wants. I cannot countenance that he is as lost as I; I think he must have a strategy in mind to get us through this, that if we quietly endure somehow we will survive.

Once, he asks me if I want to talk to a counsellor, but I refuse as I think he already knew I would. A few days later, I relent to Marc's suggestions that we get away. A long-haul flight is out of the question, but we escape showery Sydney, flying north to Darwin like migrating birds for the winter.

If either of us hopes it will somehow break the circuit, we are disappointed. It brings neither the collapse I am dreading, nor the coming together I suspect Marc is hoping for. We wander the streets and the harbour foreshore, hand in hand and a million miles apart. Over casual lunches and smart cocktails, we smile and share observations as though we are tourists forced to share the same bus. At night, the vast bed in our huge suite only emphasises the growing gulf between us.

We return after four days with tans, small gifts for family and friends, and heavy hearts, and it feels like either the end of our beginning—or the beginning of our end.

Twenty-two

Present day, early morning

'Are you awake?' I murmur, knowing he is, having sensed the cadence of his breathing change some time ago.

'Yes.'

I think we both move towards each other at the same time and then, naked, he is carrying me the couple of metres from the chaise to the long, deep couch where my sheets now carry his scent.

'This is a bad idea,' I murmur, looking up at him.

'We should stop then.' And he does, waiting, sitting on the edge of the couch next to me. In the dark, his eyes glitter and his jaw is tense. He is used to taking command, but now he is saying that the next move is mine—my decision, my responsibility, as much as his.

'You are my husband.'

'I am.' He strokes the hair back from my face.

'And I'm your wife.'

'Are you?'

215

Am I? I search his face, see myself mirrored in his eyes, but the reflection provides no answers.

'I can be your lover,' I say. It is honest at least, even if it is hurtful. 'Can that be enough for now?'

His face is grave. 'I want more, Em. I want everything.' But his fingers are moving in my hair and stroking my face.

All I can think is that, despite everything—my unsavoury history, the grubby little blackmail attempts, his disillusionment at my lack of backbone—he still wants me, at least in bed. As I desire him. But too much has been said this night for us to succumb to sex without a stab at honesty.

So, I tell him, in my halting way. 'I don't think I'm ready to be the wife you want even though I do love you, Marc, even if it doesn't seem like it—'

Leaning his forehead against mine, he sighs. 'The wife I want is the best wife you can be. That's all. I won't settle for less than that, Em. I won't let *you* settle for less.'

He puts his mouth to mine, almost tentatively. It feels strange, this uncertainty. In bed, we have always been instinctive, sure. There was never that awkward clash of limbs and noses, the nervous laughter or questions. *How was it for you?* From the start our bodies seemed to know each other, as though we had been lovers in some previous life and our physical selves still bore the imprint of the other's flesh long after our memories had been wiped clean.

I realise, with shock, how long it is since we have kissed, longer still since we've made love. We move in slow motion, sliding against each other, rediscovering the sensation of skin against skin, of hard against soft, of throaty moans and sensual, senseless words.

We are side by side on the big couch, legs tangled, his hands on my hip and back and mine in his hair. The steps of this erotic dance are languorous and known only to us, and continue on forever it seems. The seconds, minutes and hours slow to meet us, slow almost to a standstill. And finally, as delight seizes us in its relentless grip, he is inside me and we are one.

☙   ☙   ☙

April this year ...

The night of Brendan's show is here. I am dreading being on display. In deference to me, to us, he has delayed it for as long as he can. But the gallery and his agent have exhausted their patience. I think Marc has asked Brendan whether we need to be here and, of course, the answer is yes. Part of me wishes he didn't mollycoddle me; the other half just wishes he could make the world go away.

Claire has come over to help me dress; it is a new creation inspired by the works on display, a diaphanous gown, fragile yet fiery, Grecian in style, and just sheer enough to suggest at the shadows beneath.

I have lost weight; my collarbones and shoulders are more pronounced. Not quite bony, but I am down to the last layer of flesh. She makes me dust on some gold body power to suggest more than there is. My hair is loose, brushed to a pale red sheen, and my eyes and lashes are dramatically dark. A large amber band wraps around my upper arm.

'You look like a pagan high priestess,' Marc says, scrutinising me. I'm not too sure if that's a compliment. The word pagan conjures up images of people with dirty hair and bad teeth. But Claire beams in pleasure.

He turns to my friend, who is in an ice-blue satin cocktail dress with a cinched waist and flared skirt. 'Claire, you look as pretty as a picture. Ready to go?'

The show seems to have attracted more of a football crowd than a gathering of art aficionados, both in numbers and volume. I baulk at the door, telling Marc and Claire that I need a minute before fleeing to the bathroom. Locking the door, I stare at myself in the mirror. All I can see is a tall, willowy woman in a gorgeous gown. I don't feel like me. I don't feel like anyone. Even the rebelliousness, the prickliness that used to illuminate my eyes has been extinguished. They are a flat, dull green. Lifeless.

But I can act. I've been doing it all my life. As a seven-year-old, I convinced a concerned teacher that my lack of lunch was because I'd already eaten it, and ten years later, a police officer that I wasn't homeless, just sleeping rough for a school project. In the last few days I've delivered the performance of my career. Tonight I just have a bigger audience.

'Em?' He knocks on the door.

I paste a casual smile on my face and open the door. 'Let's do it.' I take his hand.

'Sure?'

I do not meet his eyes. 'Sure.' Facing a room is nothing. We've done it a million times.

'Em, it's okay if you need a few more minutes.'

I shake my head and walk past him into the vast white room where sixteen huge photographic panels fill the walls with elemental visions of a woman who is me, or at least part of me. I pause as all heads turn my way and the volume drops. Then, a smattering of applause runs through the crowd. My smile widens, I pose for the camera flashes and suddenly Emerald emerges.

When, several minutes later, I turn back, Marc still lingers by the door. I raise a questioning brow and he comes to me.

'I didn't want to steal your thunder,' he murmurs, his mouth near my ear. A shiver runs through me, and I am mortified. How can I still feel desire? I pull away from him as Brendan comes over, twittering and clasping his hands in glee.

'Perfect timing, as always. Em, you look magnificent, and Marc … a fallen angel. Those cheekbones. Those eyes! One day, I'd like to get you on film.'

I give my husband closer attention. He is extraordinarily dashing in his navy suit and open-neck dark shirt. He too has lost weight, giving him a lean, hungry and dangerous look.

'Thanks but no thanks,' Marc laughs. 'How's it going?'

Brendan beckons us in closer. 'The whispers are that the reviews will be rapturous. And my agent is juggling competing bids from some very influential collectors.' He glances at Marc. 'Are you sure you don't want one? I can arrange favourable terms.'

At that moment, I am swept away by Brendan's agent for an interview with the feature writer of a daily newspaper so I don't hear Marc's response. My grilling about what it means to be the muse of a rising star of photography and the husband of the man who made the financial markets sexy takes about forty minutes. Clearly she has been well briefed as there is no mention of anything else.

When I am free once more, I turn and she is there, Daisy Davis, red talons gripping my husband's arm as she hangs on every word. It's so blatant it's sickening. And she's not the only one making eyes at my husband. Have these women no shame?

As irritation surges through me, I debate whether to stride across the room and smack the bitch in the face. But just then Marc turns towards me, and widens his eyes in the universal plea for assistance. Aware that people are watching, I take my time crossing the room towards my husband. I smile and introduce myself to Daisy, lifting the hand attached to my husband on the pretext of admiring her ring. She takes the hint and leaves shortly after.

'Thank you,' Marc murmurs when she's gone. 'She wasn't getting the message.'

'You need to be blunt. In that kind of situation, charm is your enemy.'

He inclines his head in acknowledgement.

It is exhausting but reassuring that we have performed so well. In fact, we get right to the end of the evening without a misstep. I am just congratulating myself when it happens.

We are in a group with multiple conversations going on. Marc's arm is around my shoulders as he talks business to a man on his left. To my right, an old friend of Brendan's is casting me admiring glances and trying to engage me in an esoteric conversation.

'Oh, I'm so sorry. You don't have anything to drink. Let me get you something,' the young man says. 'Champagne?'

I smile at him, only half paying attention. 'No, thanks,' I tell him, smiling kindly. I put my hand on my belly. 'I can't drink at the moment. My babies are due—'

Abruptly, I stop, stunned. My face must have collapsed because the young guy looks at me with terror as though he has accidentally shot me. The only other person to have heard is Marc, but I am barely aware of him making our excuses quickly and firmly.

He turns me, his arm holding me up and forcing my legs to move across what seems like acres of gallery space, the crowd parting like the sea before us. We just make it into the lift before my world implodes, the dam breaks and I collapse screaming and sobbing in his arms as the agony of loss rips through me with the force of a hurricane.

I do not remember being bundled into the car or the journey home, and have only a vague recollection of being carried up to our apartment, shuddering with reaction, where Marc runs a hot shower and makes me sip fiery whisky. Even huddled in bed I am still shivering, and he curls his body around mine but still I shake.

Then the doorbell sounds, and Marc leaves the room. I hear hushed voices and then the doctor comes in. He speaks to me with kindness and concern, but I hear none of it. Marc holds my hand, there is a prick in my arm and then the tide comes in and sucks me under.

❧ ❧ ❧

Present day, early morning

One moment, I am asleep. The next, I am thrust upwards into instant wakefulness. It leaves me gasping for breath with its shocking suddenness. I am not on the chaise and it takes a moment for me to orient myself.

A rough weight is heavy on my waist and breast. Marc's right arm pins me down. His blond head is tucked into the nook between my head and shoulder; our legs are tangled together. His breath shivers across my skin, deep and steady.

Glad he is resting, I am content to lie quietly, watching the shadowy play of his eyelashes on his cheek, feeling the intimate weight of him and breathing in the heady scent of man and sex.

Our sexual reconciliation is probably the worst mistake we have made so far—and that is saying something—but maybe it can help us to navigate a way back that words cannot. The only thing I know is that it doesn't feel wrong.

Why I am awake, I do not know. After our emotional and sexual exertions of last night, I should be as deeply asleep as Marc. Yet, for some reason I am wide awake, every sense on alert.

Upstairs, a door opens, creaking on its hinges. My thoughts turn from our warm nest on the wide, newly upholstered couch to the small door revealed by the destroyed armoire. Can I hear footfalls, or is it just my imagination conjuring the sound of steps on the stairs?

My contentment has vanished, and I can no longer relax. I have to know what is up there. I have to know what happened inside this house.

By increments, I disentangle myself from Marc's clasp. At the last, I think that I have woken him. His eyes flutter open, he smiles blearily and then he slips back into sleep with murmured words too soft for me to make out. I slip my hand from his.

Even as I throw my robe around my shoulders, I am thinking I am a fool for leaving the security, however brief, of our warm tangle to go poking around in the dust and cobwebs of the attic on the hunt for a ghost.

But I have left so much undone in my life so far, abandoned so much of what I have started, I must see this through. If I can solve the mystery that has blighted this house and lay a small spirit to rest, it will be an achievement. Perhaps not one that you would put on a résumé, but the kind of quiet, uncelebrated success that counts far more.

When Marc wakes, it will be hard to resist his pleas for us to return to Sydney to work things out. I want to; I am nearly ready. But I have to do something first, and this is something only I can do.

On the way from the room, I glance at my phone. It is after six but this winter morning is a long time coming and all is in gloom. In the foyer, I turn on the lights but somehow the insipid glow just makes the house seem unusually sinister. Although my skin is still sleep-warm, I shiver.

Glancing back longingly at the drawing room, I consider curling up back next to my husband and forgetting about mysteries and ghosts until there is daylight and Marc's reassuring presence to deflect the fear.

Coward! It is time to stand on my own two feet so I sigh and turn away from the room where Marc sleeps, and start silently up the stairs. At the top, the air is colder for some reason and my skin prickles with goosebumps. I stop myself from looking down. Instead, I pick my way carefully around the smashed wreck of the armoire, wishing I had thought to put on socks or shoes.

Moving towards the door, I am wondering why the armoire was placed across it when there is plenty of wall space to the left, when my robe snags on a splintered edge of timber. I stumble, losing my balance in the dark. My foot grazes a large shard of glass, splitting the skin. I hiss in pain as blood blooms, almost black in the dim light. *Damn it!*

There is blood on the hem of my robe now too, not much but the silk is ruined. Unwilling to turn back, I tear a strip from the edge and bind my toe. Blood immediately soaks through but it is the best I can do. Anyway, all I am doing is taking a look at the attic. It will take just a few minutes.

Taking a breath, I steady my nerves, turn the handle and open the door. The narrow steps up are wreathed in darkness. I feel around for a light switch and find it; the bulb springs on but weakly. With one hand pressed against the wall, I climb the first few steps. I look back and, already, the doorway looks far behind me.

I take another few steps. Above me, the stairs seem to narrow further, closing in. I fight the feeling of claustrophobia and force myself to take another few steps. My foot hovers above the next when there is a flash, the light dies and I am in darkness.

Twenty-three

April this year ...

Two days later, I am heavy-eyed and leaden-limbed yet resolute. Claire has been with me for two hours but has just left for a client consultation. Marc is due back in thirty minutes from a board meeting. It is a narrow window, but I have had long hours to think since I woke from my stupor, and I know what I have to do.

When he returns, I am ready. This won't be like the last time I fled, the running away while his back is turned, without warning. This time I will face him. I am sitting in the chair opposite his office desk, with the idea that perhaps we can be businesslike about this. I know I can. My emotions are utterly spent; there is no more weeping and wailing left in me.

I have dressed carefully in jeans, sandals and a blazer. My hair is clean and in a topknot, my face made up to conceal my pallor. I am ready. His key turns in the lock.

'Em?'

I stand, stiffly, as he spots me in the study. He comes to the doorway created by the bookshelves and looks at me quizzically.

'You're up. That's great! Why don't we take a drive up to the shack, have a walk along the beach? I checked the forecast, windy but dry ...'

His voice tails off. He has noticed the travel bag at my feet. He looks up at me, a question in his eyes that turn slowly from warm onyx to flint. 'No,' he says flatly.

'I've decided,' I say. 'It's for the best.'

'Running away is never for the best.'

'I'm not running away, I'm getting away. I need time alone to think.'

'You can think here.'

'No, Marc.'

'You're not leaving me.'

'I need to find—' *Me* sounds too clichéd. 'I need to work things out.'

'You won't work it out by running away.'

'I can't do it here.'

'Then we'll go away together.'

'No.' I think of the Darwin disaster. 'This is something I have to do, Marc. For a while.'

'Where?'

'I don't know.' It is the truth. I have no real attachment to anywhere, no bolthole in which to lick my wounds. Perhaps the place I have been happiest is the shack, but it is his and it is not far enough away. I need distance and space to heal.

From his expression, I can see that he does not believe me. 'You must have a plan.' There is a note of exasperation in his voice.

'North.'

'How far north exactly? Are we talking Manly? Or Mongolia.'

'Somewhere in between, probably. I will find a place that feels right and stop there.'

'That's crazy, Em. Places don't feel right; you *make* them right.'

I shake my head, disagreeing, but it is too hard to explain that I have no option now but to follow my instincts.

'Em, listen. You must see I can't let you go. Not after ... what's happened.'

He still can't say it; neither of us can. Yet it inhabits us, this room, our lives.

I stand, lifting the bag. 'You have no choice.'

'I'm your husband.'

'I'll contact you in a few days or so.'

'Don't do this, Em.'

'I must do it, for both of us.'

His arms are spread across the doorway and I wonder if he will attempt to physically restrain me, but as I approach, he drops them and stands aside.

'I love you, Em.' It sounds like the last words of a dying man. 'I can't bear this after everything ...'

'Yes, you will.' I cup my hand momentarily around his left cheek and look into his eyes. 'Look after my husband for me.'

My hand drops and I walk to the door.

'Don't go, Em. Please. Stay with me.'

I walk steadily to the door. In a burst of motion he is there, his hand flat against it, slamming it shut as I open it.

'Let me go, Marc. If you love me let me go.'

After a moment's hesitation, his hand falls to his side. I touch his fingers fleetingly with mine, open the door and walk quickly through it.

෴ ෴ ෴

Present day, early morning

All I can see at first is the faint mist of my breath on the air, which is suddenly even colder—icy even. I shiver reflexively and my hand loses contact with the wall. Before I can panic, I have found it again, and this time I plant one hand on the wall at each side to centre myself before taking another step.

Beneath my robe, my heart is racing. My injured foot throbs. The pump of blood warms me a little within, reinforcing my depleted reserves of courage as I ascend another two steps. My eyes are adjusting to the gloom and ahead I can just make out what looks like another doorway. Spurred on, I continue steadily upwards, my arms still braced on either side of me.

Not only is the air icy, it seems rarer up here, as though I am at high altitude, even though I must have only climbed four or five metres. When I look back, though, I cannot see the landing, save for a sliver of queasy yellow light from far below. It looks a world away.

The stair wall has disappeared and I remain stock still until I am steady without support. I am perched on a small landing with nowhere to go but ahead, through the low doorway that matches the one at the bottom of the stairs. Something sounds faintly through the timber, a clack-clack-clack.

The sound is rhythmic until it stops for seconds at a time before starting again. Leaning close, I press my ear to the door. I think I hear the murmur of a voice.

Before I can change my mind, I bump my knuckles softly against the door. 'Louis? May I come in?'

The voice stops although the clack-clack-clack continues. Perhaps I hear footsteps, I am not sure. Perhaps I just expect to hear them. But the door does not open as I anticipate.

I turn the knob, expecting it to be locked like the room below, but it is not. Heavy and old, it opens slowly a crack under my hand. I push it open just as the first feeble glimmer of grey day-light washes through the line of pointed windows, illuminating the great sweep of the roof space save for the low corners still swathed by shadow.

Quite what I expected to see, I am not certain, but not this. Instead of a jumble of storage boxes, old papers and outdated furniture, there is a large, old-fashioned train set covering the floor. An engine moves steadily clack-clack-clack around the track until it hits a twisted rail section and overturns, the wheels spinning uselessly. Next to it lies an empty, old-fashioned pack of orange Jaffas.

My eyes dart around the attic, seeking the small figure I know must be here, but there is hardly anywhere he could be hiding. An antique rocking chair stands close to the bank of windows, and under the eaves, shelves are lined with children's toys of all kinds—tin soldiers and board games and a spinning top. There are piles of books, too, stacked haphazardly. A cushion lies on the floor between the chair and the train set, the imprint of a small body suggesting that he has just that instant risen from watching his train circle the track.

There is more dust and cobwebs than a parent would normally permit in the vicinity of their child, but in every other respect it is a well-used, working playroom.

As before, I sense him more than hear him, the softest of footfalls behind me. I force myself not to look in case I frighten him. In any case I am too terrified to turn around.

'I like your train set.'

He comes closer. '*She* broke it.' The boyish voice has a faint lisp and holds a note of annoyance.

I glance at the mangled piece of line. 'Who did?'

'The lady. She didn't want to play with me.'

'Didn't she?' I probe, wanting him to keep talking. 'Why not?'

'I don't know. She told the men she wanted to make a ... a nursery home. I heard her.'

I frown, thinking about what Robert Sanders has told me. 'A nursing home?'

'Yes. She wanted to throw all my things out. But she didn't.' The little voice is smug with childish satisfaction.

'Didn't she?'

'No. She fell.' He laughs the laugh of a child who got his way. 'She tripped over the train and hurt her leg. Then she went away.'

'And you stayed here?'

'Yes, it was quiet when she went away. When they all went away.'

'So you play up here on your own?'

'Yes, I wish I had someone to play with. Will you play with me?'

'I've never played trains before.' Slowly, awkwardly because of my cut foot, I sit down cross-legged on the floor and set the over-turned train to rights. 'How does it work?'

Still keeping my eyes averted, I can see only the quick practised movements of small hands in my peripheral vision, still carrying the plumpness of babyhood. My heart squeezes for an instant.

He quickly sets the train back in motion and we watch, spell-bound, for a minute or two until it ends in predictable disaster.

'If you let me take it away, I could see if it can be fixed,' I offer.

'No. No! You can't take it. It's mine.' The footsteps retreat to the far corner of the room.

'Okay.' I keep my voice relaxed. 'Who bought the train set for you?'

'Nobody. It was Grandpa's. He said I could play with it.'

'Was his name Brigadier St John?'

'No, it was Grandpa,' he says, in the voice of a child used to stupid adult questions. I nearly smile.

'What about the other toys? And the books?' I point to the shelves in front of me.

'My first mummy bought them, before she went away.'

'Your first mummy?' I consider asking him if her name was Evelyn and decide against it.

'Yes.'

'Did you know her?'

'Only what Grandmother and Grandpa said. She went away when I was little.'

'Why did she go away?'

'Because I was bad.'

The explanation is matter-of-fact, and spoken with such candour, my breath blocks my throat.

'Why?' I breathe. 'What did you do?'

'I was borned.' He sounds as though he is parroting something he has heard many times. 'I shouldn't have been borned, Grandmother said, so Mummy had to go away to Inkland.'

'England?'

I sense him nodding. 'Grandmother told me I could have a new mummy but she must have forgot.'

'Your new mummy never came?'

'No, and then everybody else went away and nobody came.' He sounds resigned, but a second later, I feel him at my side. He sits next to me, head leaning against my arm. 'Not for a long, long, *long* time.'

Still, I don't look down but slowly, so slowly, I raise my hand and place it on his head, feeling the soft little-boy curls under my fingers.

We sit like that for what seems an age. The sun is up now, sending a palely cheerful glow through the dusty filter of the window. I don't dare to move, thinking he has fallen asleep. But then he stirs and murmurs into my arm.

'Will you be my new mummy?'

The jolt to my heart is fierce. I must have moved because, in an instant, the weight against my arm is gone. Clouds block the fragile sun. 'I can't …' I stammer.

At that precise moment, we both hear it. Marc is calling for me from downstairs, although I cannot hear the words.

232   J.C. Grey

'I have to go now.' I stumble to my feet, scooping up my robe.

'No. Stay with me. Tell him to go away!' The little voice is sullen, the lisp more pronounced.

'I have to go to him but I'll come back. I ...'

'No you *won't!*'

'I promise!'

'Em? *Em!* Where are you?' Marc's voice is distinct now, as are the sound of his footsteps. He is on the main stairs.

'Make the man go away!'

'Louis, I—'

'*Make* him!' The little voice spits a volatile rage that fills me with fear, and the scent of oranges is suddenly overwhelming.

I rush to the door, shouting. 'Marc! Stay where you are!'

'Em? Are you okay? Where are you?'

'I'm all right. Go downstairs, Marc. I'll be down in a minute.'

'Are you in the attic? I'll come up. Shit, there's glass everywhere.'

'He has to go!' Louis hisses and it is more frightening than any roar for its venom.

'Christ! Em, there's blood. Are you okay?' His footsteps are thudding on the attic stairs and I rush towards the door to stop him.

Louis screams in fury. And suddenly, there is a terrible groaning sigh of old wood and ancient nails, and as I rush through the doorway I see that a whole section of the rotten staircase is coming away from the walls.

My disbelieving eyes meet Marc's wide ones and then he is falling, falling in a cascade of splintered wood to the landing below.

Twenty-four

April this year ...

One of the best things about a sporty little car like the Audi is that it requires you to actively drive instead of sitting back and letting the vehicle do all the work. You have to use the clutch, down- and up-shift—all of which takes concentration and brain space. It is a reasonably effective antidote to grief and panic. Walking a tightrope across the Grand Canyon might be better but all I have is the Audi.

I did not lie to Marc about my intentions. I drive north through city streets busy with afternoon traffic, both pedestrians and drivers. Cars clog the ramp onto the Harbour Bridge, inching forwards, but finally there is the glitter of water below and the wheeling of gulls against the autumn sky. The Opera House disappears behind me and before long I am on the freeway and whipping towards an unknown destiny.

They talk about white line fever, but I think it is more like driver's hypnosis, watching the white line unfold, kilometre after kilometre, stretching on, unending into the distance. I feel as if I could continue on forever, but somewhere north of Newcastle the traffic thins and I am losing the light. With daylight saving a distant memory, in another hour the light will be gone.

Noticing that I will need to refuel before too long, I turn off the freeway at an unfamiliar intersection and drive west simply because turning left is easier, eventually stopping at a service station. After filling up, I scoop up some orange juice, water and a bag of trail mix, and approach the counter to pay.

'Where am I?' I ask.

The man says something but it means nothing. Working out a plan of action is too hard so all I can do is continue on. I see signs for Gloucester and Stroud. I have perhaps heard of them, although maybe I am thinking of the English towns they presumably were named after. All I know is that I am surrounded by pretty countryside, turning dusky pink in the late afternoon light, and soon after to a dim blur.

I am not conscious of turning off the main road. Perhaps I don't and the main road has become minor. Either way, when I am next aware of my surroundings, it is fully dark. The clock indicates it is after seven. The road is a low-lying narrow ribbon. Trees crowd the overhead space so that I feel as if I am in a subterranean tunnel.

Slowing, I ponder what to do. There is no obvious place to turn so I can do nothing but continue on. Night mist drifts in fine tendrils across the road, wraith-like, lingering before drifting on. I slow further as the mist intensifies and lean forward. I can barely see five metres in front. My dream-state has vanished and I am on full alert.

Suddenly and terrifyingly, a bright and blinding light bursts through the car from behind me. Brakes and tyres shriek and an angry horn blasts. Gasping, I look away from the road to the rear-view mirror. The double headlights of a monster truck glare angrily from behind and I can see the silhouette of the driver's face, contorted with fear. He cannot stop his rig in time.

Automatically, I smack my foot hard down on the Audi's accelerator. The sporty engine responds, welcoming the sudden thrust, and leaps forward just a second before impact. One accident is averted but I am driving too fast in the mist in my panic. I nearly steer off the road, making the bend at the last moment. But I have overcorrected and the road is behind me now. I am on some kind of unmarked track.

Back on the road, the truck rumbles on. With a conscious effort to put aside my alarm at its sudden appearance behind me, I slow to a crawl. The track is dropping gently down into a valley. The Audi's tyres thud over what sounds like a wooden bridge. All around are trees, their bare branches reaching through the mist like ghostly fingers and tapping on the windows.

I almost drive straight into the wrought-iron gates that mark the end of the lane, but a gasp of wind whips the mist away at the last, and I see them with a moment to spare, rising up, black and imposing, just in time to apply the brakes.

After cutting the engine, I get out stiffly and walk to the gates. I peer through the handsome curlicues of iron up an overgrown drive. In the headlights, I can just make out the imposing portico and tall chimneys of an old house. No lights shine from the gothic-style windows, but perhaps whoever lives here is at the back.

All I need are directions. I could turn back and continue along the road but for how long? The problem is the rusty padlock looped around the gate, but when I touch the lock, it crumbles in my hands, and the gate slips silently open.

I could just walk up to the door; it is not far. But I want the car close. It is all I have now. So I drive slowly up the gravel drive to the entry, parking right in front and climbing the three shallow steps. A bell clanks noisily when I pull the cord to the side of the door.

I imagine an old crone opening the door and nearly giggle, but no one comes, even when I ring the bell again. Disheartened, I take a step back, looking up at the long, beautifully proportioned windows, curtains closed against the night.

In frustration more than hope, I thump my fist softly against the heavy door. At my touch, the lock clicks and the door opens into a dark, tiled entry.

I am not inclined to enter the shadowy house without an invitation so I call from the step.

'Hello? I'm lost? Can you help me?'

My phone chirps as it delivers another text. Marc. I ignore it as I have done all afternoon but knowing he is thinking of me gives me strength. I tighten my grip on the bag looped over my shoulder, and step inside.

'Hello?' My voice echoes around the empty hallway.

Several doors lead off the entry, only one is open. In the light from my phone I can make out a grand drawing room with towering ceilings dominated by a flaking ceiling rose. The only furniture is a shabby red chaise.

Exhaustion swamps me. I want nothing except to sink down on it and close my eyes. But I make myself retreat. I sit in the car, trying to construct a plan. I could stay inside the car, tilt the seat back and wait it out until dawn even if I can't sleep. It is the sensible option. But then I look up and the door is still open as if waiting for me. The house looks lonely in its emptiness.

What harm will it do to stretch out for a few hours on the chaise? I do not have to break in and I will face tomorrow better for some sleep. Decided, I leave the car for the second time, take the picnic rug and my weekend bag from the boot, and return to the house.

I close the front door behind me and let the calm quiet sink into me. In the drawing room, I kick off my sandals, shrug out of my jacket and curl into the chaise as I drag the rug over me.

A second later I am asleep.

❧ ❧ ❧

Present day, morning

'I *told* you.'

The little lisp comes from somewhere behind me, plaintive rather than angry now that retribution has been exacted. Whirling to face it just as the sun slips behind a cloud, I can make out a faint shadow of a small human form, slightly elongated, on the wooden boards.

'Did you … do that?' I whisper, pointing towards the stairs.

'It's not my fault. I told you to make him go.'

I think of the other accidents over the years—Robert Sanders' father, the women, the tradesman who fell from the window—and my heart clutches with fear as I turn back towards my husband's crumpled form.

'Marc?' I try to say, but all I manage is a croak. When I try a second time, my voice is a little stronger but he does not respond. He is unmoving; at this distance his face is a pale blur amid the ruin of the collapsed stair and shattered wardrobe. From up here, I cannot see if he is even breathing.

Knowing I must go to him, I move tentatively down the remaining steps at the top of the flight. But as I approach the section where the stairs have come away, there is an ominous creaking and the rending of old timbers as the rest of the staircase threatens to come away. Backing off, I know I can't leap over the gap. I would break my neck for certain. But how can I get to him?

Retreating back into the attic, I look around but the shadow has retreated.

'Are you here, Louis?'

The voice comes after a minute, that of a self-obsessed child who has no idea of what he has done. 'Yes. Will you read me a story?'

I think quickly. 'Yes, but I need your help first.'

'I want a story.' It is almost a whine.

'I'll read whatever story you want but before I can do that I need to help my husband, Marc. He's badly hurt. I need some rope to climb down to him. Is there rope here? Or sheets?'

'No.'

'Okay.' I try to think but it is hard when all I know is that Marc is hurt and he needs me to make things right. I go to one of the small sash windows, and try to tug it open. That's when I realise it is nailed down. In any case, I know these attic windows have only the tiniest of ledges and getting down to the floor below would mean edging along until I can reach the bathroom ledge and then shinning down the drainpipe.

There must be a way. 'I need to get downstairs, Louis.'

'The stairs are broken,' he points out.

Clenching my fingers into fists, I try to hold on to the panic-frayed edges of my composure. 'I know that. Is there another way?'

Feet shuffle. 'No.'

'Are you sure?'

'I don't know.'

He's not telling the truth. I am sure of it.

'If you show me, I'll come back and read you a story later.'

'No you won't. No one ever does.'

'I will. I promise.'

'Don't believe you.'

Something is nagging at me, and suddenly I know what it is—the locked room. I think of the times I sensed him behind the door and the day I caught him watching me through the keyhole.

I look around. 'Where do you sleep, Louis?'

'In my bed, silly!'

'There's no bed here.'

'It's in another room.'

'Downstairs?'

'Mmm. I'm going to play with my trains.'

'And how do you get to your bedroom from here?'

Did he have the strength to move the wardrobe at will? Maybe, but I think his power is the lashing out of a little ghost boy in anger, not a wardrobe-shifting kind of strength. In any case, I would have seen him coming and going from the landing. No, there is another way down—and I have to find it right now.

Back at the top of the stairs, I peer down at Marc. He hasn't moved. 'Marc! I'm coming. I'm going to find a way to reach you. Just hang on.'

There is no response but my promise to him bolsters my determination, and I stride back into the attic, ignoring the shadow crouched by the train set, looking around, trying to orient myself so I can search in the right place.

If there is a secret stairway, it must be towards the front, south-western side of the house. I go to the wall but there is no obvious door. Carefully, I move my hands over the faded wallpaper but there is no ridge to indicate the presence of a doorway.

From Louis, there is silence. I sense him watching me carefully from where he kneels on the floor, pretending to play. He is a ghost, I remind myself with a sinking heart. Most likely he needs nothing as prosaic as stairs or doors to get from floor to floor and room to room. He probably just floats through walls and floors.

'Please help me, Louis,' I plead softly, looking at where his eyes would be in the shadowy head. I try to imagine them a soft brown, with a remnant of innocence and goodness lurking behind the resentment and hostility. 'I'm sorry that other people didn't play with you or read to you and it made you cross, but Marc is a good man and we have to help him.'

He is very still as he listens. At long last he speaks. 'I want to play with your little book with the buttons that play music and have pictures.'

Confused, I frown for a second and then figure he means my mobile. Of course!

'It's a little phone. You like it?'

He nods. 'I made my name on it. There was a king named after me.'

I think of Louis XIV and would have smiled if things hadn't been so dire. 'I think it was the other way around,' I tell him. 'It's downstairs. If you take me down, I can phone for an ambulance and then you can borrow it. We can find out more about the king with your name.'

'Okay.' He shrugs and his shadow drifts across the room. I don't see what he does, but suddenly a wall panel glides open.

Peering into it, I see a child-size flight of stairs twisting downwards. I let him go first, and in a few seconds we are standing in a small windowless room containing a bed, a chest of drawers, a chair and a paint-chipped rocking horse that must have been vintage even when Louis was alive.

'Okay, I just need to get help and then you can play with my phone.' I will show him how to play games on the mobile, I promise, as soon as Marc is safe. I will do anything he wants once Marc is safe. Crossing to the door, I twist the handle. It is locked.

There is a sound behind me. I spin around as the rocking horse begins to move. Swish-swish-swish.

'You need to open the door,' I say, my patience in tatters. 'So I can get my phone.' He says nothing but his shadow moves faster on the rocking horse.

'Louis!' I am angry now, and afraid. I am so close to Marc with just a locked door between us. I have no idea how badly he is hurt, but every minute—every second—might count and I am at the whim of a sulky child who is not even alive. 'Open this door!'

'No!'

The rocking is faster.

'Open this door this minute!'

'No!'

'You promised! We agreed!'

'You'll go away.'

'But I'll come back,' I tell him again. 'I'll come back and read to you.'

'You won't.' He sounds so full of misery and hopelessness that I can't help feeling a shred of pity amid my fear for Marc.

I only have bits and pieces of his story, but enough to work out that he was an embarrassment to his family and shut away, promised a new mother who never arrived. And then, somehow, he died. Only those who have experienced it firsthand can understand the confusion and powerlessness of a mistreated child.

'Please, let me out,' I whisper, desperately. 'Please, Louis. I'm scared my husband will die and I love him …' My voice breaks. 'Please, Louis. I'll give you my phone, do anything if you'll help me.'

As, I watch, tears streaming down my face, the rocking slows and eventually stops. The shadow climbs off and comes to me and leans against me, mumbling something into my leg.

My hand touches those ghostly curls as I listen, and stills as I begin to understand what he wants. And when he is done, I nod and stutter 'yes' because I have no other choice.

We stand there a moment longer until I realise his head is no longer under my hand and footsteps are retreating back up to the attic.

I want to say something else but I am not sure what. In any case, it is too late. My eyes fly across to the door from the room. It is ajar.

Twenty-five

Present day, nightfall

Marc sleeps peacefully in the small hospital at Gloucester. One side of his face is a mess of cuts and bruises. The biggest of the bruises indicates a fracture of his left eye socket, which is causing some concern. He is also likely to suffer nausea and a hell of a headache when he wakes as a result of the concussion he suffered, and his ribs are badly bruised. At the moment, though, the drugs mean he can get some sleep.

My hand tightens unintentionally on his and he murmurs a little in his sleep until I loosen my grip. I lean forward. 'Marc, I love you. You know that, right?'

It is not the most elegant declaration of feelings, but it is true. I think he has always known how I feel about him. Even when I was not sure, he was—at some level, at least. But I need him to know that I know.

These are the first words I have said to him without an audience since the ambulance officers arrived at the house, although I have barely left his side throughout the ordeal of the day. Even when Yvette burst into the room, followed by Gordon, I removed myself only as far as the corner.

'You!' Yvette turned to me once she had assured herself that her son was alive, fur coat swirling around her. 'How dare you show your face after all you've done? You are responsible for this, do you hear me?'

Gordon had intervened, apologising as he led Yvette, sobbing delicately into a handkerchief, from the room. After a while I went out to find them both, sitting and staring at the floor. I touched her shoulder and she looked up at me.

'You're right, Yvette,' I told her. 'I'm to blame for this. You'll never know how sorry I am for that, and for putting you through this.'

Yvette hadn't even looked at me although Gordon offered a wan smile. I returned to Marc's side and a while later Léo arrived with Sylvie, and I gave them all half an hour together with Marc while I spoke with the doctor and tried to make sense of what he was saying so I could report back on his condition.

Now they have all gone, although Gordon and Yvette are staying not too far away and will be back here for the start of visiting hours tomorrow. But right now it is just the two of us, and the hospital sounds are few as everyone turns in for the night. No one has kicked me out so I am staying.

I sit back in the chair, feeling the weight of the day across my shoulders, and yet such lightness of heart that Marc was not more seriously injured. He could have died. I know it. He could have died, or broken his neck and ended up paralysed, which—for someone as vital as Marc—would have been worse than death.

The doctors seem unwilling to confirm categorically that there is no permanent damage to his eye. They will run more tests over the coming days, but I think their hedging is more to do with insurance than a belief that something is actually amiss.

I wonder if Léo or anyone has called Will and James. I have not thought of it until now. Someone should tell them. My phone is in my free hand and I glance at it to check the time. It is a little after nine. I could call them now—

The thought goes out of my head as I realise I have broken my promise to return to the house. I have not even thought of Louis since I emerged from the little unlocked room and sprinted to Marc's side. After that, all I could think of was the long minutes ticking by—forty-nine of them—as I waited for help, and tried to make Marc comfortable without moving his head.

Then when the sirens sounded, I had to leave him to open the gates and after that I hovered anxiously as they checked his vital signs, fitted a neck brace and then lifted him onto the stretcher. Though they assured me he was stable, I drove every kilometre of the journey to hospital with my fingers clenched on the wheel of the Audi, whispering an incantation that he would be all right.

Everything in me has been focused on my husband but now I know he is safe my thoughts travel back to the house.

I wonder if he waits, the ghost boy, peering out of the window of the master bedroom and down the drive, wondering if I will return, as realisation dawns that he has perhaps been abandoned yet again. Or if he searches the house, looking for the phone I promised him. Or does he sit cross-legged on the floor of his attic playroom, a book lying by his side that I promised to read to him?

My mind wanders back through this morning's encounter with Louis, and when I check online, I find out that what he told me was not as shocking as it sounds now. Unmarried mothers in the fifties and even later were still commonly sent away to have their illegitimate children, which were then adopted out.

Marc stirs a little and murmurs something that sounds like my name. I touch his face gently on the side least damaged. He settles back but then half-wakes again. I find a nurse but they tell me he is fine and that I need to go home. I pretend to do so but when the coast is clear I double back and perch on the edge of the bed trying to calm him.

Each time I speak, his face relaxes and his breath eases, but when I stop, his restlessness returns. I tell him he is in hospital, my fears for him and his family's loving concern, and about the sweetly gay nurse who I am considering setting up with Brendan, if it can be arranged.

And as the night settles over us, I tell him things that weren't in the private investigator's report—that alerting the authorities to my stepfather's brutality wasn't just the action of a protective sister, but vengeance for Vanessa and for what he would have made me do if I had stayed. I'm glad that Vanessa is doing well now. I speak of the day I left Marc, the mist that had brought me to the house, and how I'd found some measure of peace within its walls.

'I thought the nameplate said *House of Lost Souls* until I looked again and it was Lammermoor House, as clear as day,' I whisper. 'Perhaps that's what I saw because that's what it is—a place where lost souls go until they are found again.'

I tell him about my insecurities, particularly about my underwhelming career. I explain about the blog and the vintage clothes and my plans for a website, my dilemma about how to make it pay. He knows about the garden, but I fill him in on the steps I have taken to return it to splendour. And I tell him about the repairs that are needed to the house and my plans for the interior.

'It's been a sad house for a long time,' I tell him. 'Something happened there more than sixty years ago, something terrible. I think a child—a small boy—was hidden away for fear he would shame his family. I haven't pieced it all together yet but somehow he died.'

I look down at Marc. He is still except for his eyelids, and I wonder if, wherever he is, he can hear and understand me.

'Afterwards, the house was abandoned,' I continue. 'From time to time, some people went there with plans to turn it into this and that, but each time something went wrong. There were accidents and people got hurt. And eventually no one went there anymore, until it was almost forgotten.

'And then I came.'

I think of the open door on that dark night when I had been lost in heart, mind and soul—the way it had seemed to invite me in, to rest a while.

'And I stayed, even though I suspected, almost from the start, that I wasn't alone—that there was something else, a shadow left behind.

'People warned me about the house, said I should run from it. But I felt safe there and I had nowhere else to go, so I stayed and stayed. And I worked in the garden and made my plans, and I rested and ate and, little by little, I found myself.'

My eyes open wide as Marc's hand tightens a little in mine as though he is responding. But when I say his name, he does not answer. Sighing, I reach forward and skim a hand through his hair. It still has blood in it so I go into the bathroom to find a damp cloth.

When I return, he is muttering again, so I clean the blood from his hair and go on with my story.

'The spirit in the house and I, we seemed to have an unspoken agreement to live companionably in the house, although he was curious about me and—when I was feeling better—I began to feel curious about him. I think he is a boy of about five or six, named Louis, and that his mother was a young woman named Evelyn St John, who gave birth to him out of wedlock and was quietly shipped off to England.'

I laugh low. 'It sounds very Victorian, but it happened. As late as the seventies, single women were still routinely being pressured to give up their illegitimate children.

'Last night when you arrived, Louis had just confirmed his name to me. It was a big step for him as he had been let down by so many over the years. It was a sign of trust. And then you came, and I think he became angry that he'd lost my attention.

'Instead of responding to his gesture, I was with you. The destruction of the armoire was him dealing with his anger—and maybe a lure to get me away from you. Or maybe he wanted to show me how he had been kept hidden from view.

'When I went up there this morning, it was the first time I'd done more than sense his presence. I could see his shadow and feel him when he leant against my knee. He wanted me to stay with him.'

Will you be my new mummy?

I falter. In my head, I can hear his lisp as he asks the question that stops my heart, and makes me want to hold him close. Even now, with time to think, I am not sure if my response was to Louis' innocent question or because something in me that I can't even name believes the little ghost can in some way make up for the two tiny souls that are beyond me.

Marc frowns in his sleep, so I continue, not wanting him to move his face unnecessarily.

'But you called me, and I wanted to go to you. And it made Louis angry that I wouldn't stay with him, and when he is angry, things happen.'

I hold my breath as Marc's eyes move beneath his lids, hoping he will wake and smile at me. But eventually he is still again, so I stroke his hand and resume, explaining about the fall and how he came to be in hospital. I tell him that he will be all right and that his parents will return tomorrow.

'While they're with you, there are some things I need to do. You see I made a promise.' Uttering a brief laugh, I smile at him. 'I know I haven't often stood by my promises, but I'm trying. I don't know what will happen, but I have to try.'

'Em.'

His voice is faint but clear, although his eyes are still closed. Slowly, so slowly, his right one opens a crack.

'Marc.' I brush away a single tear. 'There you are. I was so worried.'

'Em.' He says something else that I can't make out so I lean close.

'You found what you were looking for,' he murmurs and I realise he has been listening.

I smile into his good eye. 'Yes. Yes, I think I have.'

'Good.' He smiles and then his eye closes, his hand relaxes in mine and he sleeps as I watch over him.

ஃ ஃ ஃ

Present day, morning

It is still early when I park the car in Lammermoor and hope that Robert Sanders' hardware store is open. It is, although when I open the door and walk in, he is not in the shop. Instead, the younger man who served me the first day I came in here when I bought the padlock sits behind the counter.

He looks up quizzically and offers a polite smile.

'Can I help you?'

I give him a tight smile. 'Actually, I was wondering if I could have a word with Mr Sanders.'

He looks confused. 'I'm Kevin Sanders … but you must mean my father. Just a second.'

Before I can say anything he moves out from behind the counter and that is when I see he is in a wheelchair.

He disappears through a doorway and, even as I hear him call for his father, another piece of the puzzle falls into place. When Robert appears alone a minute or two later, I look at him with sympathy.

'Your son,' I say. 'Kevin. He was the one who fell from the window.'

His eyes slide away but he nods.

'I'm so sorry.'

Again he nods and neither of us speak for a moment. Then Sanders sighs and starts to talk.

'He was just a boy then. Not long out of school and needed work. The new owner of the house, Mrs Banks, had plans to turn the house into a boutique hotel. My father tried to warn him. I did, too.' Sanders' voice breaks and he stops to collect himself. 'Next thing we knew he'd been rushed to hospital.'

'What happened?'

'Stupid. Just a silly thing.' Sanders shakes his head. 'He was working on a ladder, sanding a window frame in one of the bedrooms. Something startled him and he fell.'

'Did he ... did he say if he felt it was deliberate?'

Sanders shakes his head. 'Always said it was an accident. Just an accident. But after everything else ...'

'I'm sorry.' It seems such a useless thing to say but Sanders nods and makes eye contact. 'Heard you had some trouble of your own.' The tone of his voice screams *I told you so.*

'Yes, there was an accident.'

'You look all right.'

'I wasn't the one hurt, but my husband was.'

'As I said, accidents happen in that place.' He sounds a little like Louis. *I told you.*

'That's not what I came to talk about.'

'I don't have anything more to say.' He turns his back on me and begins stacking shelves.

'You see, that makes me think you know more than you've told me.'

He grunts.

'You were a young, impressionable boy back in the late fifties,' I muse. 'Proud when your dad took you to work at the fanciest house in the area. And when you saw the beautiful Evelyn, you fell a little in love.'

He snorts, keeping his back to me. 'That's ridiculous. I was seven or eight years old.'

'She was polished, shiny, a creature from another world. It's no surprise you had a crush on her.'

At that he turns. 'Maybe I did. So what?'

'And then, after Evelyn treating you like a little brother for months and the dazzle of the party preparations, suddenly you weren't allowed to go to work with your father in the school holidays anymore. No chance to say goodbye to your goddess. But I think you tried, didn't you?'

Sanders laughs. 'You have a very vivid imagination, Ms Reed.'

I drag a stool up to the counter and make myself comfortable to show him I have all the time in the world to explore this. 'I'm right though, aren't I?'

'What if you are?' He spends several minutes lining up products on the shelf behind the counter, making sure the display is perfect, before sighing. 'All right, look I went there. One evening when I was supposed to be in bed, I crept out of the window and walked from the town all the way to the house. Fat lot of good it did. I never got to speak with her.'

Disappointed, I feel my shoulders slump. I had been so certain he knew more.

'Saw her though.'

My eyes shoot up to meet his. 'You saw her? How long after the party was this?'

'Not long, a few weeks.'

'Was she all right?'

A faint smile curves his mouth, and his eyes are blurred with memory. 'She was glowing, more lovely than ever. But I hadn't picked my time very well. I thought I might catch her out in the garden. She'd told me she liked to walk there after dinner, when the scent of the summer roses was strongest. But she was in the house with her parents. I could hear her father shouting and her mother crying, and I crept as close as I could to hear what they were saying.'

I hold my breath, wondering if my theory is close to the mark.

'I didn't understand it, only that her parents were angry with her and that she was being sent somewhere.'

'To England?'

'No, to Sydney. When the Brigadier told her she had to go, she was furious, and stood up. She pushed her chair so hard it fell over and that's when I saw that she was—'

He stops abruptly and puts his head in his hands. Even now, more than half a century later, his disappointment is palpable. The goddess was mortal after all.

'Pregnant?'

Sanders nods. 'My mother was expecting my sister at the time so I knew what it meant when a woman's belly starts to grow.'

'So she was sent away to Sydney to have her baby. Did she come back?'

Sanders clutches his hands together. 'A while later, I heard my father tell my mother that he thought he'd seen her there one day and he was sure there was a baby in the house. He'd heard it crying. Not long after, the story about Evelyn moving to England started to get about.'

'So she was packed off overseas to put the past behind her and little Louis stayed under wraps at Lammermoor House,' I murmur.

'Who?' Sanders asks.

'Louis, Evelyn's son.'

He looks surprised. 'I never knew his name. I didn't think much about it after she was gone. Lammermoor House wasn't the centre of my world anymore. And then Dad was injured.'

'In the garden.'

He nods. 'Dad was burning leaves one autumn. He … well, it got out of control.'

'That must have been terrible, for him and your family.'

'He lost a leg.' Sanders looks around. 'Couldn't work as a gardener any more so he opened the shop. I took it over in the eighties, and now Kevin helps out. I'm sixty-six. I've been thinking I'll retire soon.'

'How long had your father worked at Lammermoor House at the time of the accident?'

Sanders thinks. 'A good while—ten, twelve years, I suppose.'

'He would have burnt leaves regularly, as part of his duties?'

Pursing his lips together, Sanders frowns. 'I don't know what you're getting at, Miss.'

'Yes you do. How did the bonfire get out of control?'

'He said the wind changed. He took his eye off the fire, and the wind blew a spark onto his clothing. It was an accident. There's no reason for it to be anything else.'

I look closely at his face but it is closed. I don't think I will get any more from him today, or probably ever. Sometimes, the full truth is just too hard; I know that only too well.

Getting down from my stool, I glance through the dusty windows. The street outside is busy with people shopping and running errands. I need to be on my way, to do what I have returned to do.

'The accident, the fire, it was in 1965 wasn't it?'

Sanders nods. 'Yes.'

Louis would have been six years old.

'I'm sorry,' I say again.

'Not you who should be sorry, but there are some who should.' His bitterness doesn't sound as though time has softened its edges. 'My father worked for the St Johns for more than a decade and when he was injured, that was it. No help, no nothing. Not even a card when he was in hospital.'

'They don't sound like very warm people, the Brigadier and his wife.'

He gives a hollow laugh. 'You could say that again. When I was a boy, I probably blamed Evelyn for being weak, for letting herself be taken advantage of. But now ... well, I reckon she was just after a bit of love. Who doesn't want that?'

As I close the door of the hardware shop behind me, I wonder if Evelyn found the affection she sought, either with Louis' father or later in England. I hope she did because otherwise the terrible price her little son had paid was all for nothing.

Twenty-six

Present day, morning

I do not know what I am expecting to find when I drive in through the open gate of Lammermoor House. It seems that after yesterday's dramatic events, the house should—in some way—have changed irrevocably, that it should have been razed to the ground in the incendiary aftermath of a child's rage. Or, alternatively, that yesterday has served as an exorcism of sorts, lifting the heavy weight of sorrow contained within its walls.

As I head up the driveway, I notice with surprise that the shrubs I cut back such a short time ago are already tipped with the spring green of new growth. The air is milder too, for winter.

The front door is ajar, which is just as well as I had forgotten to pick up the house key yesterday in my rush to follow the ambulance. When I walk in, I could be doing so after nothing more than a shopping trip to town. It feels exactly as it has done for the weeks and months I have lived here—of dust and damp and of a gathering of shadows, waiting to be released.

I close the door, firmly, and stand on the tessellated tiles of the entry, listening to the sighs and groans of the old house. All appears as I left it. I put my head around the door of the drawing room where the couch is rumpled from my abandoned night with Marc. Heat quivers through my body. Given all that has happened since, maybe sex was not such a bad idea after all. Perhaps our instincts know more about love than our rational minds.

After shaking and folding the sheets and blankets, and piling them up on the chaise, I put my fully charged mobile phone on the table to fulfil my promise to Louis. Then, I pick up Marc's bag and place it in the entry hall so that it will be found easily, even if I am not able to take it to him myself.

As I wander through the house, there is no sign of the little ghost. In the kitchen, the fridge hums and the cold tap drips. I turn it off tightly. I open the back door and stand on the long verandah, looking out over the garden. Sunlight pierces through the cloud cover, one of those 'hand of God' moments that makes it seems as though the mortal world is being blessed by the immortal one.

I am not one to believe in signs, but today I may make an exception. Perhaps this is the end—and even if it is, every end marks a beginning, doesn't it?

Inside, I climb the main stairs to the first floor, trailing my hand along the smooth bannister, feeling the give of the wood beneath my feet, wondering if I am setting myself up for disaster. But if the ghost boy wants to punish me some more, he does not take his opportunity to repeat yesterday's near-tragedy. Perhaps he has something else planned, but probably not. Small boys are not usually planners, I suspect.

Before me, the narrow stairs to the attic reach up into the gloom. I cannot even make out the top from here in the greenish light. I shout his name, but only the house responds with a faint echo.

Picking my way through the detritus of smashed wood and glass, I go into the master bedroom dressing room and try the door to the little bedroom. It is locked. I knock and call his name.

'Louis? Are you there?'

I crouch down and put my eye to the keyhole, but from my limited view, the room appears to be empty and the rocking horse is still.

'Louis, if you open the door I'll read you a story.'

The door remains firmly shut, though I wait for some minutes, and eventually I leave. Perhaps he has forgotten. Like the child he once was, perhaps he has forgotten his demand and my promise and is absorbed in his little attic world, busy playing with his train set or sitting cross-legged on the floor trying to sound the words to his storybooks.

After poking my head into the bathroom and the other bedrooms, I return downstairs to fetch a broom and spend the next hour piling the wood from the armoire and stairs into a heap, and sweeping up the broken mirror. It reminds me that I need to clean the cut on my toe. In fact, I need to shower and change my clothes, having borrowed the jeans and shirt I am wearing from the nursing staff after turning up at the hospital dressed in a robe.

Downstairs, I wrap the glass in newspaper and place it in the bin. Then I collect clean clothes and take a long hot shower. The cut stings but in a good way. I wrap a clean tissue around it and carefully pull on a sock to hold it in place, before dressing in my own leggings and loose brushed cotton dress.

When, I have put on a laundry load, including the borrowed garments I head for the library, thinking to find *Jane Eyre* to take to hospital to read while Marc sleeps. I open the door and freeze.

I had thought the rest of the house untouched by the child's fury. How wrong I have been.

It is as if a whirlwind has been through it. Books have been spilled from the lower shelves and lie in heaps on the floor, pages and jackets hanging loose. The curtains have been wrenched from their rail to fall in tatters, and chairs up-ended. The reading lamp has been knocked from the table, the bulb smashed against the hearth. On the window-seat, the stuffed bear sits, its belly gaping and stuffing spilling out, as though it has been disembowelled.

'Louis.' I breathe his name as if he might still be in the room, but of course he is long gone, and I have no way of reaching him unless he chooses to be reached. I rush across the hall to the drawing room, but my phone sits where I left it. He is keeping his distance, rejecting all my overtures. Sulking, perhaps, now that his fury is spent.

Sighing, I phone Gordon and learn that Marc has been awake and spoken lucidly to the doctor, who has whisked him away for a CT scan.

I tell my father-in-law I plan to return later in the afternoon so that he and Yvette can head back to Sydney if the tests show nothing sinister. Even if they are clear, Marc will stay in hospital tonight but may be well enough to be discharged tomorrow or the following day. I remember to phone Will, who as usual is with James. They are more than a little surprised to hear from me and there are none of the usual jokes when I tell them about Marc's 'accident'. They promise to drive up tomorrow.

When I am done, I return to the library to start putting it to rights. There is nothing I can do about the curtains, so I throw them in the bin, along with the shattered light bulb. It does not take me long to right the chairs and lamp, and return the books to the shelves.

Near the bottom of the pile, I find the military book with the bookplate, and shake my head. It is a book written for an adult, not a young child. The more I think about the Brigadier, the more I despise him. He seems to have not had a clue about rearing a little boy.

Poor Louis. I imagine him, as a five-year-old, anticipating the great occasion of his birthday. Perhaps he was hoping for a bicycle or a go-cart or a board game, and instead he gets a book he cannot even read. I can see his face alight with excitement as his grandfather hands him the gift, the eager unwrapping and then the disappointment as he realises what it is. Perhaps that is why it is down here with the other adult books, and not in the attic playroom.

At least someone had bought him the ragged children's books that sit on the bookshelf in the attic—his grandmother perhaps, or had Evelyn sent them for him? And he had the Brigadier's old train set. But really it wasn't much; nothing at all for someone condemned to spend more than half a century as a six-year-old.

I slot it next to the other military books, and stoop to pick up *Jane Eyre*, which is splayed beneath it. As I lift it, I notice a yellowing envelope beneath, addressed to Miss Evelyn St John at this address. Sitting in the chair, I unfold the letter, inside which is another written on different paper.

The first is dated 22 March 1958, and is from a Lance Corporal Paul Patton.

Dear Miss St John

By now, you will have heard the sad news and circumstances of Lewis Crichley's passing in Malaya last month. We had served together since his arrival in March and, although he had not been a soldier long, he showed real promise and commitment. The jungle is as much the enemy as anything, and a cut can easily turn septic if it's not watched. I'm just sorry it happened to a top bloke like him.

Please accept my sincere sympathies for your loss. If it is any comfort, he talked about you all the time and thought the world of you.

I found the enclosed part-written letter to you after his other effects had been returned and thought you should have it.

Once again, my deepest sympathies.

I refold it and open the letter that Paul Patton had enclosed.

Dearest Evie

How are you? Hope the oldies aren't getting you down.

We've been seeing some action here. Lost a truck the other day, with some minor injuries. Gerry's sporting a broken finger that he's rather proud of. A war wound, he says! The blokes who were in World War II just shake their heads and tell us we don't have a clue. We probably don't.

Don't worry about me, though. I'm far too cautious to cop it. The others laugh at me, but I reckon it pays to be careful—especially now I've got a girl in Aus to come home to.

You are my girl, aren't you, Evie? I showed the blokes your picture and they reckon you're a top sort. I know you are!!

I was looking forward to being a soldier so much and continuing the family tradition, but now I can't wait to come home to you. How do you think your dad would react if we told him we were going steady? I'm sure he expects you to do better—him being a commissioned officer and my dad being just a quarter-master—but times are changing aren't they?

If

It ends there but in my mind I see the young soldier's letter-writing being interrupted by his mates or the dinner bell or being called on duty, intending to get back to his letter in an hour or a day or two. Before he can do so, he suffers a minor scratch or cut, and that is that—such an insignificant thing, yet how big its ramifications.

Evelyn, just nineteen, would have been devastated, a toxic mix of grief and shame, something I know all about.

She probably would have known she was pregnant by then and been feeling nervous about telling her parents. With Lewis dead and only weeks until her shame became public knowledge, it wouldn't have been too hard for the domineering Brigadier to convince her to let him sort things out his way. And so she ended up sentenced to a future in exile—and her son to a life locked up out of sight while his grandparents tried to organise a discreet adoption that never happened.

It is hard not to feel intense disdain for the St Johns' treatment of their confused little grandson, concealed like a dirty secret for long years. Yet, they, like all of us, were products of their time, of their experiences. They would have grown up in an era where children had no voice and no rights.

Fleetingly, I think of my own background. Perhaps we have not come as far as we may think.

Perhaps the St Johns thought they were being kind, keeping him safe from ridicule. Perhaps they had tried in their own way. There is the train set in the attic and the old rocking horse, the book of military history, however inappropriate. They were ashamed of their grandson but I suspect they did not hate him.

I wonder if anyone ever told Louis about his dad. I rather think not. Perhaps it is time he knew his dad died serving his country, if he is willing to talk with me again. Maybe it will make a difference, I don't know.

Folding the letters, I tuck them back inside the book and place it in my bag. My phone has still not been touched, so I take it upstairs and stand at the base of the steps up to the attic.

'Louis,' I call. 'I have to go out for a little while to see Marc but why don't you pick a story for us to read later? I'll bring my phone with me and we can find out some more about those kings. I'll be back in a while.'

Not sure if I have achieved the right tone of adult calm, I pick up Marc's bag and walk out of the house, shutting the door behind me, wondering what reception I will get on my return. I can only hope that Louis will take me at my word.

As I drive towards the gate, I glance in my rear-view mirror. I think I see a shadow at an upper window, watching me leave. He lifts his arm and I realise he is waving me goodbye.

❧   ❧   ❧

Present day, afternoon

When I get to the hospital, the matronly nurse on duty in Marc's unit is outside his room, hands on barn-like hips, glaring angrily through the doorway at James and Will, both of whom are wearing fright wigs.

'The patient is not to laugh!' she tells them.

'But nurse, laughter is the best medicine,' James points out.

The glare intensifies, and I intervene. Dumping Marc's bag on the bed, I rummage in my wallet, find a couple of twenties and ask the boys to buy lunch for us all.

Will gives me a kiss on the cheek and waves away the cash. James grins idiotically at me. A moment later, they have vanished to the café. The nurse stalks off, mollified, and I am alone with my husband who is sitting in his chair, dressed in a robe and looking somewhat piratical with an ice-pack over his left eye.

'Hey,' he says, smiling.

'Hi.' I lean into him and press a kiss to his right cheek. 'You're looking good, all things considered.'

'No thanks to those two.' He runs a hand over my bottom. 'How could you sic them on me in my fragile state?'

'Not that fragile,' I point out wryly, removing his hand in case PDAs are also against hospital regulations.

He grins. 'The spirit is willing, but the body is on the weak side.'

'Probably just as well. I don't think that nurse would approve of hanky-panky.' I look around. 'I thought your parents were keeping an eye on you.'

Marc rolls his eyes. 'Mum was overreacting a bit so Dad took her home.'

'It's not overreacting to be worried about your child. It's normal. How did the tests go?'

'Fine. They did a scan. No lasting damage, provided I keep my head still while the bone heals. No sudden movements, hence no laughing.'

'I'll keep that in mind.' I crouch down in front of him, stroking his cheek. 'Headache?'

'Yeah.' He grimaces. 'But it's eased off a bit since earlier.'

'I can't tell you how relieved I am that you're okay.'

'Me too.'

Our eyes lock and something passes between us. We are okay, I realise. We have survived this fire, and perhaps something stronger has been forged in it—something that can endure what is to come.

'You seem different,' he says, taking my hand.

'The prospect of losing a husband does that to a woman.'

'Is that it?' He asks and when I sit back on the bed to study him, he continues. 'I had this dream last night.'

I wait for him to go on, but he is silent. It is my turn.

'You were pretty out of it,' I tell him. 'They gave you some really good drugs. It seemed like a good opportunity to tell you stuff I probably wouldn't if you weren't off your face.'

My joke falls flat; his face remains serious. 'You can tell me anything.'

I shake my head and he pulls gently on a strand of my loose hair until I stop. 'This story is a bit … wild—probably enough for you to get me sectioned.'

'It's a bit fuzzy but I think most of it sunk in.' He frowns. 'You said the house was a place where lost souls found themselves. And that you weren't the only lost soul in it.'

He has summarised things so neatly, no wonder he is so effective in business. Business! Oh God, another call I should have made and haven't.

'Marc! The office.' I fumble for my phone and nearly drop it. 'I'll call them now.'

His warm hand closes over my cold fingers. 'Don't worry. They knew I'd be away for a few days, and Dad spoke to Toby this morning. Everything's under control. They'll be fine for the next day or two.'

'That's good,' I mutter lamely.

'And right now, I'm far more interested in your haunted house than I am in spreadsheets and risk profiles.'

I can't tell if he is teasing me or not, but his eyes are firmly on mine. I shift under that steady, one-eyed gaze. 'Your house,' I remind him. 'You bought it.'

'For you. It's yours, Em.'

'Then, will you trust me to try and fix it?'

Marc is silent for a moment. 'We're not talking about plumbing and carpentry here, I take it.'

Pressing my lips together, I shake my head. 'No.' I give him the letters I found this morning and wait as he reads them both.

'The Malayan Emergency,' he says at last. 'Dad's Uncle Iain fought in that one, I think.'

'Oh?'

'He came back in one piece.' He looks up. 'Go on.'

'So, I'm thinking Evelyn's predicament would have made her vulnerable to her old-fashioned domineering father.' I tell him what Robert Sanders remembers of those times. 'Once she was out of the picture, there was no one really to care about her little boy.'

'What about the grandmother?'

'Perhaps she did what she could. He can write, after a fashion. Someone must have taught him.' I get up and pace, my mind so jumpy, my body won't stay still. 'But after however many years of marriage, I'm assuming she was pretty much under the Brigadier's thumb.

'I still don't know what happened to Louis, and until I do I can't help him—and the house—to lay things to rest.' I almost don't dare to look at him, it sounds so ludicrous. 'Still don't want to have me admitted?'

'No.' He gives me a wry smile. 'I may be a boring suit, but even I know that there are more things in heaven and earth ... et cetera.'

'You trust me then?'

'You, yes. But a tantrum-prone ghost kid with supernatural powers? No, absolutely not. Em, you said last night there had been other ... accidents?'

'It's true.' I tell him what I know about Robert Sanders' father, the broken leg and asthma attack. 'And then Kevin Sanders, Robert's son, fell from an upper window, and has never walked again. Individually they all seem like accidents, but collectively ...

'Marc, I was there yesterday.' I tighten my grip on his hand. 'Yesterday, at the precise moment Louis exploded with rage, the stairs collapsed. I can't let this go on.'

'But why you, Em? Maybe we need an expert. I don't know, a medium, perhaps, or an exorcist.'

'He talks to me, Marc. Only I can do this.'

'But why?'

I close my eyes, trying to find the right words. When I open them, he is looking right into my soul.

'Perhaps because I understand what it is to be lost.'

Twenty-seven

Present day, late afternoon

We argue back and forth for half an hour. Eventually, Marc sighs, looking tired, and rubs his head.

'Then wait until tomorrow and I'll come with you.'

'No, absolutely not. Not yet.'

His jaw firms and he begins to push himself from his chair, but the effort costs him. He presses a hand hard to his head and staggers. 'Jesus, my head.'

'Sit down and stay still! Do you want to lose your eye?' I ease him back into his chair.

Eyes closed, he rests his head against the chair back. I think he has fallen asleep, but a moment later, he opens his eyes again.

'In my phone, there's a name. The investigations firm Mum used. They might be able to trace Evelyn St John. She might still be alive.'

At his suggestion, I gasp. Of course! It hadn't even occurred to me. She would be well into her seventies but she could easily still be living.

Just then, the boys arrive back with pizza, the nurse following them, complaining that junk food is inappropriate for her
patient.

She takes one look at Marc's white face, and orders the rest of
us out of the room. We munch soberly on pepperoni pizza as we
wait for her to emerge. When she reappears, she gives us a thor-
oughly professional ticking off, and tells us Marc is sleeping again
and is not to be disturbed for the rest of the afternoon.

'I suppose we should get back to Sydney,' Will says when she
has disappeared down the corridor on her crepe soles. Why are
practical shoes so ugly? 'We have to get back to work.'

James looks at me, his expression unusually serious. 'You'll stay
with him, won't you?' he asks, an edge of accusation in his voice. I
am used to being found wanting by Marc's family but not by these
two. It is a salutary reminder of my epic failures.

'You won't … leave?' Will adds. 'He needs you, you know,
even though he's so together.'

I almost start to cry at that but I cannot make promises I may
not be able to keep. 'I love him,' I tell them huskily.

It seems to be enough because they nod, hug me and head off.
After they've gone, I make the call Marc has suggested and then,
for a long time, I sit with him, torn between a husband who needs
me, and a haunted house that needs me perhaps just as much.

Eventually in the late afternoon, his phone vibrates. With
surprise, I see it is the investigations firm calling back. I hadn't
expected any answers so quickly. I get to my feet to take the call
outside the room. I am so engrossed, I barely notice a nurse go in
to Marc. When I return a few minutes later, the blind is drawn,
the room is dim, and Marc is sleeping peacefully on his back, his
chest rising rhythmically.

I lift the hand on the blankets and place a kiss on his palm. His
fingers curl, reflexively, as though he is holding it there.

'I'll see you soon,' I whisper as I leave the hospital room, and I hope that I am telling the truth.

ə.   ə.   ə.

Present day, evening

Returning to the house after dusk—a house that has been the scene of countless tragedies—I am jittery with nerves and the hospital's horrible coffee. I do not know what to expect. If the little boy blames me for Marc's unexpected arrival at the house, he has the power to wreak a terrible revenge. But just maybe, the last months that we've shared the house will count for something.

It is a clear night, the stars just starting to wink on overhead as I unlock the front door and turn on the insipid light. If I have my way, the house will soon have bright white lights, I vow. No more murky lighting.

'Hi! I'm back,' I call, without thinking, and then realise how stupid I must sound. But I don't know how to play this. All I can do is trust my instincts.

As expected, there is no response. After hanging my jacket on the bannister, I head into the study—trying to ignore the disembowelled bear—and light the laid fire. With flames leaping, it seems more cheery. Turning on lights as I go, I switch on the stove and set some soup to heat up, before going into the laundry and hanging my washing on the rack to dry. Even as I run through these homely rituals, I am conscious of all this seeming a strangely domestic precursor to what may come. But if he watches me from the shadows, perhaps this is what he wants. A normal home, a family.

While it is warming up, I go through to the dining room. I am a little hesitant in case Louis has been here during my absence but nothing appears to have been disturbed. Was it only two days

ago, that Marc and I stood here while I tried to explain about
the clothes and the blog, hoping it didn't sound hopelessly
amateur.

Picking up the notes I have made for future blogs, I take them
and my soup into the library where the fire is blazing nicely. As I
eat, I review the notes. I've made some good points, I think, and
some not-so-good ones. But something is missing. It is not quite
me, and, really, I think I'd rather shoot myself than come over as
earnest as some of the ridiculous efforts out there.

Marc's words at our wedding spring to mind. *I married you
for your wicked mouth.* At the time, everyone laughed because of
the sexual inference—probably because Yvette had made sure her
gold-digger theory had wide exposure—but we'd both been clear
he meant my caustic tongue.

That was what was missing! Irreverence. There is a fine line
between edgy and bitchy, but if I can maintain the balance, it
will be a style blog that cuts right through the crap to reach real
women from all walks of life. Excited, I don't even finish my soup
before I have scribbled another two pages of ideas and thought
bubbles, scenarios that I think will get a strong response, perhaps
even make people laugh out loud. Who says fashion can't be funny?

Chewing on the end of my pen, I think I have really hit upon
an exciting concept. Now all I need to do is make it fly—and make
it pay. Tomorrow, I will ask Marc if he can suggest a way I can
make a living from it. Perhaps the exercise will occupy his mind
enough for him to agree to stay at the hospital for another day—

My phone rings from somewhere in the house. Dumping
everything, in case it is Marc or the hospital, I fly through to the
kitchen, where I last saw it, but it isn't there. I can still hear the
ringing, faintly now, from upstairs.

'Louis, wait!' I take the stairs two at a time, and bolt into the
main bedroom and rush to the dressing room, expecting to find

the little door locked. It is wide open and I walk inside to find it empty. But I can hear faint footfalls moving up the secret stairway to the attic. Scared that Louis will shut the wall panel at the top, I race up and burst into the attic.

The little shadow turns with a gasp and drops the phone, which skitters across the floor towards me. I can see Marc's name on the screen, and then all goes silent.

Neither of us moves for more than a minute. Then I reach forward and pick it up. I type a brief text to Marc. *Trust me.*

Then I open a web browser and hand it to Louis. Our hands touch and it is softer than the touch of human flesh; it is there and not there. Strange.

'Spell your name,' I tell him.

Carefully, he does so. I walk over to him, seeing the list of results appear. 'Gently press the words in blue at the top with your finger. The Wikipedia page for Louis XIV appears almost immediately, and the little shadow is absorbed. He sits on the floor cross-legged, until the screen goes dark.

'It's broken again!'

'No, the light just goes out after a while to save power. If you touch the screen every few seconds, it will stay on.' I sit next to him, find his page for him and he continues reading.

'Too many long words,' he says at last. 'But he was a famous king, wasn't he?'

'Very famous. But I don't think your mother named you for the king.'

'She might have.'

'I think she named you for your father. His name was Lewis.'

Louis lisps his father's name.

'His name was Lewis Critchley and he was a soldier a long time ago in a place called Malaya.'

The little ghost appears to be considering this. 'Did he die?'

'Yes,' I manage. 'He died before you were born. That's why you never knew him. But I think he was a good man.'

The shadow turns to me, and I know what he will ask me next. I think I am prepared.

'Did my mummy die too?'

'Yes, she died, too,' I whisper. 'She died in England in a car accident.' There is no need to tell him she was on the way to church to be married to another man when the bridal car was in an accident. 'It was a long time ago.'

He sits, still clutching the phone, trying to take it all in. I cannot tell if it makes a difference to him to know this.

I get up and wander to the bookshelf, thinking to pick a book for him. There are so few, and most of them are a little young for him. I pick one, a vintage edition of Dr Seuss's *If I Ran the Zoo*, and I'm about to ask him if he would like me to read for him.

Flipping open the cover, I see an old-fashioned bookplate.

This is the property of Bobby Sanders.

One by one I check the other books. Around fifteen bear either Robert's name or Michael Sanders'.

'Do you remember the gardener who used to work here?' I ask Louis, who has found the ringtones and is playing them one by one.

He looks up. 'He was nice. I used to watch him from the window.' He gets up and walks to one of the windows that are nailed shut, staring down. 'I wished I could go outside and help him sometimes, but I wasn't allowed. Sometimes, he would wave to me, and sometimes he would leave books for me in the shed.'

'You weren't locked in here all the time?'

He looks at me and then back out the window. 'I don't know.'

It is his usual answer when he is not telling the truth.

'It's all right, Louis,' I tell him. 'You weren't bad. I'm glad if you went outside into the fresh air sometimes.'

'I wasn't supposed to. Grandpa said I had to stay out of sight or I would grace the name. But he was old, and Grandmother. Sometimes they forgot to lock me in.'

'And one day, Mr Sanders, the gardener, he made a big pile of leaves to burn,' I say. 'You watched him, didn't you?'

Louis nods. 'He made it go on fire, and I wanted him to show me how he did it. So I went downstairs very quietly so no one heard me and ran out into the garden.'

'And what happened?'

'I didn't mean to do it.'

'I know you didn't.'

'I ran up, and he was so surprised, he dropped the leaves and there was a whoosh, and his leg was on fire.'

I close my eyes. How terrible for them both, is all I can think.

'And I went into the fire to help him. But it was hot and it hurt me a lot. And then it didn't hurt anymore. So I went back to my room before Grandpa found out. If I was bad, I couldn't have a new mummy.'

I want to cry for him. 'But Grandpa and Grandmother, they didn't come to your room or to the attic again. Did they?'

He shakes his head. 'I waited and waited but they didn't come. And then they drove away and I didn't see them again. My new mother didn't come either. No one came, not for a long time.'

'You must have been lonely.'

He nods. 'After a long time, some new people came a few times—but I didn't like them. They wanted to throw my things away and knock down the house.'

'So you stopped them.'

Again, there is that shifty jitter. 'I don't know.'

But I do.

'Louis, I think you tried to do a very brave thing and help Mr Sanders when he was hurt. But you accidentally died in that fire and that's why your grandparents couldn't see you anymore.'

Whether or not he understands I am not sure but I can only try.

'If you can come outside with me now, I'd like to show you something.'

'I can't go outside. I'm not allowed.'

'Well, you can watch from the back porch,' I tell him, and we troop down two flights of stairs and into the kitchen, bright after the dimness of the rest of the house. He is almost invisible here but I can feel his shadow following me as I cross the room. I turn the key, open the door wide and step out into the starry night. My breath turns to steam in the cold night air, and I shiver.

Taking the torch from the window ledge, I switch it on, directing its beam across the garden to near where I'd found the train carriage all those weeks ago.

'Is that where the fire was?' I ask him.

'Yes.' The whisper is reed-thin as though sucked up into the night.

I walk over to the spot, beyond the herb garden, to a place thick with leaves from the overhanging trees. 'Here?' I call, but he does not answer and I cannot make him out on the verandah.

With my bare hands, I sweep aside the leaves that have piled there over the decades. It takes only about ten minutes to find what I am looking for. A small mound, with a simple wooden cross.

LOUIS
October 1958–May 1965

I sense him next to me, and I reach out my hand, which he clasps. It feels less substantial than the last time I held it.

'Is this me?'

'Yes,' I say. 'When you're ready, you can come here and you won't need to be alone anymore.'

'All right,' he says. 'Until then, will you stay with me? You promised.'

He is telling the truth. In the moment I made it, when Marc lay so still and pale, I would have promised anything.

'I'll visit often,' I tell him. 'Is that enough?'

After a second, he nods.

I'm not sure how long I stand there by the small grave but at some point I realise I am alone, and there is a moment or two of hush, as though the garden and the surrounding woods and river are paying their respects.

And then I head back inside to call my husband and tell him that I think everything will be all right.

Twenty-eight

Ten months later, evening

I am standing in front of the bathroom mirror, pretending to consider various hair styles. We are about to enjoy an evening out, courtesy of my new gig as an occasional radio host. Terribly old media, I know. But it suits me. I have found that, while I don't particularly like being seen all the time, I do like being heard.

My first few pieces for *Small Poppies* attracted a fair bit of attention and my own website, *Chartreuse Says*, is developing a growing following. It is still a work in progress but I love it. I have taken Marc's advice and introduced an irreverent tone to my writing that helps people to have fun with style rather than be slaves to it, and the absence of advertising means my advice is trusted.

It also means that it costs me rather than pays me. However, a few weeks after the website launched, a radio host Claire knows invited me on to her show for an interview, one thing led to another and now my wicked mouth is getting a workout interviewing all sorts of guests, mostly on matters of style but sometimes on other topics. Listeners call in for advice sometimes, too, and

I like giving it—and getting paid for it. Thinking about other people is good for me.

People sometimes comment that it must be hard to do style on radio, a non-visual medium. I disagree. When I describe a look, each listener interprets it in her own way, layering something of herself, her personality, on top of my ideas. Instead of one look, there are thousands. Having said that, I have been offered a casual spot on lifestyle TV. I'm considering it.

It is not the kind of stable, consistent work that perhaps I originally thought I needed to do to be taken seriously, but I am happy nonetheless.

At the moment I am not thinking of work; all my attention is on my husband. The hair thing is just to conceal the fact that I am staring at him as he stands behind me, his arms around my waist, watching my reflection. His eye is fine although his looks are not untouched by the accident. He has a three-centimetre, scimitar-shaped scar across his left cheekbone, which makes women want him even more, me included. Bastard!

'Do you like this look?' I ask, scooping my hair up on top of my head. 'I'm wearing that silvery mini-dress from Claire's new collection.'

'Mmm,' he says with an absent-minded air. His gaze drops a little and he frowns. His hand caresses my midriff over the silk slip I'm wearing.

'What?'

His hand has stilled and when he doesn't reply, I glance down and see what he sees. My belly is no longer flat.

I inhale sharply and almost forget to exhale. When I do, it comes out in a whoosh. I meet his eyes in the mirror. Mine are wide; his are febrile with shock and excitement. We have not used birth control for months, leaving it up to nature to decide what would be. When nothing happened after a few months, I suppose we just thought it wasn't to be and put it out of our minds. We have been too happy with what we have to regret what we do not.

Our evening out forgotten, I perch on the toilet while he hands me one pregnancy test after another—four in all from the stash that is probably well past its use-by date. Or perhaps not, because one by one, definitive lines appear. I am completely, utterly, unambiguously up the duff.

'Christ,' Marc says, sitting down heavily on the side of the bath. 'How did this happen?'

I give him a look.

'You know what I mean.'

'I don't know. I suppose I haven't been paying much attention, and I haven't been very regular since … the girls.'

'Are we ready for this?' he asks.

I shake my head. 'I have no idea.'

'Let's keep it to ourselves for a while,' he says. 'Except …'

I know what he wants to do. He will want to stand by the remains of our little girls and tell them the news.

'Tomorrow,' I say. Tomorrow, we will take colourful flowers to the small grave with the headstone identifying Pea and Nut. We have talked about giving them proper names, but Pea and Nut is all we have ever called them so I think they will stay.

'Sure?' Marc asks, knowing I still do not find it easy.

In the mirror, our eyes meet and hold. I nod. 'Yes.'

Epilogue

Marc thinks we should be able to tell each other anything; I think some things should remain secret—and my deal with the little ghost is one of them.

The day of Marc's accident, I had to make a promise. I had to give the little ghost what he wanted—a mother. I think I have given him more than that. I have given him the truth, and a way to move on when he is ready. And until that day, I have given him a family, at least part-time.

Marc does not know this, or at least I have not told him, but perhaps he suspects it because he fought me only briefly when I told him we would be spending regular time at Lammermoor House. It may just be that he trusts me with certain less cerebral things, the way I trust him on business matters.

We sold the apartment in Surry Hills and—when Marc cut his days in the office to three a week—decamped to Palm Beach. It is cramped but we plan to extend it just a little to use as our city base. Long weekends and holidays we spend at Lammermoor House.

At first, Marc's appearance at the house was greeted with dis-pleasure: slammed doors, broken crockery and stolen keys. But we set the rules and acceptance quickly followed, bringing with it sweet moments that we both cherish: a flower left on the kitchen table, a lost cufflink found and returned, the light touch of a small sticky hand from time to time, accompanied by the faint scent of oranges.

When we decided to restore the house, we spoke simply and clearly about our intentions, knowing a shadow stood eavesdropping just inside the kitchen door. It seemed to work; no tradespeople have fallen from the window or been knocked out by falling timber. Robert Sanders has even dropped by once or twice to advise on the garden and admonish me for overwatering the hydrangeas.

The house has responded to being cared for and inhabited again. It has emerged from the shadows—gracious, welcoming and a family home once more.

The house has back its soul, as do we.

Marc is nearly the old Marc except that now he knows loss, he can never *unknow* it, can never be quite that innocent again. I, however, have changed beyond all recognition. Oh, occasionally I'm my old vain, self-centred and shallow self, but you'd probably like me a little more. I know I do. Even Yvette tolerates me, and I have spoken to my sister Vanessa on the phone. Perhaps one day we will meet up. I'm not sure.

When our son Charlie was born, Marc was worried about how his arrival would be received by our little ghost. I was too, but less so. Marc's peacekeeping gift of a modern train set delivered to the attic was a masterstroke, greeted with distant yet gleeful whooping. He's a smart man, my husband. Have I ever told you that?

Sometime after that day, little Louis came to me in a dream, holding the hands of two small girls. He whispered goodbye and since then I rarely see him, except as the faintest of shadows sitting quite still in the tree that overhangs the small garden grave.

Then, just when I think he is gone for good, I catch the sound of two sets of feet on the stairs to the attic, those of my sturdy toddler son as well as footfalls slightly less earthly. And in the wake of Charlie's infectious chuckle, the echo of another child's long-ago laughter lingers like mist in the air.

Acknowledgements

First and foremost, deepest thanks to Harlequin Australia's Rachael Donovan for taking a chance on this book and its troubled heroine— and for being such a collaborative and supportive presence through- out the book's development. Thanks also to Harlequin's editorial team for all the wise and constructive feedback; this book is vastly better for it. I'd also like to acknowledge the influence of all the authors whose heroines don't fit the mould. And to the readers who go along for the ride—especially when you're not sure where you're heading—you rock!

Author's Note

While Lammermoor House and the town from which it gets its name are creations of my imagination—as are the characters in this book—I hope they live and breathe for you, as though they were real.

talk about it

Let's talk about books.

Join the conversation:

 on facebook.com/harlequinaustralia

 on Twitter @harlequinaus

www.harlequinbooks.com.au

If you love reading and want to know about our authors and titles, then let's talk about it.